CW01472287

TAINTED LOVE

Sinful Souls
MC Book 3

Amo Jones

Tainted Love
Sinful Souls MC Book Three

Amo Jones

This book is a work of fiction. Any references to real events, real people, and real places are used fictitiously. Other names, characters, places and incidents are products of the Author's imagination and any resemblance to persons, living or dead, actual events, organisations or places is entirely coincidental.

All rights are reserved. This book is intended for the purchaser of this e-book ONLY. No part of this book may be reproduced or transmitted in any form or by any means, graphic, electronic, or mechanical, including photocopying, recording, taping, or by any information storage retrieval system, without the express written permission of the Author. All songs, song titles and lyrics contained in this book are the property of the respective songwriters and copyright holders.

Formatting by Swish Design & Editing
Editing by Swish Design & Editing
Cover design by Amo Jones
Cover image Bigstock Photo

© 2015 Amo Jones
All rights reserved.

ISBN-13: 978-1517763879
IBSN-10: 1517763878

Note: This story is not suitable for persons under the age of 18 as it contains strong sexual content and explicit language. This book also contains upsetting content, which may set off triggers for some people.

*If the word "Fuck" offends you, please don't read this book.

Welcome to the messed up and broken world of Kalie-Rose Reynolds and Ade Nixon

DEDICATION

To all my alpha loving addicts, may this give you
the hit that you crave.

ACKNOWLEDGMENTS

Simon—My partner in crime, the Clyde to my Bonnie, and the love of my life. I could not have done all of this without your undying support. You have been the truth to my words and my number one critic. I love you so much, and I cherish the moments you have had to (at times) take up both roles, as mother and father while I locked myself up in my writing cave. I love you - *Always and Forever*.

My four little people—My four little critters who are the light of my life. They have tolerated at times a moody mother when all I wanted to do was write, but they enjoy all my guilt gifts and privileges once I'm finished a book, though. So it's a win-win.

Isis Te Tuhi—Thank you for always being the ear to my troubles, for going through the emotional rollercoasters of all these stories with me, you are my caramel soul sister. *The one and only, Mrs. R.F.*

Kaylene Osborn—My lovely editor, thank you for all that you do. You're more than my editor, you always go above and beyond with helping me through whatever I may need. I appreciate you and all that you do so much.

My Readers—My beautiful readers, I love you all. Keep reading and keep writing those reviews. Each of you has contributed to me pushing through my rough patches. You make it all worth it, each and every one of you.

The Bloggers—Thank you to all the lovely bloggers who have been there from day one, and the new ones who have just started reading my stories now and sharing your honest reviews. You are all amazing and I thank you for taking the time out of your busy lives to read my book. I hold the utmost respect for you.

Lastly, thank you to all who have had to endure my yapping as I got excited about a plot in one of my books and all I wanted to do was talk about it. I know I talked your ears off, *so thank you.*

TAINTED LOVE

*Sinful Souls
MC Book 3*

PROLOGUE

KALIE - ROSE

I attempt to open my eyes, but they refuse to open. All I feel is the pounding in my head.

Boom, boom. Where is that sound coming from? Where am I?

I try to open my eyes again, this time succeeding. Everything is black.

"What the fuck," I mumble.

I think over my jumbled thoughts, trying to think of the last thing I remember.

"Vicky's wedding," I whisper.

"Kal? Kal, is that you?"

"Alaina?" I gasp in shock.

"It's me, babe," she quietly replies, her voice hoarse and dry.

I attempt to move off the bed, but I feel like an anchor is weighing me down. Using all my strength, I push myself up and stand off the bed, only to fall to the ground when my legs give way.

"Fuck!" I scream out in frustration.

"Shhh Kal, if they hear you they'll come back."

I begin crawling across the cold hard concrete floor.

"Alaina? How long have we been here?"

"I don't know. You've been out for a few days. I lost count. I'd say a week, maybe more."

I pause my shuffling. "How have I been asleep for a week?"

"They've been drugging us with something. More you than I. They found me fascinating, being Zane's old lady."

Continuing my shuffling, I keep my hands feeling around in front of me. Feeling cold chains, I follow them up until they lead me to one of Alaina's hands. They are cold and stiff, she feels like death. I keep feeling around her until she winces.

"What did they do to you, Lain? Who are they?"

She pulls her arm out of my grasp. "It's going to be okay, we just have to be strong until the boys arrive."

The metal door swings open and a dark shadow looms. I swallow down and look at Alaina. Now there's light shining through the doorway, I can see her.

I wish I didn't.

I wish I never looked her way.

My stomach coils over, as little more than bile spews out of my mouth.

CHAPTER 1

KALIE - ROSE

I have always loved my job, being a professional dancer has its benefits. I'm not the type of dancer you may be thinking, though. I'm the type who keeps her clothes on—well, for the most part anyway. The only downside is never being able to set down roots because I'm constantly either in Hollywood or in Coronado. I've just finished shooting a music video for some drop kick wannabe player who thinks his dancers are his personal escorts. They're not always like that, just the new younger artists. They seem worse than the ones who have been around long enough to earn their respect.

I'm heading back to my apartment in The Hills where I live with my best friend, Carter. It's only around the corner from the studio so I walk most nights taking in the sights and sounds around me. Carter is amazing and so easy to live with. We've been friends going on ten years now. I do hate his obsessive OCD disorder, and his need to bring home different men every day of the week.

Yep, you guessed it—Carter is gay.

Walking into my apartment and pulling my headphones out of my ears with R-Kelly's song *'Cookie'* beating through them, I throw my jacket on the counter.

"Carter?" I yell out while checking the fridge for food.

Walking through to the living room with last night's cold Chinese food in my hand—cold food always tastes nicer than hot food—I see Carter coming down the hallway.

"How's it going, baby girl?" Pulling me in for a hug, he unlatches himself from me when I hear shuffling come from his bedroom. I look to him with my eyes narrowed.

"Again? God Carter. It's going to fall off soon you use it that much."

He laughs at my comment, stealing some of my food.

"Mm-hmm baby girl. Not all of us are able to have sex only the once."

Licking my lips and smiling at his comment, not because he's fun*ny, because he's not*, but because it reminds me of Ade. Ade was my random one night of first-time sex. One night two years ago, and he *ruined* me. I haven't been able to go anywhere near sex since. I date, yes, but they all eventually leave when they discover that I'm not the slightest bit interested in sex with them. It's not from the lack of trying, believe me I've tried, but those piercing blue eyes, strong square jaw and his intense, possessive stare has haunted my dreams more times than I can count. Which has resulted in other men just simply, not meeting his standards. To say he set the bar high is an understatement.

"Carter!" I scorn him. Picking around the honey soy chicken in my dish.

"Do you even know this one's name?" I ask with an eyebrow raised, as he walks behind me to head back to the kitchen.

"No," he answers directly as he flicks his blond, perfectly styled hair back across his forehead.

When we first met, I used to call him JB, because his hair looked as if *Justin Beiber's* hair stylist had styled it—he hated it, to say the least, which resulted in me loving it.

"Oh well, I hope you wash it twice a day. Just sayin'!"

He spits his drink out and looks at me. "Kalie-Rose! That's not something I expect to hear come out of your mouth."

I laugh while I head over to join him in our large open plan kitchen. Our apartment is nice and relaxed. It's actually a loft, complete with brick walls, and big glass windows overlooking the street below. The area is all open plan downstairs, where the living room and kitchen are located. There are also two big wooden pillars centered in the middle of the large area, between the living room and the kitchen. The stairs leading you to both Carter and my bedrooms and the one bathroom. The bathroom is where all my framed Lakers singlets are hanging nicely in their glass frames. Bryant, Clarkson, Young, and Randle—they all have a spot.

"You got some mail today, in the top draw." He points as he pops open a bottle of Veuve Clicquot.

I slide the drawer open and see a silver envelope with my name written in delicate cursive writing. Looking up at Carter, he's staring at me, waiting for me to open it. I bite down on my lip and rip the envelope open. A whole lot of confetti spills out everywhere and I pull out a simple card that reads:

Will you be my bridesmaid?
Vicky xo

"Fuck," I curse a little loudly as I slam the note onto the bench.

Why couldn't she just ring, or text me. Ever the theatrical princess is my Vicky.

Carter walks over, picking up the card. He begins laughing under his breath.

"Oh, baby girl."

Pulling me under his arm, I push off him and huff out, walking back into my room and swearing profanities under my breath. Stripping my clothes off, I slide into my sheets and close my eyes as I relive a crazy night two years ago…

Two Years Ago

I was blasting Beyoncé '*7/11*' as I zoomed onto the highway. I have a massive love for music, all kinds. But in my line of work, I guess I heard more hip-hop than anything else. I was ready to get out of Hollywood for a lifetime after my boyfriend of two years had dumped me for being a virgin. I guess he was sick of trying, can't say as I blamed him to be honest. So right now, I was driving to my family's house in Coronado to meet my best friend, Vicky. I hadn't seen her in a few months, but whenever I did, it was as though nothing had changed. That shows true friendship. I was singing along with my long, light, caramel brown hair flowing freely behind me, and I felt like getting a little wild. I'd always been the good girl, the innocent one. I felt as though I needed to be exposed. I felt like something deep inside me needed to be unleashed. I felt like I need to be tainted.

I pulled up to my family home and made my way inside. It was overly large, especially for the amount of time my parents actually spent here. But they refused to sell the place for—as my mother put it—sentimental reasons. I used to spend some weekends there, mostly when I felt the need to get away from Trevor. As soon as I walked in the front door, I got a text from Vicky.

> Vicky: *Are you almost ready? I can come over in ten.*
> Me: *Ready when you are ;)*

Boy was I ready. I needed to let loose, and there was no one better to help me with that, than Vicky Abrahams. When I saw her car pull up, I walked out my door.

"Hey, Vick!" I squealed, pulling her in for a hug.

"Hey beautiful lady, you ready for a wild time?" She wiggled her ass and threw her hands up.

I laughed. "I wouldn't be here if I wasn't."

Shutting the front door and locking it, we walked down the steps.

"We could walk, it's not far?"

She nodded her head. "Good idea."

"So, how have you been?" I asked.

"Good. Man drama with Jesse, but meh, what's new."

I shook my head with a smile. "You're such a man eater. You could even give Carter a run for his money..." I paused and thought about that for a second. "Actually, no. He's still worse than you."

She laughed. "I guess. How are my brothers?" I brought my glasses down from my head, blocking out the LA sun. *And maybe hiding my thoughts.*

"Um, Dominic is great, he's awesome actually. Jacob is still a little off the rails, but he's good, running his empire and all that. I did see him driving a new Ferrari, complete with the latest blonde of the week in the passenger seat."

She laughed. "So not much has changed there then."

I shake my head. "Nope, not at all."

"I'm still rooting for you and Dominic you know," she said, hooking her arm around my elbow. I shook my head and laughed. "I know. I know you are."

We walked into the local bar with the smell of cigarettes and beer hitting my senses. The need to lose control took over my body like a wave of rebellion. I was sick of being a virgin, this much was true. However, I at least wanted it to be with someone I felt sexually attracted to. I'd never had that with Trevor. It had always felt more like a business transaction every time we were together. I didn't know how we'd lasted so long to begin with. I wanted to do all things that I'd never thought of doing. Before I had a controlling boyfriend, I had controlling parents so this would be the first time I'd felt a sense of freedom. When I was little, both my parents were Mormon. Therefore, they were very, very, strict. Now, not so much. Quite the opposite actually. They still had their beliefs, but they were more like normal parents now. Apart from my mom, she was a little crazy.

I was walking straight to the bar when I felt Vicky stop behind me. I turned to see her purring at a large group of bikers in the corner. I rolled my eyes. I couldn't take that girl anywhere. Even her vagina needed a GPS. I envied her in a way, she was so free-spirited and didn't care what people thought. Vicky's motto was *'If you don't feed me or fuck me, then your opinion doesn't matter.'* Yep, that was our Vicky. So I thought nothing of her perving. Me on the other hand, I had never been one who liked to be the center of attention, and I'd never really paid attention to what was going on around me. Not a smart trait to have when I thought about it.

When we reached the bar, I slumped down onto the bar stool, placing my handbag on the bench.

"So," she said, dropping to the stool. "Why so glum?"

I ordered our drinks and picked up some mixed nuts that were sitting in a glass bowl.

"My ex dumped me," I said with a shrug.

"Oh well, let's find some new toys to play with then."

She began to look around the room, her eyes landing directly on the bikers. Typical bloody Vicky Abrahams. I looked between her and the group before I started clicking my fingers in her face to gain her attention.

"Vicky, I swear to God you and Carter are soul mates."

She laughed, taking a sip of her drink. "Anyway, so he left you, must be a good reason."

I laugh. "Mmm, very." I threw up four fingers to the bartender, signaling shots.

"What? Are you going to tell me he left you because you're a virgin?" She scoffed at her own words, which were laced with sarcasm. I closed my eyes and picked up the drink that had been placed in front of me, pounding it back fast.

"Oh shit, *no way*," she exclaimed.

I drank my two shots before ordering two more. The pretty young bartender looked at me like maybe I'd lost my mind. I probably had, I wouldn't know. I think I was drunk.

"I know it's hard to believe because I'm only twenty-one. Who is twenty-one and is still a virgin? I just didn't want to. I don't do anything that I don't want to do. Besides, my parents always pushed the whole *no sex until marriage* bullshit down my throat when I was a child. Who knows, maybe that impacted me too?"

She stared at me as if I was an alien before picking up her shots, shooting them back and ordering another round of drinks. "You mean, who is twenty-one, still a virgin, and look the way you do?" She scoffed in disbelief, throwing back her drink. "You're on your own with that one."

I skulled the new drink in record time and placed it down in front of me, signaling for more, and ignoring the judgmental eyes that came from the young girl behind the bar. *Please,* when she had her big girl panties on, she would understand why people resort to drinking. She should wear pink lace, though. It would suit her skin tone and definitely needed to be Victoria Secret.

Yep, I'm drunk.

"Okay, so now that we have established my known *innocence* can we move on to drinking more," I said to Vicky as I threw back my—I'd lost count, but I was starting to feel the effects of the alcohol.

She nodded her head, lifting her drink in the air. "That we can do."

"Wait," she paused mid drink, "Oh God. Please don't tell me this is your first time being drunk?"

"Well, I've tried drinking before, but yes, this is the first time I've been...what's the term? Buzzed." I laughed to myself briefly before shutting my mouth when I realized I was one of those stupid drunk girls.

"It's fine Vicky, it's spring break!" I said, swinging my hands up in the air.

"Fuck it, let's dance," she retorted. We pulled each other up off the stool, dancing and laughing our way over to the dance floor. Glancing quickly over to the table, I saw that all eyes were on us. *Weird*, I thought to myself. Before going back to doing my own thing.

It wasn't long before a hot guy with dark blond hair came over and started to chat up Vicky.

Actually, scratch that, he was not just hot, he was sexy, I guess, in a way. They were chatting to each other, but I couldn't hear their conversation, I was too busy dancing my moves around to a rock song.

Vicky pulled on my top. "Come on."

After he had lured us over to his table, I looked around, attempting to pull my eyes into check, and try to at least act sober. I couldn't help but feel as though I had a set of eyes on me at all times, I could feel a magnetic pull, and it was something I'd never felt before. The feeling was intense. When I meet the eyes of one of the guys who were sitting at the table, it confirmed my suspicion.

Holy shit.

He was out of this world good looking. He had a square defined jaw, tattoos running up his neck and down his arms. I couldn't tell how tall he was from where I was sitting, but if I had to guess, I would have said he'd definitely be over six foot, and he was huge. Like Hulk, smash muscle—huge. He looked at me with bright blue eyes that were so blue, they could pass as contacts and dark, thick lashes. I drew my eyes down to his piercings, one nose ring, and two lip rings that were sitting next to each other. And just as I was looked at his lips, I saw his tongue draw out and lick across his lower one. Smirking at me, while showing a tongue piercing and straight white teeth that were framed by dimpled cheeks. I couldn't deal with how hot this man was. Couldn't even put together the words that would justify him. I would have said he could be a model, but when you feel the energy that surrounds him and how he held himself, you just knew, that there was not a model-like bone in his sexy damn body.

Before I knew it, I noticed I'd been staring a little too long and began feeling that familiar pull that I felt deep in my belly because I'd felt it before. I'd just never been interested in giving it away— until now. I dragged my hungry eyes away from him before I embarrassed myself. There was no way this man would ever be interested in me, I was not experienced enough for him. I carried on sipping my drink, glancing around the bar and then at the men sitting at this table. They were all good looking in their own way. My eyes stayed a little longer than what was necessary for a guy with shoulder-length hair and a beard—there's something seriously sexy, alluring, and dangerous about him. But he didn't appeal to me the way the beautifully tattooed and pierced monster appealed to me. Something stirred in my belly, telling me that these men were no good, but I was on a mission.

I dragged my eyes back to—I think Zane said that his name was Ade. Dropping my eyes to the leather vest he was wearing, I noticed below where it read *'Vice President'* on the front left, there was a 1% patch and then a crossbones patch. A cut, I think that was what they called it. A cut was a leather vest that all men who were a part of an MC wore. It identified membership of their respective club and territorial location.

Bringing my eyes back, I was surprised to see him still looking at me and with so much intensity that it made me squirm. Those eyes were going to haunt me. When I looked into them, I felt the darkness seeping from the depths of his irises, and it terrified me. It was as though they had seen things that no one should ever have to. I was a strong believer in the saying, *"Your eyes are the windows to one's soul,"* and this man's soul, felt almost demonic. Judging by the way he was looking at me, he was beautifully menacing. I looked away quickly, drinking my drink and pulling myself out of the trance he had trapped me. A trance that he managed to hook me in without so much as speaking a word to me.

I really am drunk.

Everything was beginning to spin a little. I noticed out of the corner of my eye that Vicky and Blake were all over each other, I roll my eyes to myself. She hadn't wasted any time at all. They stopped what they were doing, Vicky stood, straightening herself up.

"Do you want to come?" she whispered into my ear.

I looked at her feeling a little confused. I didn't want to go, especially if I was going to be third wheeling it.

"Where?" I asked. Feeling like my plan to get rowdy was stepping into desperate territory.

Blake pulled his face down between Vicky's and mine, looking into his lazy eyes and—my God, this man had player written all over his face.

He simply replied, "On Vicky's face."

My eyebrows shot up as I laughed at his crass mouth and Vicky's eyes roll to the back of her head. I took a second glance to Ade, who was sitting opposite me, only to see an almost naked skank spread out across his lap.

Gross.

I looked back to Blake. "Okay."

Walking into the hotel, Vicky tried to give me a pep talk. Obviously, I didn't want to do anything with Vicky, but I did with Blake, just for fun. I promised myself a good time, and that was what was going to happen…I hoped.

CHAPTER 2

ADE NIXON

Dirt. That was all I was fucking thinking with this slut's tongue down my throat. *Why had I done it?* The feelings Kalie was giving me had me feeling fucked-up. I was never *that* interested in fucking a girl, especially with just one glance. What I did for the club and the COA (Confederation of Assassins) had me shutting my feelings off a long time ago. Although, my childhood also had an impact on my feelings—or lack thereof.

Below my Vice President and 1% patch was a crossbones patch, which meant that I did the majority of dirty work when it came to our enemies.

Was I proud of my kills? *No.*

But did I care? *Fuck no.*

And that was why I needed a distraction from those fucking alluring green eyes. They pulled me in, hook, line, and sinker. Her eyes were like lasers, melting through the ice wall that had been present most of my life, and that scared the fucking shit out of me.

I pushed the slut off my lap with such force that it had her stumbling to the ground, and looked up to Zane, who had a cocky smirk on his face.

"What?" I spat at him.

"Oh, nothing bro, nothing at all." He tipped his drink up to his mouth around a smile.

I narrowed my eyes at him before noticing that Blake, Vicky, and green eyes were gone.

"Fuck," I grunted to myself. "Where did they fucking go?" I asked around the table.

Harvey laughed. "Bro, Blake took them both. Fucking felt that shit right down into my soul."

I pushed my chair back and made my way out the door while listening to the chuckling coming from the boys behind me. I'd deal with them later.

I began dialing Blake's phone on my way out.

Fuck, I was going to kill this fool if he had touched her.

KALIE - ROSE

I was standing in front of the bed when Blake handed me a glass. I had taken a long drink before he pulled my chin up to meet his lips. When his warm lips touched mine, I felt the alcohol take over. The kiss was hot, I guessed. Trevor and I had never really kissed. As stupid as that sounded, I had no point of reference to go by. But I was always too scared because kissing always led to him trying to get me naked.

I moaned into Blake's mouth as I felt myself slowly warming up to the situation. He picked me up, wrapping my legs around his waist and threw me onto the bed. I laughed as the alcohol hit me at full force.

I wanted this to happen.

"Have any limits?" he asked both of us. I was spread out on his bed, Vicky was still standing.

I nodded my head. "I'm a virgin, and I want to keep it that way. Anything else, I'm fine with," I replied with certainty.

I thought over my words, I really hoped he didn't take that too literally, it didn't mean he could go back door. I meant that I could play with him and he me.

"Are you sure you want to do this, Kalie? You can stop anytime. Okay?" he responded, which took me back a little. I warmed up to him even more because he was actually a decent person.

"Thanks, Blake, but I'm sure."

I continued looking at him, internally working myself up to get this started. He nodded with a small smile, throwing Vicky onto the bed with me. Standing for a few seconds, he looked at us before crawling up the bed and over the top of me. I swallowed, sliding myself down the silky sheets.

What have you gotten yourself into Kalie?

He had his fists on each side of my head, smiling down at me. Cocking his head to the side, he pushed my legs open with his, which resulted in his groin pushing into me, right between my legs. My face heated instantly from the bold move, and just when I thought this situation could not get any hotter, he leaned down to my neck, licking me from my collarbone up to just below my ear, then bit down. He raised my dress above my head while beginning to pull my bra and panties off. Slowly he started sucking on my nipples. I was panting a little again.

He moved over to Vicky, beginning to undress her, sucking on both her nipples and pulling her panties down her legs. I watched as his head began to go lower down to her sweet spot. When he latched on, her head flew back. I took that as my cue to—do something. So I got in between his legs and took him deep in my mouth. Oral sex was about as far as it ever went with my ex Trevor and me. Never thought I'd hear the day when a man complained about being sucked off too much. It was what we'd done instead of sex, it did get old fast with him, though. I went down on him more than he did me. That was okay, considering he wasn't very good at it. I had to constantly remind him that my clit wasn't fucking chewing gum.

After hearing Vicky come out of her daze, I popped him out of my mouth and moved back to the head of the bed. Blake moved his body back to mine, opening my legs.

Please don't chew.

Please don't chew.

And just as he was about to go downtown, his phone rang. I slumped my head back, blowing my hair away from my face. I needed a release. The look Ade was giving me earlier was directed right at my center.

"What?" he snapped at the person on the phone.

"Oh yeah? Is that right, *Ade*?" He chuckled, looking over at me.

"Oh, trust me, brother, I'm almost one hundred percent positive she'll be worth it. Looking at the position she's in now. All pink and wet, waiting for my tongue to slide all over that sweet pussy. Oh, and did I mention she's a virgin?" He laughed while throwing his phone back onto the bed. I couldn't believe he'd just outed me as a virgin. *Fuck.*

"I can't believe you told some random guy about my virginity," I said as I was pulling on my dress.

"Trust me, baby, he's not going to be some random guy for much longer."

I was pulling my hair out of the back of my dress when the door burst open with Ade storming directly toward me in all his beautiful glory. Even when he was mad—*and boy was he mad*—he was still beautiful. He picked me up and threw me over his shoulder.

"Oh my God. What are you doing?" I protested as he began walking out the door. "Seriously? You're not going to grunt or bang on your chest too, are you?"

He didn't answer, so I decided I'd wait until he put me down. This was so humiliating.

Once we reached the underground car park, he placed me down to my feet. I brushed my hair out of my face, narrowing my eyes at him. Which was brave considering he was a whole foot taller than I was and wider than the average heavyweight bodybuilder.

"What the hell was that about?" I asked him.

He matched my stare and I noticed his jaw ticking.

"*That,* was me saving you from the biggest mistake you *almost* made."

I laughed at him. "Why would you actually care? *I don't even know you!*" I yelled.

He walked to his bike, passing me his helmet.

"Get on the bike Kalie, I'll take you home."

I shook my head vigorously. "Nope. There's no way I'm getting on that," I replied. I'd always been terrified of bikes. I witnessed a bad car accident one time that involved a bike, and ever since that time, I've not managed to be near them. Not that I'd actually had the opportunity arise. He looked to me, so obviously annoyed.

"It's this," he waves to his bike with a bored expression, "or you're staying with me. What will it be?" he asked.

I felt as though that had a double meaning.

"I'll stay with you."

I watched as his face softened a little. He took hold of my hand and led me back to the elevator.

Well, you've found trouble now, Kalie.

Walking into his room, I was feeling a lot soberer than I wanted to. I guessed that was a good thing, now I could appreciate him more through calm eyes. I looked down at my hand and saw he was still holding onto it.

"You want anything to drink? And by drink, I mean water," he asked while walking into the kitchen, leaving me standing there awkwardly in the living room.

"Yes, please."

He walked back into the living room, handing me a glass of water, and then looked down at me.

"You get into an awful lot of trouble for a virgin," he said casually, putting his hands into his pockets.

"Hmm…I came here a little reckless, I guess," I responded, taking a few small sips of my water.

He walked over to the sofa, patting the spot next to him. When I didn't move, he rolled his eyes and I swear to God that it was the sexiest eye roll I'd ever witnessed.

"Sit down, Kalie."

Walking to the sofa, I sit beside him.

"Why did you come and take me away from Blake and Vicky? You know, I sort of wanted to be there," I said a little too honestly.

He chuckled and narrowed his eyes at me. "Don't ask me that."

I widened my eyes at his clipped tone.

"Why were you feeling reckless?" he asked, spreading his legs out in front of him and running his index finger across his upper lip.

Goddammit, the man was delicious.

"I just got dumped. It seems my virtue is sort of getting in the way. I wanted to get it over with if you will. Not with Blake, though, with someone...hot. He has to be..." I trailed off because actually, I wasn't making any sense. I was sort of sounding like a predator, or worse—sounding like Vicky. "Let's change the subject. Why did you come and play hero with me?" I responded, licking my lips nervously. He made me nervous.

Looking at me with his jaw clenched tight, and his eyes narrowed, he smirked, placing his drink down on the coffee table in front of him.

"Want me to help you with that?" he asked mischievously with a half-smile.

I snort. "What? Are you serious?" Taking a long, nervous, pull of my water, I looked up.

Shit! This was not part of the plan.

However, I came here on a mission. He was hot, that was a plus. Sure, a biker was never part of my plan, but I needed to get this taken care of. At least I knew he wouldn't expect anything from me, he screamed *'emotionally unattached.'* He was, well, he was perfect. I wished I could've said that we have some sort of great chemistry or some romantic crap like that, but we just didn't. I just wouldn't have minded having sex with him, even if it was my first time. Hell, I thought it would be better than most, with their *sometimes-tragic* first-time stories.

He studied my face for a few seconds before smiling and looking down to the floor with a shrug. "Sure, why fucking not." His eyes were glistening with mischief.

I smiled, putting my glass on the table, shrugging back to him. "Okay."

He laughed and grabbed onto my hand, pulling me over to him. He brushed a few of my stray hairs away from my face.

"You sure?" he asked out of complete sincerity.

I gulped and nodded my head. "Yes, yup. I'm sure."

Wrapping his hand around the back of my neck, I glanced down to his plump lips. He must have seen me looking because he half smiled. Showing perfectly straight, white teeth, then he swiped his tongue over his lips. Smiling I looked up into his eyes, right before he brought his lips to meet mine.

His lips were perfect, warm and soft. He ran his tongue over my bottom lip, before dipping it back into my mouth to dance with my own. He laced my tongue with his, in soft strokes, feeling the ball from his tongue ring brush over mine. I moaned into his mouth quietly, noting that I was more worked up about this man than I was with Blake and Vicky. I was horny, that was a given. It was hard not to be when this perfectly sexy, rough, bad boy, was licking and sucking on my lip as if it was his favorite ice-cream.

He began to undress me, slowly removing my clothes. I dropped my arms and let him run the fabric over them until my dress fell to the floor in a pool at my feet. I pulled his MC cut and T-shirt off, eager to see him in all his naked glory.

When I finally did have him naked—apart from his loose jeans, and red and white, flat baseball cap. Which, by the way, only added to his swagger—I almost gasped out in complete awe. I knew right then, that every male I'd seen before him, and every man I would see after would look like shit in comparison.

Sweet Lord have mercy.

His whole body was entirely covered in ink, and underneath all of that art was a damn masterpiece of a body. I was never one to admire a man's body, or pick one man over another just because he had a six-pack. But that, right there, I would have thrown myself under a bus for.

Okay, that was a little melodramatic.

However, he was extremely attractive. So much so it blew my mind. How was it fair for one man to have the body, the face, and the danger that all women secretly craved? I was stunned.

He slowly walked to the bed, unbuckling his belt and undoing the button of his jeans. I looked over to him while wiping my lips because they were feeling a little swollen by this stage. He took a slow sweep of me, from my head down to my toes before licking his lips and nudging his head toward the bed. I walked to him in my black lace panties and bra.

"Why are you so eager for this?" I managed to squeeze out.

He chuckled, throwing his head back, showing me his perfect smile.

God, I want to know how those rings felt in-between my legs. I was not even going to lie.

He looked back down at me. "Eager? I wouldn't say that, babe. You said you were on a mission, and I'd hate for some selfish loser to show you any less of a good time."

I laughed at his honesty because it was refreshing. I couldn't stand men that sweet-talked you in an effort to get into your pants.

He reached down and picked me up, so I wrapped my legs around his waist, my arms around his neck.

"I'm just going to go out and ask this, but has anyone ever told you how extremely good looking you are?" I asked. My head tilted so I could look over his chiseled face.

He shook his head with a small smile. "I've never had *good looking*. No."

He brought my face down to his, kissing me again and moving me onto the bed. He made his way over the top of me, settling in between my legs, kissing me down my neck. I felt the metal of his tongue ring slide down my neck, and I started to pant embarrassingly hard with need. I always thought that sex, for your first time, would be rushed and dysfunctional, but Ade seemed to be taking his time, enjoying me, by slowly ravishing me. He ran his hand over my bra, slipping it underneath and squeezing my nipple. The pain had pleasure in it, which was confusing. *How could something that should hurt, feel so good?* These feelings were all new to me. Trevor wasn't interested in doing foreplay activities. Unless he was getting sex, he said there was no point.

Ade slid his hand around to my back without breaking our kiss, unlatching my bra in one swift move and throwing it to the floor. I threw my arms up above my head as he leaned up on his elbows, looking down at me.

"You're gorgeous. You know that, right? I wouldn't do this if you weren't. Shallow? I know. But it is what it is."

I laughed. "Oh boy, you're brutally honest. You do know that, right?" I answered and he smiled a slow, sexy smile.

"Well yes, I've been told that many times."

Bringing his face back down to mine, he slowly slid his lips down to my breasts, sucking on one of them while tugging on the other with his fingers. I arched my back and bit down on my lip. He began going down lower...and lower...

Please don't chew.

Please don't chew.

...slowly, licking and nibbling his way down.

Once Ade's mouth landed on my most sensitive and almost untouched part of my body, I could feel his expertise. This should have worried me, but it was hard for me to think of anything else when the way his tongue slid up and down my slit was the most intense feeling I'd ever felt. I moaned out in pleasure, grasping the feeling of his wet tongue expertly sliding up and around my clit in pressured circles. When I felt his finger slip into me, then push on my front wall inside me, the feeling intensified.

He stopped, and I almost wanted to kick him in the face. He looked up at me, eyes hooded and his hat flipped backward.

"Get up on your elbows, Kalie. I want you to watch this go down," he told me with a smirk.

After I'd propped myself up on my elbows, my hair sprawled out in front of me, I watched him in fascination. Throwing my head back as he made my body explode in front of my very eyes, I bit down on my lower lip, sucking in a breath as my body tensed around his finger.

"Let it go, baby," Ade grumbled from between my thighs.

As if on command, I exploded around his fingers.

Coming down from the best oral I'd ever had, he stood, pulling his jeans down and making his way back up to me, pushing me with his body to lie down on my back. He placed a single soft kiss on my lips, wrapping his fingers with mine, and then popping them above my head. I felt his thick head at my opening before he eased his way into me slowly. Once he felt the barrier, he looked down at me.

"You good?"

I nodded my head, unable to create any words as he pushed into me in one hard thrust. I cried out a little and bit down onto his shoulder. I was sure

I'd drawn blood because it fucking hurt that much that I didn't care.

"Fuck," he mumbled, letting me slowly widen out for him as much as I could.

"I need to move now, babe. You good with that?"

I nodded my head again, unable to speak. The pain—*oh my God, the fucking pain*—fucking hurt like a motherfucker. It was nothing like what I'd read in my romance novels.

Yeah? You don't say. And billionaires looked like Donald Trump in real life, definitely not like Christian Grey.

There was no warming up then having a mind-blowing orgasm. Lies, all lies. All I wanted to do was push him out of me, so I could go home and cry about how painful it was.

Shit.

"Give me a minute," I squeaked, scrunching up my face. He laughed a small laugh.

"That sore, huh? You wanna stop?" he asked. Not in an *'I'll be an asshole to you if you said yes'* kind of way, but in an *'I couldn't really give a fuck'* sort of way.

I shook my head. "No, definitely not. Sorry. I guess this isn't how things usually pan out when you take a girl home."

Blushing with embarrassment, he swiped my hair out of my face and caressed my cheek.

"Maybe not, no. But if you want me to stop, tell me now. And be honest with me."

I looked into his eyes, and I didn't know why, but I got the feeling he was not usually this nice with his '*girls.*'

"Thanks, but I'm good." I smiled up at him.

Noticing it felt a little better down there, just a little uncomfortable, I began to grind against him. He groaned a deep guttural groan into the crook of my neck before pushing back into me softly. He slowly pulled out and I swear to God it felt as though there was a razor blade down there. I winced but swallowed the pain. By the third thrust, I felt the pain start to dissipate and pleasure began to take over. Grasping onto my thigh, he hitched it up onto his hip and pulled me in, deeper and deeper. His sex skills were insanely perfect. It was as though he was built to pleasure women.

God must be a woman. There was no way a man would create someone like Ade.

With every thrust and every hit, he rubbed his thick head against my g-spot; noting that something did not feel natural down there. He pushed in softly, and pulled out, the rhythm in which he was caressing my walls was addictive. With every extract of his long thick piece, I felt the pull of pressure when he slid out of me. I began to feel that familiar climb, my breath hitched and I attempted to suck in air. He brought his face down to mine, pulling my lip into his mouth.

"Don't fight it, Kalie. Come all over my cock, baby."

Holy fucking shit.

My toes curled and my eyes rolled back when I reached that perfect peak of my orgasm. I rode it out, letting it take control of my body. With my body shaking while I came down, I felt him pulse inside of me. He dropped down, leaving his weight on me briefly before rolling off.

Out of insecurity, I pulled the sheet up to surround me.

CHAPTER 3

"Are you okay?" I asked.

If I could, I would have told him that it was the most amazing experience I'd ever had. I could not have asked for a better first time.

"Yeah, I'm good," he replied in a clipped tone.

He pulled his jeans back on and stood from the bed, looked at me while he threw his red and white flat baseball cap back on. I tried not to perve too much at him, but my God, he looked incredible. His eyes were set in stone, with absolutely no emotion in them whatsoever. And I internally winced from the look he was giving me.

"I can go?" I questioned, looking around the room for my clothes. His face fell and he stopped what he was doing.

"Don't. Just give me a minute. I shouldn't have done that, it was a weak move. Get into bed. I'll be back in a second." He came over, kissed me on the head and walked out of the hotel room.

Should I have told him to put a shirt on?

He shouldn't be walking around in low, dark denim jeans, with nothing else on but his flat baseball cap. He would give women a heart attack. That encounter was weird, the man did not care about how blunt he was, and he sure as hell didn't care about hiding his true feelings. He was more than a little intimidating.

ADE NIXON

Closing the hotel door, I walked out to the lobby and made my way into the reception area. Noticing a young blonde behind the counter, I nudged my head up to her.

"What's up? Where can I get some ice?"

I watched a blush spread across her face. Licking her lips before pulling her tongue back into her mouth, she swept me from head to toe. I watched the movement of what she was doing and I had to laugh to myself.

Why chicks think doing that shit was cute, was fucking lost on me. It just made me want to choke them—how I chose to choke them was a different story. I smiled at her when she reached my eyes again.

"You can get some at the bar," she responded, tilting her head to the side.

I tapped the counter a couple times and began walking over to the bar. After grabbing a bucket of ice and some vodka, I made my way back into the hotel room.

Opening the door, I saw Kalie lying down. She was still awake, but looked a bit out of place, because she was. I'd never been with someone as innocent as she was, and I was not talking about her virginity. I'd taken a few of those in my teen years. No, I was talking about her as a person. She was so pure and innocent and it shone through her. She was like a fucking angel. Way too good to be in my bed. I'd taken advantage of the situation, because, well, I was me.

She gets up from the bed, her light brown hair was sitting naturally around her make-up-less face. She was so fucking beautiful that it stirred something deep in my dark soul, and that alone was a lethal combination. I closed the door behind me.

"Hey!" She smiled, sitting up on the bed. "What's that?" she asked, pointing to the bucket.

I half smirked at her. "Oh, this?" I raised my eyebrows. "This is your next orgasm."

Her eyes bugged out, and I couldn't help but laugh at her. She was fucking cute.

"Relax baby. You still sore?" I asked. Trying to look like I gave a fuck, which I didn't.

She shook her head with the same shocked look still on her face. My smirk turned into a slow smile while maintaining eye contact. I licked my lips and started running my eyes up and down her body.

"Lie down. This is not over till the sun comes up."

Walking over to her, I dropped the bucket and vodka down on the table. Unbuckling my belt buckle, I crawled over her body on the bed. I looked down to her plump, perfect, pink lips and her tongue came out, licking the bottom one. My eyes turned dark as I looked up at her, running my thumb over her bottom lip.

"Don't do that."

She dropped her lip and started to pull my jeans down. I let her—it would've been rude not too. When her eyes fell to my dick, I saw her face register with understanding.

"What? What—"

"It's a Prince Albert."

She looked up under her long lashes in shock.

I burst out laughing. As soon as she noticed that I was making fun of her, she smiled.

"Don't laugh at me. I'm serious. Is that not sore?"

I shake my head. "No, it's not. Come here."

I dragged her down the bed by her legs, and she screamed out in laughter. Wishing I could have said that laughter had reached into my heart or some corny shit like that, but all it reached was the nerve endings to my dick. I dragged my face down her body, not missing a single breath every time I licked her skin. I flipped my hat around backward, popped her leg onto my shoulder while spreading her other one open. Flicking my tongue over her clit and circling it around in perfect, slow, circular motions, her back was arching off the bed. Pushing her tits up in the air, and showing her chest levels rising and falling, she grabs my shoulder. And just when I felt her pussy clench around my tongue, I stopped.

"Oh my God!" she moaned out in frustration.

Placing her legs back down and smiling up at her, I pulled her back down the bed. Then I picked up some ice cubes out of the bucket and began slowly dragging them down her body, over her perfect fucking tits and down over her clit before slipping them up into her pussy. She yelped out at the contact of ice sliding inside her before lying back down and letting me have my way with her.

Taking a long pull of the vodka, and then pouring it over her tits all the way down to her pussy, I took another drink. I squirted some vodka into her mouth from mine, kissing her briefly. Before licking all over her body, and following my trail of vodka, I rolled her nipples a little roughly, and then slammed into her in one hard thrust. Her eyes shot open at the sudden contact before they rolled back into her head. Flipping her over onto her stomach, and pulling her up by her hips so she was face down and ass up, I then ease my way back into her again. This was the sexiest fucking view I'd ever seen, and I'd seen some amazing stuff. Her curves were fucking perfect, a little waist with the dog bone shape.

Wrapping her hair around my wrist, I pounded into her deeply. I let go of her hair and grasped her neck with my hand, applying light pressure and testing her boundaries. She let me have it, calling out a soft, "Yes," as her permission for me to continue. I gripped a little tighter, my whole hand wrapping around her tiny neck. The wetness of our sweat rubbed over each other, and just as I felt her tense up around my cock, I flipped her back over and pushed inside her missionary position. Starting slow, I pushed in so deep that she could feel me rubbing up against her clit. Bringing my head down, I sucked on her nipple, and with my other hand I grasped onto her hair. I felt her pussy tighten up around me, and her fingers were digging into my shoulder. Lifting her leg up, I propped it on my hip and ground into her until she was screaming and I'd emptied myself into her tight, sexy, sweet pussy.

I rolled off her and got up, pulling on my jeans but leaving them unbuttoned. "You sore?"

She turned red and nodded her head. "Yeah, I am."

Leaning over the bed, I grasped her chin a little tightly and pulled her to my lips. "I'll run a bath for you."

Before she could protest, I walked into the bathroom and began to fill the bathtub. I sat on the edge, pouring in the bubble bath that was situated on the side of the tub, and I think about what just happened. I'd had sex, a lot, but I was safe, always wearing condoms and getting check-ups every month or so. Sex had always been *just sex* for me, nothing more and nothing less, just a simple deed you were doing for each other to get to where you wanted.

With Kalie though, it was a little different. Different in a way that I didn't want to hurt her when fucking her brains out. I usually needed to cross some sort of line, it got my dick hard to see a woman grovel on her knees with a gag in her mouth. I wanted to take care of Kalie though, that was why I was in there running this fucking bath like a pussy whipped bitch.

She walked into the bathroom with the sheet wrapped around her small curvy figure, her long sex hair messy around her face, cheeks pink and her emerald green eyes shining brightly. I smiled a little smile and patted the bath tub's side.

"Get in the tub."

She smiled and pulled her bottom lip into her mouth. For the first time ever, I found that little motion the sexiest fucking shit ever.

"Are you coming in too?" she asked shyly.

I tilted my head at her. "Do you want me to?"

She looked away with a shy smile and nodded.

I pulled down my jeans and got into the bath, running my wet hands over my hair and making it stand up. I didn't usually wear it this long. It was not long, as in ponytail long, but it was long enough to look messy every time I didn't wear a cap, and it stuck up in natural fucking spikes. It basically was annoying.

She dropped the sheet and I ran my eyes over her body slowly from her head, down to her toes, and then back up again. When I reached her eyes, hers drifted to the side and looked down to the ground.

"Don't be shy, Kalie. Your body is fucking banging. It's what wet dreams are made of. Now get in the fucking tub."

She quickly walked over and sunk into the tub opposite me. When I noticed she was staying as far on that side of the tub as was possible, I rolled my eyes and latched onto her hand pulling her over to me. She screeched at the water flowing over the side of the tub, making me laugh. She turned her back and lied straight out in front of me. Kissing her head softly before grabbing the soap, and squeezing some into the palm of my hand, I started washing her.

"Where are you from?" I asked, running my hand over her smooth, toned stomach.

"Um, Colorado but..." I slide my hands over her tits slowly, squeezing her nipple tightly. "I live in Hollywood Hills at the moment," she answered as her breath picked up.

"Oh?" I said sarcastically. "What do you do in The Hills?" Sliding my hand down the front of her, and rubbing up her thighs, her chest moved up and down rapidly.

"I was—I was a...um...a dancer. *Shit.*" I held my thumb to her clit while sliding two fingers inside her swiftly.

"Something tells me, you're not a stripper."

"Nope, no way. Street, hip-hop, whatever you want to call it. I dance for my clients in their music videos." She began grinding against my hand, and a smile pulled at my mouth.

Atta girl.

"That's pretty fucking hot."

I slid my fingers out of her and she spun around to look at me, obviously flustered.

"That's not fair," she responded, almost pouting.

I brought my fingers to my mouth and ran my tongue around them while smiling at her. "Don't pout, baby."

She moved to turn around and lie back on my chest, but I picked her up, spinning her back around to face me. She spread her legs open on either side of me and slowly lowered herself on my dick. I leaned my head back on the bath, and biting down on my lip. She followed the motion before bringing her face down to mine, licking and sucking on my lip. I grasped her hips and slowly guided her into riding my cock. Wrapping her arm around my neck, she got into the motion of things and begun to ride it like a pro. Gripping her hips a little tightly, with every pull of her pussy it brought me closer and closer. I looked up to her, wrapped my hand around the back of her neck and pulled her face back down to mine while licking her lip and pulling her tongue in with mine. I felt her clench around my dick, so I reached up and grasped her neck, pushing hard thrusts into her. In one movement, I felt her pulse all around my cock while it twitched its release inside of her. She let go and slumped all her weight on me. We laid there for a few minutes while catching our breath.

"The bath's cold," she said from on top of me, her voice vibrating through my chest.

"I know," I replied a little hoarsely.

I cough. "Come on." Tapping her leg.

She peeled her body off me, stepped out of the bath, wrapping a towel around her body and letting her bun down. I stood there for a few seconds just watching her before I followed suit. We both slide into bed, and I pulled her up against me kissing her head. I had this foreign need to take care of this girl, like a delicate flower or something precious.

What the fuck was that?

It was a good thing that this would be the last time I'd see her, she made me feel things that a man in my position should never feel.

CHAPTER 4

KALIE - ROSE

Attempting to open my eyes, I fail. They were sticky shut and I couldn't feel any of my limbs.

"Holy crap," I groaned while trying to move myself out of the bed, but I gave up.

I looked over to Ade and noticed that he was still crashed out. My God he was perfect. I knew girls said that about every man, but this man really was. His hair was dark, sitting messy and perfect up around his head—short, but longish on top. He had the most amazing jaw structure that I'd ever seen. Tilting my head to the side, I looked at his long lashes that flowed out along his face.

"Oh my God," I whispered. "You're out of this world."

His nose ring, two lip piercings and the mass off tattoos added to his intrigue. He was the man that every woman wanted. He was worth the danger you knew surrounded him. I blew out my breath, making my hair fluff up and his blue eyes suddenly opened. He took hold of my hips, pulling me over so I was straddling him, and nudged his head into my neck. I squealed out in surprise, slapping his chest. Being extremely ticklish and sensitive, and I hated being tickled. I don't find it funny and I don't find it cute. I will punch you in the face if you tickle me.

He wrapped his massive arm around my waist, pulling me down and kissing me briefly.

"I gotta go, babe. Hate to leave you like this." My face dropped for a second before I could collect myself. "No, of course, I'll go wake up Vicky."

He paused for a second, his face going serious. "I could take you home, and then I'll go."

I laughed, jumping off him, and beginning to collect my things together. And by things, I meant my panties.

"Don't be stupid, they're only a few doors down." After putting my clothes back on, I looked over to him on the bed where he was spread out under the white sheet. "Thanks, though, really." I was confused as to what I was supposed to say to him.

Should I thank him for accepting my virginity?

Or thank him for accepting my virginity, then fucking my body into oblivion?

I just knew that there would be no other man in my life that would match him. He was too perfect. He laughed while getting up and making his way to me.

"Why are you thanking me Kalie?" he asked while brushing a strand of hair off my face. "For robbing you of you of your virtue?"

"Hardly, I gave it to you on a silver platter."

I laughed and began making my way to the door until I felt my hand hit the door handle and I turned.

He looked over at me, eyes narrowed and a half smile appeared on his face.

"Bye Kalie."

I smiled at him. "What's your real name? Is Ade short for something?"

His eyes darkened for a brief second.

"Aiden," he replied coldly.

"Okay, bye Aiden," I said, and before he could protest me using his real name, I shut the door behind me.

ADE NIXON

Sixteen Years Ago

"Aidan! Get the fuck in here boy," my pops yelled at me from the bar in the clubhouse. I always hated it when he'd had too much to drink. But when I came here, I knew I always saw Zane and Blake and I looked forward to that fact.

"Yeah?" I asked nervously as I ran into the bar.

My dad was a hard man. He had been known to throw in a beating every now and then.

"Pincher over here seems to think that you couldn't take Zane down in the ring." He laughed, bringing a cigarette up to his mouth to light. He had smoked all his fucking life. Why hadn't one of those cancer sticks killed him already?

"I want you to prove him wrong."

Pincher looked over to my dad. "I wasn't meaning to actually put them in the ring. It was just a statement." My Uncle Pincher and his big mouth—he was harmless, and probably cared more about me than my own father did. I never really bonded with him, I'd never met anyone from his side of the family either, he was like a ghost to me.

My dad laughed while lighting his smoke. "No such thing as a statement, brother. Go wrap yourself up, Son."

I looked over to Zane and nodded my head. I really didn't want to fucking do that. We fight, yeah, but not each other.

I hear my Uncle Pincher yell, "He's just a boy, Frank. They both are."

Frank, my dad, laughed. "Thirteen's not a boy, thirteen is basically a man. After he's done knocking Zane's block off, he can take Cindy into one of the back rooms. Break him in right."

I looked over to my Uncle Dave and he smiled. Uncle Dave was the president of Sinful Souls MC and Zane's dad. I knew he wouldn't do anything to *actually* hurt one of us, so I thought that this must be okay.

Walking into the back room I started getting the wraps out when Abby came in with a sad look on her face.

"Don't be sad, Abby. I won't hit him too hard." I winked at her.

She shook her head. "Don't joke about this, Ade." She walked up to me, taking the wraps out of my hand as she began to pull them out and wrap them around my wrist. I looked into her eyes.

"What's wrong, Abby? How's this any different to the fights we usually have? I love Zane like a

brother. There's no way we could kill each other."
She smirked a little and brought her green eyes up
to meet my blue. "I'm not worried about you,
bear..." I laughed at her nickname for me in
between her pausing, "I'm more concerned about
Zane. If you beat him, Uncle Dave will be
disappointed. Zane has a lot to live up to in the
club."

I looked at her, pulling my hand out of her
grasp. "Are you asking me to throw it in for him?"

She sighs. "Yes, Aidan. Look at the bigger picture
here. We all know you can beat him with one
punch, but there's more on the line than pride."
She patted my shoulder. "Please just think about
it," she finishes as she spun around and walked
out.

For an eleven-year-old, she sure packed a lot of
knowledge. She was street smart, the kind of street
smart that only comes to you by living in hell. I
ripped off my shirt and warmed up my body. I had
always been a buff young fella. When I started
walking, Dad had me sparring with him.
Continuing out to the ring, I saw Zane standing to
the side with a blank look on his face. He knew
what my hands could do, he'd seen it firsthand
many times. It was at that exact moment that I
knew I could not let myself win. Walking up to him

and punching fists, I started bouncing around his body, light on my feet.

"Do it," I mouthed to him.

I knew once I let this happen, my dad was going to beat my ass, but I would rather get my ass beaten than let Zane have the shame over his head. He looked at me sideways, narrowing his eyes in confusing.

"Do. It." I mouthed again with a little more pronunciation while bouncing around in front of each other.

Understanding sets in as he drew his hand back, and like every other time this happened, the movement played out in slow-mo in my head, which resulted in me being a lot quicker than your average Joe. I let it hit me, his fist connecting square with my jaw. That was the first time I'd ever been touched in a fight that didn't include my dad. I was getting back up when I heard Aunt Annabelle yelling while walking up to us.

"David Mathews! Get those boys out of there now! I don't care what you do with your club, but if you throw my boys in that ring again, I'll cut your balls so deep you will be pissing out your mouth for a week. *Are we understood*?"

For the first time ever, Uncle David looked like he'd just shat himself. The thought made me laugh. Aunt Annabelle was gentle and graceful. She wore cardigans and had a soft angelic face. Therefore, the words that had just come out of her mouth shocked me.

"Come here boys. Aidan, come and get cleaned up hon," she said, dragging us out of the ring.

She turned her head to my dad and pointed her finger. "Frank Nixon, you should be ashamed of yourself. You may be Sargent at Arms of this club, but he's your *son*. You sick, twisted, man." While storming off with both Zane and me on her heels, it was at that moment that I knew Aunt Annabelle must be an angel. *A potty-mouthed angel.*

Present Day

Pulling my mind out of my brief memory lapse, I make my way back to bed. I don't know why hearing my full name triggers memories, maybe it's because my dad always used it—he made it filthy. Up until I was thirteen, I was Aidan Nixon. Now, I'm just Ade Nixon. Stepping into the shower, I let the water run down my head.

Fuck! Kalie is fucking out-of-this world-beautiful. I've never seen a woman with such raw, natural beauty. She doesn't even realize how bloody outstanding she is. I lean my head against the glass door, rubbing my hands through my hair, and before I know it, I'm stroking myself at the thought of her eyes looking up to me. I squeeze around my dick, thinking about those sweet, plump lips wrapped tightly around my cock. Her head bobbing up and down, and then just as I blow my load all over the glass, I think of those fucking eyes looking right up at me.

Those fucking eyes, they had me in a second.

"Fuck," I groan, turning the shower off.

What the fuck was that about? I haven't jacked off since I was thirteen.

Wrapping a towel around my waist, I walk out to my room and get changed. After throwing on my clothes, I gather my shit, ready to make my way back to Westbeach. I need to put myself under as many bitches as I can to get over this weekend. Kalie is going to haunt me forever—good fucking thing I'll never have to see her again.

KALIE - ROSE

Present Day

I wake up to Carter's annoying fucking alarm going nuts in his room.

"Carter!" I scream from my bed, trying to put my pillow over my head. I just want to go back to sleep and dream about Ade again. Spewing profanities, I get up out of bed and storm into Carter's room.

"Carter! Your fucking alarm is killing me!" I yell, walking to it and smashing it on the ground.

I look to the bed and see he's yet again, not alone.

Rolling my eyes. "Carter, I'm serious about the *falling off* thing. However, if it doesn't fall off, I might just cut it off. Sort your fucking alarm out. I don't shake my ass in front of MTV cameras all night to have to wake up to your psycho ass alarm." Storming off back to my room, and on my way there, I walk past the bathroom mirror and see my crazy hair all over the place. I groan just as I hear Carter laughing loudly.

"Shut up, Carter. You have no idea what the struggle is like with thick hair."

He laughs again before yelling, "Sorry, baby G, the only thick thing I'm experienced in, is the cock."

I slam my door, hard. I love Carter so much it hurts. But right now, I could slice his eyeballs open with a skillet knife.

What can I say, I love my sleep.

I slide back into bed, closing my eyes ready to pick up where I was so rudely interrupted. But after tossing and turning and trying to go back to sleep, I realize can't.

"Fuck my life," I moan getting back up out of bed in a little bit of a better mood.

I know I need to call Vicky, see what's going on with the wedding. I've seen Pipper a few times, but they were all times that she had come to The Hills, I haven't been to Westbeach in years.

"Fuck," I put my head into my hands.

I should have known that this was bound to happen. I was hoping I would at least have a boyfriend by now.

Can you hire wedding dates?

If not, I'm going to start a company.

You could make a small fortune out of that.

CHAPTER 5

ADE NIXON

"What do you think you're doing?" I say to Gretchen.

Gretchen is walking pussy. She means less than shit to me, but sometimes she gets her wires crossed.

"Ade, don't be mean," she pouts while placing her arm back across my chest. I scrunch up my face in disgust. I hate pouty, whining bitches.

I remove her arm and discard it over her side. "Get out, you know how this goes."

"I've been doing this same song and dance with you for years, Ade." She rolls her eyes and gets out of the bed. "One of these days, baby, you'll see that I'm right for you. For this life," she responds, pulling her long blonde hair into a ponytail before she shimmies her skinny ass back into her tight leather mini skirt.

I laugh, getting up and throwing on my jeans. "I will *never* make a whore my old lady. Get that through your over-peroxided head." I look at her with a glare. "Get out!"

She storms off, not even bothering to put the rest of her clothes on.

Making my way down to the bar, I need to find Zane. The last mission he had me on didn't end well. I pull out a seat next to him at the table.

"How did it go?" he asks.

"Not good," I reply, lighting up a cigarette. "He pissed me off. So I cut off his dick and shoved it down his throat, and then I shot him."

Zane looks over to me. "It was meant to be a clean kill, Ade. What happened to *clean kill*."

I look at him, blowing out smoke. "That became irrelevant once I found out that he raped a fucking sixteen-year-old girl. Fuck that, he got that shit easy."

Zane laughs, shaking his head. "Pull it in brother."

I stub my smoke out and look up to Ashley, our barmaid. She's been working for us for a few years now, no one has touched her, and we won't. She's too good a cook and bartender to let her go, but the girl has killer legs, though. She walks up to me in her tight little top and tight skirt. I bite down on my bottom lip and lean back on my seat, tilting my head to try and get a better look.

"Beer," I say, slowly dragging my eyes up to meet hers, hooded with need.

She looks and smiles her broad smile at me. "Hey now, don't be giving me those 'come fuck me' eyes, Ade Nixon. There's only so much of that I can take before a girl breaks all the rules." She winks and makes her way back to the bar. I'm still gazing at her with a smirk when Blake comes to sit at the table.

He laughs. "Bro, can you keep it in your pants for one whole week?"

I tip the bottle up to my lips. "I have no intention of doing that. Not all of us are whipped, so I don't *need* to keep it in my pants," I say while looking at both him and Zane.

They both laugh before Zane says, "Really? I seem to recall Alaina whipping you and I both, at the same time."

I laugh and shake my head. "Touché. How is my girl?" I ask, smirking at him.

I love playing this game with him. It's always been too easy to work him up where Alaina was concerned. He and I have both loved her from day one—which never happens for either of us—but he was *in* love with her. At first, I wanted to fuck the shit out of her, but that was before I recognized the bond she and I held. It was more of a brother and sister bond. One where the brother will occasionally eye fuck you every now and then. It then turned into one of my favorite things to do when I saw how worked up Zane would get.

He narrows his eyes, throwing me a disgusted look. "Back down, Ade." I laugh, tipping my drink to my lips.

"She's fine. Landon is keeping her on her toes, though."

His face lights up, talking about Landon and Alaina. Landon is Zane and Alaina's son and he's one fucking cute little dude. *Because he looks like his mother.*

"I'll come around and see her tonight," I say taking another pull of my drink.

Blake shakes his head. "I wouldn't. Vicky has her on all sorts of duties. She's turned into a mad woman planning this wedding. I thought that was what bridesmaids were for," he answers shaking his head. I see his face change, turning into a full Blake smirk.

"What Blake, spit it out," I say looking directly at him.

He laughs a loud roar of a laugh, clutching his stomach. I look to Zane, who looks like he may just hit Blake if he ever laughs like that again.

"Brother, you are in for a treat." He takes a long pull of his drink.

"Kalie is a bridesmaid."

Well, that wiped the smile off my face.

Fuck.

KALIE - ROSE

"Get this one!" Phoebe yells from the other side of the store.

I look over to it and scrunch up my face. "Phoebs, I don't want to look like I'm one of his whores."

Her face drops, along with the short skimpy dress she's was holding her hand. I walk over to her and pat her shoulders. "I'm sorry, what I meant to say was that it's a little short. I don't want to flash my vag to a whole club of bikers."

She laughs, putting the dress back on the rack. "No, you're right. Maybe I should get it," she answers, while admiring it on the rack.

I step in between her and the dress, shaking my head. "Nope, no way. Your brother is bad enough with you being around bikers...let alone, dressed in *that* around bikers."

She rolls her eyes. "He's literally the most annoying brother in history. He could even give Jacob a run for his money, and Jacob is fucking bad."

I laugh while we are walking out of the one hundredth shop we have been in today.

"That's true. Jacob loves his sister. He's been a bit better since Blake, though," I say, pulling my glasses down over my eyes.

"Yeah, I guess. I'm bringing Slade to the wedding." She smiles, in awe of her boyfriend.

"Is this the first time Blake is going to meet him?" I ask, stopping in my steps.

She nods her head. "Yes, I'm a little worried about that." She raises a single finger in innocence.

I laugh. "I'd be more than a *'little worried.'* At least, he's not a biker. And, at least, he's not Ryder Oakley." I laugh, shaking my head.

Her face drops to a frown. "Yeah, I guess."

Not many people know about Ryder and Phoebe's hot affair they had a couple of years ago, it ended quite badly so it's a good thing Blake doesn't know about it. Ryder Oakley is the biggest rock God of our time. Not only can the man sing, but he can play any instrument that's placed into his hands. He's the complete package. All tall, tattooed, muscles, and with the most sultry eyes I've ever seen. He's a big-time player, though, always with different women, and the paparazzi follow his every step.

"We'll get some lunch, and then I need to hit the gym. I'm dragging it out for as long as I can before I need to be in Westbeach."

She laughs. "Oh boy, this is going to be good. I've heard that he's been a little bad with the ladies lately. I think you have nothing to worry about."

She's referring to Ade.

I pull the door to our favorite café open. "Yeah, you're probably right."

I hope he doesn't remember me. What's the chances of him remembering me? He's probably been with hundreds of girls since then.

Dropping my shopping bags on the table, I twist my hair up into a messy top bun while I make my way into my room to throw on some workout clothes. My job alone would give any woman enough workout time, but all the extra exercise I do is for the sole purpose of eating more. You know energy in vs. energy out and all that.

"Carter, you home?" I yell while I strip down to my bra and panties, replacing my black lace bra for my sports one.

"Damn girl, if I were straight I would be tap'n that ass," he says, leaning against my doorframe.

I roll my eyes. "You and I both know that isn't true. I'm so scared about tomorrow that I'm going to sweat all my problems out at the gym."

He walks in to help me with pulling on my tight tank top. "Why are you going so early? Isn't the wedding this weekend?" I pick up my yoga pants and jump around, trying to get them past my fat ass.

"Yes, but Vicky is having a meltdown and begged me to come down earlier to help with all the things she needs help with. Also, it's the hen's night on Friday and there's no way I'm missing that."

I bend over to pick up the mess from clothes I left on the floor and Carter smacks my ass before replying, "And…what if Beyoncé called and she needed you on her video?" His eyebrows are raised.

I slip my shoes on and pick up my keys. "Then I'll need to tell her to call Sophie. She's just as good as me."

He scoffs. "No, she is not. Last time you gave Sophie to one of your clients, she went all diva on them."

Carter doesn't like Sophie, they constantly fight when we're all together. It's exhausting to say the least.

"It's fine, Carter, I'll be back in two weeks. But right now, I need to hit the gym."

I make my way to The Pit, Vicky's brother Dominic owns it. He and I are—well, we are close. I walk in through the big sliding doors and greet the receptionist, who doesn't like me by the way because she thinks Dom and I are seeing each other. I've given up caring what people think about our friendship years ago. Swiping my card, I smile at her anyway before making my way to the second level, where all the cardio equipment is located. Punching in forty minutes on the treadmill, I run my little heart out. Every level of the gym is surrounded by glass. There are no walls, so people walking past can always see inside. It was Dom's idea of making women feel safe. I look to the hallway and see Dom walking down when he sees me, he smiles and opens the door. Turning my treadmill off, I pull my earphones out of my ears.

"Hey, I thought you'd be in Westbeach by now?" he asks, pulling me in for a hug.

I shake my head, taking a drink of water. "I've been sort of putting it off, I guess."

He raises his eyebrows. "Oh? Why might that be?"

I take a seat on the treadmill. "I may have...slept with Ade a couple years ago. Wish I could say that I regret it, but I don't."

Looking up at him, I see his jaw clenched. "Why didn't you tell me earlier?"

I look down to my hands. "Um, I'm not sure. I guess it just never came up."

Looking up at him again, I see he's clearly upset by my confession.

He smiles and pulls me up by my hand. "Fucking bikers."

Wrapping my arms around him for a hug, I laugh. "Fucking bikers is right."

Walking back into my room while I'm checking my phone, I see there's a text from Alaina.

Alaina: *Hurry up, get here already girl. Please. I think I'm going to kill her.*

I laugh, typing out a quick reply before throwing my phone back to my bed and getting into the shower. The water is cascading over my body and I feel more alert than I ever have before. Maybe it's because I'm going to see Ade, or maybe it's because I haven't had any sex since the last time I saw him, which hasn't bothered me until this point. Running soap all over my body and letting the sweet smell of apples and cinnamon swim up my nose, I slide my hand over my stomach, throwing my head back and moaning as I run my hand over my clit. I stop and my eyes shoot open in surprise. Quickly I turn off the shower and get out, wrapping a towel around me.

What the hell was that about.

Wiping the fog away from the mirror I look at myself. *Have I changed much in two years?*

My hair is a little lighter, caramel brown and hanging long with a slight curl at the ends, dropping right down to my waist. It contrasts off my fair skin and green eyes. My skin may be fair, but I tan easily. That would come from my Brazilian heritage, I'd say. Leaving my towel on, I head to the kitchen to pour a glass of wine. There are no straight men living here, so I'm safe. I hear a knock at the door.

"Who is it?" I yell from the kitchen where I'm putting the wine back into the fridge.

"Open up Kal, it's Dom."

I pause briefly. "Be there in a sec."

Sprinting up to my room, I throw on a big, oversized T-shirt before heading back to the door and pulling it open. He's standing there looking me up and down. Dominic is a very, *very,* good-looking man. He's all protein shakes and iron, with brown hair. He keeps the top long and slicked back, with the sides shaved. He has deep brown eyes and a five o'clock shadow. He's got his head screwed on and we get on like a house on fire, but for some reason, I've never made a move on him.

"I just need to do this real quick," he mumbles as he wraps his hands around the back of my neck, pulling me into his kiss.

At first, I'm shocked, so I don't kiss him back. I know I should stop, but to be honest, I did always wonder what it'd be like to kiss Dominic Abrahams. He pulls back, clutching my face in his hands, looking observantly into my eyes.

"Dom? Are you okay? Did I do something wrong?" I ask in shock and confusion.

He laughs, running his fingers over my cheek. "I kiss you, and you think there's something wrong with you?" He shakes his head. "No Kalie, you're perfect."

I swallow down my confusion. "Do you want to come in and talk about what that was about?" I ask, pointing my thumb toward inside.

He shakes his head. "Nah, I'll leave the rest up to you."

I cough nervously, my eyes searching around the place. "Dom, what am I supposed to do with that? You just kissed me, unexpectedly. I mean, I know we've been flirtatious at times, but I thought that was just our friendship?"

He runs his eyes over my face, studying me intently. "I've always wanted more, Kal. I just didn't know when to make my move."

I cross my hands across my chest. "Okay, we need to talk. Have you been drinking? Come in." I pull him inside and close the door behind him.

"Sit down, Dom. I'll get us a drink."

Walking into the kitchen, I pull out two glasses and fill them with wine. I have a feeling this night is going to be long. Moving back to the couch I pull my legs underneath myself and take a drink looking up to him.

"How come you never told me before?"

He looks to me. "Because, I thought I had time. Obviously not," he seethes, rolling his eyes.

I move over to him some more. "Is this because of Ade?"

He shrugs. "Yeah, I guess it is. I can give you time if that's what you need Kal. Just don't cut me off." I take another sip of my drink and nod my head. "I wouldn't cut you off anyway," I say smiling at him. He pulls me under his arm and kisses my head.

"We could be something great Kalie, I can promise you that."

CHAPTER 6

My speakers are blaring and I'm singing along terribly to Akon *'Right Now,'* dancing along as much as I can with my window all the way down. Then I realize the irony and hit skip on my iPod, changing it to Akon *'Dangerous.'*

What the hell is up with all the Akon songs? Fucking Carter.

I feel like I've slipped and fallen back into the early 2000's. However, I dance along anyway blowing out all my troubles.

"You can do this, Kalie. He won't even bat an eye."

Before I left, I had the dilemma of what I was going to wear. So I opted for not caring and put on some tight skinny jeans, my Chuck Taylors, and a tight, white singlet. I really, *really,* do not want to attract any unwanted attention. My hair is falling down my back in it's natural curls at the ends. I put on a little blush and mascara, and that's it. My nerves are running at one hundred miles an hour and I feel sick.

Damn, Vicky Abrahams.

I pull into the gates of the address Vicky sent me, and I think I might actually spew. My tummy flips when I see all the bikes lined outside the garage.

"Holy *fuck*," I gasp in shock.

Noticing a young guy come up to the gate glaring at me, I wince at the look he's giving, but I get out of my car anyway.

"Hey, I'm one of Vicky's bridesmaids," I say to him, looking a little uneasy.

Maybe I should have called Vicky before coming, but she told me to meet her here.

"Oh, right. Sure darling, come this way," he says dropping the evil glare and smiling. He's cute. All blond, blue-eyed, and baby-faced. He nudges his head toward the building opposite the garage.

Closing my door and run my hands up and down my arms, I try to ease the tension. "Okay, sure."

I begin to follow him into what I'm guessing is the clubhouse. There's a huge deck sitting around what looks like a bar. Walking up the steps that lead us into the bar, the young man pushes the door open, and I'm left standing there—obviously out of place. All that's in here are bikers and—prostitutes? I'm guessing by their attire. It's loud because of the music blaring, and the talking and drinking. Pulling on the young man in front of me—who's wearing a patch like everyone else, except under 'Sinful Souls MC' it reads, 'Prospect,'—I look at it confused. It must mean something, but I honestly have no idea as far as motorcycle clubs go. I could be walking into a snake pit. On the other hand, if any of these big men pack like Ade, it's probably an Anaconda pit.

"Is Vicky in here?" I ask, eager to get the hell out as soon as possible.

He nods his head. "She's up the stairs. Wait at the bar."

Following him to the bar, and looking to my left and see a couple making out. Well, what I would say more like having sex on one of the couches in the corner by the pool table. The girl gets off his lap to escort him to a room—I'm guessing.

And that's when I see who was under the barely dressed skank.

Ade?

Fuck.

ADE NIXON

Having Gretchen rubbing her shit all over my leg is getting old.

"Let's go," I say smacking her bony ass.

She gets up off me and pulls on my hands to lift me up. I give her a disgusted look before getting myself up to follow her out, and that's when I see her. Kalie is standing at the bar with Travis, looking as fucking beautiful as ever. I swear to God she looks hotter than she does in my dreams. *Holy fuck!* She's in a simple tight singlet, tight as fuck jeans that wrap around that fucking perfect ass, and Chuck Taylors. So fucking simple, but yet so fucking sweet. Gretchen feels my pause so she tugs gently on my hand. I look at her with a scowl and pull my hand away from hers.

"Don't fucking do that...ever again." Pushing her out of the way, I walk up to Kalie.

"Hey, I didn't know you were going to be here today," I say, studying her eyes and face. She looks at me like I have three heads.

"Why would you need to know Ade? It's fine, go back to what you were doing. I'm just going to order a drink and wait for Chucky's bride."

She turns her back to me and walks away to the bar with Travis on her tail. I grab Trav's cut and pull him to me.

"Fuck off! Stay the fuck away from her." Travis looks between Kalie and I confused.

Harvey stands from the table. "Trav, that's Kalie."

With that simple statement, I watch understanding set into Travis' eyes. Good. I won't need to kill the little fuck.

Travis looks at me, then looks back to her again. "Sorry bro, didn't know."

Ignoring him I make my way to the bar with her, pulling out a seat and ordering another drink. She looks at me from the corner of her eye.

"Go back to your whore, Aidan."

Laughing at her, I run my tongue over my bottom lip and see her eyes follow my movements. Something tells me, her sweet little pussy still aches for my cock.

"What if she's not my whore? What if she's my old lady?" I ask her, just to work her up.

"What? Your mother? Yeah, that's *clearly* not the case," she states rolling her eyes as she brings her glass to her lips.

I laugh, loudly. I'd forgotten that she doesn't have a clue about our way of life. An old lady is higher than a *'wife'* in our world. When you're crowned an old lady by one of the brothers, you hold all the power over them. They are the highest rank that any women can gain with one of the brothers. It's not to be taken lightly, and if something goes down? We, as an MC will kill for them, lay our lives down for any of the old ladies. They hold a deep level of respect in the MC community. In saying that, Gretchen is no fucking way an old lady, especially not fucking mine.

"What? No. In your way of understanding, my *wife*?"

I see her whole body still and she pales. "Fuck, I'm so sorry Ade. I didn't mean that, I'm going to go." She pulls back off her seat and dashes out the door so fucking fast that I can't catch her in time.

I stand and make my way out the door watching. She glances at me briefly before sliding into her car. Gretchen comes up to me, and wraps her hand around my arm, just in time for Kalie to see us together. I push Gretchen away and walk toward her car, but she reverses quickly and pulls out, driving off down the road. Gretchen moves to me again, placing her hand on my back.

"Get your fucking hands off me, Gretchen. You need to get the fuck back into that whore zone you're trying to escape from."

She huffs and drops her arms to the side. "Why are you so mean, Ade? And who was that?"

Swinging the door open I walk back to the bar where Vicky is now standing with her hands on her hips.

"What the fuck did you do to my bridesmaid, Ade Nixon," she seethes.

I keep walking out the back door to the yard, slamming the door shut behind me. A few moments later, I hear the door open and Zane walks out.

"What's with Kalie, brother? Whenever she's around, she has you all worked up."

I shake my head. "Fucked if I know. Keep me busy."

He narrows his eyes at me. "You sure?"

I nod my head, looking out to the large yard in front of me. It's only used for family events. It's equipped with everything including a playground and a bonfire.

"All right then." He pulls out a yellow folder from under his cut, passing it to me.

Placing my drink down in front of me I pull out a simple paper that has a photo of a man, a name, and his whereabouts.

"This from the Confederation of Assassins?" I ask, looking up at him.

He shakes his head, placing his hands in his pocket. "Was a personal request, from a reliable and safe source."

I narrow my eyes. "Are you sure? I don't usually do personal requests."

"I know. Felix handed it to me."

"Felix? He wants me to do his dirty work?"

"Nah, it's not for him. He said it was a request from a trusted friend."

I raise my eyebrows. "You trust this?"

"He's a brother. We are to trust him, even if something feels off."

I nod my head again, picking up my drink and downing the rest. "Be back soon."

Pulling up to the bar where my new target is supposed to be, I shift on my seat. This is how I pay my way and it's how I've managed to have a large chunk of cash under me. All the rest of the brothers have actual investments, not me, though, I'd rather do this. Ending someone's life is much easier than running a business. *Fuck that!*

Sitting outside the bar, I wait for Justin Littleton to come out. I never know what these people do, that's not how it goes. I just get the slip, do the deed, then I get paid. I've killed for free, this is child's play. Lighting up a cigarette, I lean against my bike and wait. Once I see him walk out of the bar and get into his Mercedes, I start up my bike and follow closely behind him to the outskirts of Westbeach and into an industrial zone. I shut off my bike, take my helmet off and glance around at my surroundings. I've been here before, I'm sure of it, everything is all too familiar.

Sixteen Years Ago

"Where are we going, Pops?"

My dad had me riding passenger on a run he needed to do. My mom said that the club was clean, but I knew better. I may have been young, but I was not stupid.

"Shut up, Son. This doesn't happen. Got it?"

I nodded my head, looking out the window at the passing trees. "Yeah, I got it."

He pulled up to a warehouse and drove in. Looking around and into the large doors, which were open, there were cages everywhere inside. Fighting cages.

"Get out, Son. You have a fight," he said pulling open his door.

"But why?" I asked, getting out of the car.

He knelt down to my level and I watched the pure evil in his eyes, that same darkness some said they saw in mine.

"This is about something else, Son. The club does not know about this and does not need to know about this. You go in there, fight, and then that's it. Got it?"

Nodding my head, I followed behind him. My father's accent was still strong, even though he'd lived in the US since he was a boy.

Walking in, I saw three other big men. One was smoking a cigar with gold teeth. He noticed me and bent down to my level.

"You must be Aidan. Roger here is going to take you to get ready, Son."

Roger grabbed onto my hand and pulled me toward a room that was to the far right of the cages.

He pushed me in. "Be out in that cage," he pointed to the center stage, "in five minutes." Then slammed the door shut.

I ripped off my top and started doing pushups, single hand pushups, plyo pushups, diamond pushups, every single push up you could think of before I started swinging and practicing my jabs. I was not nervous, I never was. That was not out of cockiness, that was out of the certainty of knowing when my fist landed on someone, it could be deadly.

Five minutes passed and I made my way to the ring. I looked around and saw another MC, not the

Sinful Souls, though. I was sure that they were our enemies. My dad would never be a traitor, though. He and Uncle Dave had been brothers since they were young boys, he wouldn't do that to him. I stopped gazing and jumped into the ring. When I saw my opponent come in, my body automatically became alert. This man was in his twenties—at least. He was all muscle and standing at around six foot tall. I was big for my age, but this man was a fully-grown adult. I looked to my dad, and he nodded his head. Instantly, I fucking hated him. The ref came to the middle of the cage.

"You know the rules folks. There's no tapping out, and the only way you leave this cage is in a body bag."

He threw his hands down. "Fight." He quickly made his escape outside of the cage.

A fucking deathmatch? That was what he was putting me into with a grown ass man? Even for him, that was an all-time low. I pulled my head up to the man just as his fist connected with my jaw, throwing me back against the cage. The pain that I felt on my jaw was excruciating. This was why I didn't let people come close enough to hit me. But that was a blind shot, and I now knew that this man was a coward. Standing up just as he was walking over to me, he swung his right hook again and I automatically realized that he didn't use his left hand as much as his right.

Blocking his swing with my right hand, I pounded his face with my left. I'm ambidextrous, my left hook was just as lethal as my right. He fell back onto his back and I jumped on him, pounding his face, putting force into each blow. Each time my fist connected with his face I felt a bone crunch. There was blood pouring out all over the place, all over my face and hands, so much that I could taste the metallic-like substance in my mouth. I saw the ref get into the cage, and in the heat of the moment, I grasped his head and twisted it with such force until I hear that *snap* sound and I knew he was dead. The crowd went deathly quiet. I got up breathing heavily with blood all over my skin. Looking over to my dad, who had excitement gleaming in his eyes, I just stared.

I pointed at him. "We are done, and this is done."

Then I walked out of the cage hearing the commentator yell through the microphone, "That my dear friends, is Ade 'The Executioner' Nixon." I continued walking back to the room. That was the first time I'd killed someone. It both excited and frightened me all at the same time. However, it only frightened me because I liked it. And that was how the Executioner was born.

Present Day

Walking into the familiar building, nothing has changed, there are still cages scattered around everywhere with the main cage right in the center. I glance at it, remembering my first kill at the tender age of thirteen. I guess to average people, it would sound appalling, but to me, it's just another childhood memory. I carry on, following the footsteps of my target and when I reach the door he just walked through, I stop, listening in to what's being said.

"Justin, do you have our fighter?" I hear the familiar voice say. That familiar voice was the same man that had the gold teeth and cigar, that I remember from all those years ago.

"I do. He's being imported in from the UK. Fucking big bastard too."

I hear a cigarette lighter spark. "How old?"

Justin pulls out a chair. "Twelve, maybe a bit younger, but imagine the pot on his head if he wins. It would be like Aidan Nixon all over again."

I hear the familiar voice laugh. "That was a once in a lifetime event, the biggest pay day of my life."

Kicking the door open they move across the room with raised guns, only I have both my fully automatics already drawn on them.

I laugh a guttural laugh. "You know, it's sweet, that little conversation I just stumbled in on."

Gold teeth drops his weapon. "Aidan?"

I laugh again. "It's Ade. Take a seat and carry on with your story, I was rather enjoying myself." I smile at them both.

Justin laughs. "Who the fu—"

Bang.

I shoot him, right in the head. Which results in his blood splattering all over the place, the old gold tooth fool included.

"What's your name? I never did catch it," I say, leaning back in my seat, propping my knee onto my other leg.

He sits uneasily on his chair. "Bruce, Son. Why don't you drop the weapon so we can talk? Justin was my main line of business, and you just shot him. Now I'm very angry. You won't like me when I'm angry."

I chuckle. "Now..." I sit forward with a cocky smile on my face, "the fact that I'm sitting here with my weapon drawn on you, and you're sitting there with nothing, tells me that I don't give a fuck whether you're angry or not."

He narrows his eyes. "What is it you want, Son. Revenge? Is that why you just killed my right-hand man?"

I smile. "That's not why I killed him. I killed him under orders, but I'll kill you for free."

Now he laughs, clipping his cigar and rolling it around his mouth. "You won't get away with it, Son. If anything happens to me, I have people just as powerful ready to fill my shoes and take down anybody that's taken me down. Now tell me, do you want that sort of heat on your shoulders?" he asks, spitting out a bit of tobacco from his mouth before continuing, "Also, do know this. For that little outburst which resulted in you shooting my man here," he points to the bloody mess on the ground, "I'm going to hunt you down myself. So either way, Son, you won't win this."

I stand up and walk around to his table where he's sitting. "You think I care? I don't fucking care at fucking all. I have nothing to lose. So, you tell me…" I bend down, bringing my lips to his ear before whispering, "What can scare a man who has nothing to lose?" I draw my gun up, watching his eyes set into understanding at my quick movements, and fire a whole round into him.

Once I'm done, I'm once again dripping with blood. I take the cigar from his lifeless fingers and put it into my mouth, puffing on it. Making my way to the back, I find a shitload of gasoline containers. Taking hold of them, I start pouring the gasoline all over the place, starting from the center cage. I walk out, stand at the doorway and look into that cage for the last time ever before I flick the cigar into the middle and watch the whole warehouse burn down in flames.

CHAPTER 7

KALIE - ROSE

I'm walking in a hotel room that I decided to get instead of staying with Vicky when my phone rings. I notice it's Vicky, so I answer.

"Hey Vick, I'm so sorry."

She laughs. "Don't be sorry, girl. Are you okay?"

I huff out and drop to the bed. "I think so. I can't believe I insulted his partner, Vick. Fuck! I called her a whore."

Vicky pauses briefly then laughs down the phone. "Kalie, relax. That *was* his whore. He's just being typical Ade. He was kidding."

I shoot up of the bed. "Pardon? He was kidding? I am going to kill him. Seriously."

Vicky giggles. "Come back to the clubhouse. He's not here right now anyway. We can have a drink and bounce some ideas around for the hen's party on Friday."

"Okay, I'll be there soon."

Hanging up my phone I grab my keys. I'm so going to give him a piece of my mind when I see him. I don't care how monstrous he is.

Pulling up to the gate, Travis lets me in this time with a small smile. I get out and smile back.

"Thanks, for letting me in without the scary stare downs."

He laughs. "Yeah, no problem, Kalie. Come, I can take you in."

I walk up to him, and we make our way to the bar.

"So, you're new?" I ask.

He nods his head. "Yeah, I guess you could say that."

"How old are you? Don't they have age restrictions on who can patch in?"

"I'm old enough, sweetheart. Come on."

He takes hold of my hand and pulls me in through the door. At first, I think nothing of the hand-holding gesture. I thought it was a nice thing to do. However, that was before I saw Ade storming across the floor making his way to us. Quickly, I pull my hand out of Travis' grasp. I don't know why I did that, probably has something to do with the death stare Ade is currently giving Travis.

Also, I don't really want to see a homicide today, or any day.

"Hey, sorry about—"

He cuts off my apologies. "Go and sit at the bar with Vicky, Kalie."

My eyes widen, he still hasn't looked down at me. His eyes are too busy glued onto poor Travis.

"Ade, leave him alone. He was just helping me in," I say standing in front of Travis.

I feel Travis' hands go around my shoulders, and a growl comes from Ade's mouth.

"Go sit down, darling. It's cool," Travis says as he winks at me.

Making my way to the bar, I give Ade the stink eye on the way. I pull out a seat and Vicky's laughing.

"Well, I'll be damned."

I look to her. "What the fuck is his problem? Does he live in a cave too?" I ask.

I hear Zane laugh from the other side of Blake. "Good. It's about time he got a taste of his own medicine."

Vicky orders me a drink quickly while I watch Travis make his way back to the pool table and Ade make his way over to us. He bends down and kisses me on the head.

"Hey, now what were you saying?" he asks casually. Like he doesn't need to explain what just happened.

He looks down at the man that's next to me. "Move."

The man moves, grabbing his beer before Ade sits down on his seat.

I laugh. "You've got to be kidding me," I say taking a drink of my drink.

"What? What did I do?" he asks innocently with a smirk.

I raise my eyebrows and smile. "Well, I thought for a start, that you would not even remember me. Actually, I was sort of counting on it."

His eyebrows cross. "What do you mean *'you were counting on it?'*" His eyes narrow, giving me his panty-wetting evils.

I smile, blushing at his stare. I would drop my panties in a heartbeat if he ever looked at me like that again. "Um, never mind." I pull my lip into my mouth and look ahead of me.

His eyebrows raise and the corner of his lip pulls up. "I still make you uncomfortable?" he asks with a glorious smirk running along his lips.

I cough. "Um..."

Vicky leans in to shoot him daggers. "Leave her alone, Ade. Go work your magic on someone else please, or have you slept with all the girls here?"

Putting my drink back to my lips, I'm not going to lie, that disturbs me. I'm not on a high horse, but I know that Ade was different for me. I also know it probably has something to do with the fact that not only did he take my virginity, but he's the sexiest man I've ever seen, and I have seen a lot of sexy men. The way he worked me over that night has me orgasming in my sleep and waking with wet panties, on more than one occasion.

Ade looks around the bar and smirks. "Yeah, I think I have."

I look to Vicky before yelling, "Shots! I need shots. *Right now*." I point to the bench.

Vicky laughs and bends over the bar to grab the vodka from under the bench.

Blake grunts and slaps her ass. "Babe, sit the fuck down. You're giving everyone a show."

"It's on my side anyway," I state as I lean over the bar to reach underneath. "There," I say, sitting the bottle on the bench.

I look at Ade to see him biting down on his lower lip with his face scrunched up, covering a smile.

"Damn. Shit!" he mumbles while adjusting himself.

I stare at him shocked while bringing the bottle to my lips and taking a long pull before pouring shots.

This is going to be a long two weeks.

Slamming my fourth shot onto the bench and ready for another, Vicky says, "So, I hear you've been spending a lot of time with Dom?"

I laugh, pouring more vodka. "Yeah, I guess I have."

She looks at me eyebrows raised. "Any reason why?"

I shake my head. "No, we're still very much friends. We did have a moment the other night, but I'll tell you about that when Ade isn't killing me with his stare," I say looking pointedly at him.

He narrows his eyes then throws his arms up. "I didn't say anything."

I laugh, taking another drink. "You smell like cologne, mixed with gasoline."

He looks at me and then looks back at Zane. "Spilled some gas on me when I filled up. I changed, but it must still be there."

Shrugging my shoulders, I continue my reckless drinking while Vicky and I make plans for this weekend. Every now and then, I feel Ade's leg brush up against mine and my body stiffens. Every time I stiffen, I hear a cocky chuckle come out of his mouth. *Asshole.*

Amo Jones

Right now, I'm well and truly drunk. Unlike my sex life, I've been drunk many other times since spring break. I'd rather spend nights drinking wine by myself in my undies while eating pizza than hitting the clubs.

"Let's dance," I say to Vicky, pulling her up onto the dance floor.

"Not on the pole, Kalie! I mean it," I hear Ade shout out from his seat, and I roll my eyes at him.

"No, do go on the pole, Kalie. I'll sit down there and watch you do your thang," Zane responds, smirking at Ade.

I have no idea what they are on about.

Vicky laughs. "Oh, don't worry, Ade. What this girl does on the dance floor, will have strippers jealous." He narrows his eyes in interest.

She makes her way to the sound system and mumbles. "I'll make her." Then she comes over to me with a killer smile on her lips. The next thing I hear is The Weekend *'Or Nah'* blasting through the speakers. She sits on a seat and points to herself.

"Do me, come on. You know you want to."

I smirk, looking to Ade, and then shrug. Dancing is something I love to do. Sometimes I have to rub up on famous men for their video clips, so I'm pretty sure I can do my best friend. Slowly I dance and adjust myself to the beat, giving Vicky a lap dance to the dirty lyrics of the song. It's somewhat empowering to know that you can bring a man to his knees just by shaking your ass around him. Following the baseline behind the song, I drop myself low and push my ass into Vicky's lap. I don't even get halfway through the song before I see Ade stand from his seat with a smile and make his way to me.

He pulls me into him. "Really? Do you *really* think it's smart to shake that fine ass all over the place*? Here*?" he asks with a mischievous twinkle in his eye.

I shrug. "Right now, I don't really care."

He grabs onto my hand and pulls me toward the exit door.

"Ade Nixon, I'm getting real tired of your caveman shit with my bridesmaid," Vicky yells from the dance floor. Ade turns around and flips her off.

We move outside and a shiver runs over my body. *Why the hell did I not bring a jacket?* He takes off his black and white flat cap, pulls his hoodie off, and throws it on me before placing the hat backward onto his head. He's in his usual, at least I think it's his usual, white T-shirt with his MC cut over the top, loose fitting jeans that hang off him nicely, and black army combat boots. The flat cap gives him an edge, an edge I'd happily jump off just to view that face on top of me while I'm feeling his dick pushing into me. I bring my drink up to my lips, a smile playing on them. I can be a little naughty when Ade is around.

"Thanks," I say, smiling at him while taking another sip of my drink.

"I finally get you alone," he replies with a smirk, sitting on the second step and leaning back on his elbow.

I laugh. "I think that scares me a little," I say while taking a seat on the second step with him.

He looks to me and cocks his head back. "Who me? Fuck no! I'm not scary at all." Sarcasm laced through the tone of his voice.

I laugh again. "I really was hoping that you wouldn't remember me."

His face falls serious. "Why? I usually don't. You though? There's no way I'd forget, that ass is etched into my skull for life," he replies playfully.

I smack him on the shoulder. "Stop," I say laughing and taking another drink while looking out to the dark night.

"Are you going to ask me if I have a boyfriend before you continue to play caveman with me?" I ask raising an eyebrow.

He laughs and looks at me, running his pierced tongue over the two rings I'm familiar with on his lip. "Nope, I wouldn't care if you did."

I feel like an idiot, of course, he wouldn't care. This is Ade we're talking about here. "Right, sure."

I stand from where I'm sitting. "I'm going to call a cab, head back to the hotel."

He's still looking out deep into the backyard, so I turn to walk away, but he grabs onto my hand with his. I look down at him, heart racing and thighs clenched.

"I'll take you, Kalie," he says looking up at me. I sigh out in annoyance. He's so perfect it hurts.

I chuckle nervously. "Yeah, have you forgotten? I don't do the bike thing."

He shrugs, getting up from where he's sitting, still not breaking hold of my hand. "Then we'll take my car. I've been keeping it here until my house is built anyway." I look to him and he narrows his eyes, smirking at me. Always the mischievous shit, he is.

"Okay," I respond quietly. Following him back through the bar I see everyone staring at us.

I look to Vicky. "He's going to drop me off at my hotel."

Her face drops. "Why don't you just stay with me?"

I place my hands on her shoulder. "Because love, I might kill you if I have to live with you for the two weeks leading up to your wedding. I do love you, though."

She laughs. "I have been sort of bad, hey? And who told you? It was Blake wasn't it?" She whips her head around to Blake, and if looks could kill, he'd be dead on the ground.

I shake my head and laugh, saving him from his future wife's wrath. "No, but I'm going to go. Text me tomorrow what the plans are. Okay?"

She nods her head and hugs me before I begin to make my way out the door to where Ade is standing there waiting. When I'm almost at the door, I can feel someone burning holes into my head. Turning to the right I see that same blonde I saw Ade with on my first night here. She's sitting there looking none too happy. Ade sees that I've stopped and looks at who I'm looking at before walking up to me and pulling me in under his arm.

"Baby, you gotta cut the jealous crap or this is just never going to work," he says smirking while kissing my head.

I laugh and shove him away from me. "Shut up." We walk to the garage together, and he punches in a code, making one of the seven garage doors open up and revealing a big, beautiful shiny car. I walk over to it and run my hand over the metallic gloss black paintwork.

"1970 Dodge Charger RT," he answers my unspoken question.

I look up to him and smile. "It's beautiful."

Popping open the door, he gets into the driver's seat, roaring the beast to life.

"So, you're the whole package, huh? Mr. Bad-Boy-Biker, who has tattoos, piercings, and drives a V8? I'm impressed," I say humorously.

He laughs, putting it into first gear. "Impressed enough to open those sweet little legs for me again?"

I snap my head to him in shock, only to see him laughing inwardly.

Laughing, I shake my head. "You are something else, Mr. Nixon."

CHAPTER 8

The drive there is slow, but I learn that Ade's dad died when he was young, along with Zane and Blake's dad. A few months after their deaths, his mom died too. He didn't say how, but I can see it is a touchy subject. As you would expect. Zane's mom, Annabelle raised him since then, and the rest is history. I can see how much he loves Zane's mom just by how he talks about her. We pull up to the hotel and I take off my seat belt.

"Thanks, for the ride."

He yanks up the handbrake and turns the car off. "Have you eaten?"

I shake my head. "Ade, it's two in the morning. There's no way I can eat at this time." I stop briefly before continuing, "You can come up, though if you want. I mean. Shit! Hang on. Give me a minute to rephrase that. I'm not offering sex, but you can come up," I say, blushing bright beet red.

I can hear him holding in his laugh, so I look up to him, watching his hand covering his mouth, trying to contain his laughter.

"Don't laugh at me. I...oh God. How do I say this without sounding like a complete nerd."

He shakes his head, pulling the keys out of the ignition. "Stop begging me, I said I'll come up. Geez," he replies playfully, and a little loudly. I widen my eyes at him when I see a few people stare from outside.

"Ade! Fuck!" A small laugh leaves my mouth. I love how he can be playful with me. Opening my door, I round the car to lead the way to my room. Walking into the lobby, we take the cart to the top floor in silence. When we walk down the hallway, he laughs from behind me.

"This is all a little similar."

Turning around, I catch him smiling. "Yeah, yeah, don't get any ideas."

I also need to keep telling myself this. He tests all my limits.

Walking in, I turn the light on and flop my jacket over the sofa while taking my shoes off.

"Want a drink or anything?" I ask him as he makes his way to the sofa.

"Nah, I'm good. How long are you here for?" he asks.

Pulling out a bottled water from the fridge I answer, "Two weeks. I came a little earlier for the hen's party this weekend."

I make my way to the sofa and sit down next to him. It's a little quiet so I turn the television on, leaving it on some stupid infomercial that they have running at this time of the night. Looking to my left, I catch him staring at me. His perfectly pouty lips on that strong, defined jaw, and those eyes? Not just the color, but the shape. They're so seducing. His stare alone could make me wet. Is— is making me wet.

I blush. "What?"

He gives me a half smile. "You're still the most beautiful girl I've ever seen."

I cough out my water that I was drinking. "Ade, that was really sweet, if it was true. I told you, no sex."

He laughs. "I didn't say that to get down your pants, Kalie. If I wanted in that pussy again...trust me, I'd be down there."

I raise my eyebrows at him. "Oh really."

He smiles. "I'm serious. And I promise I will not have sex with you. *Yet.*" He continues when he sees that my face hasn't changed, "I'm dead serious. Come here." Patting the spot next to him, I crawl over and get under his arm. We must stay like that for a while, it's so warm and cozy, that I fall asleep.

ADE NIXON

After a few minutes, I look down at Kalie and see she is sleep. I kiss her head and slowly get my arm back from under her, before standing and picking her up to carry her to her bed. Once she's tucked in, I write a note for her saying to text me with my number on it. I walk out of the hotel, lighting a cigarette and getting into my car. Roaring her to life, I pull out and make my way to my apartment. It's temporary until my house has been built, but I can't have my car and my bike there. One of the two always needs to stay at the clubhouse. I walk into my apartment and throw down my keys, walking into my room, undressing and scrubbing up in the shower before getting into bed. I toss and turn for hours thinking about those bright emerald green eyes, before I drift off to sleep, haunted by the demons of my past.

Fourteen Years Ago

The crowd was cheering as I made my way into the ring. I'd thrown myself into fighting, not for status anymore, but for money. Since my dad died, my mom had become a zombie. She never ate or left her room, and I had to regularly check on her to make sure she was still alive. Her soul died the day my dad died.

I bounced around on the soles of my feet, waiting for the ref to stop talking.

"To the right, we have the undefeated…Ade *'The Executioner'* Nixon! He's known for his one-hitters. So watch out folks, this may be a quick one."

The crowd cheered for me and it was fucking pathetic. I got it, I'd been fighting in the ring since I was thirteen, so I was used to it, but I was fighting outside of the ring much, much, earlier than that, though. My opponent smiled at me, probably hoping his poker face stayed strong. I smirked back at him and the whole crowd erupted again. It sounded like the crowd was filled with women, by all the squealing I could hear. This was an underground fight, but there were people of all ages there too.

"And to the left corner, we have Steven Luger with twelve wins under his belt and one loss. He's not to be under-estimated folks. He has a mean right hook."

Well, I have a mean both hook. So we'll see how this goes down.

We punched fists, and then I started walking around him, watching his step. I dodged his hook and placed all my weight into my left jab. My fist connected with his jaw and I could feel the crunch of his jaw under my knuckles.

Crack.

His body fell straight to the ground. The crowd went deathly silent briefly before the screaming started again, and when I looked down, Steven looked dead. His coach ran in along with a couple of his other members. I shrugged and walked out of the ring and back to the dressing room to gather my shit. I walked past Tommy, grabbing my earnings from his outstretched hand.

"You know, Ade, you're going to need to let them get a hit in soon. Or no one is going to bid against you."

I laugh. "Yeah, we'll see."

Walking out into the crisp air I slipped onto my bike. The bike was my dad's, but when he died, it was handed down to me. I fucking hated him and what he'd put me through as a kid, but I'd keep the fucking bike, it was beautiful.

I pulled up to our average home that was on the middle-class side of town. Shutting my bike off, I began walking up the steps, opening the front door. I closed it behind me and walked into the kitchen. I flicked the light on and looked to the ground. That was when I saw my mother lying there in a pool of blood with slashes across her wrist, legs, and neck. I ran over to her and checked her pulse.

"Mom?"

I shook her, but she was not responding. I ran to the phone and dialed 911, then I called Zane. After making the calls, I dragged myself down the wall and just looked at her. I should have felt sad, but if anything, I was angry. What sort of selfish bitch would take their life when she had a kid? I would never do that to my kid. I stood from where I was sitting, running up to my room and started packing a bag, throwing the things I'd need into the black rucksack.

Fuck this house! I'd burn it to the ground with my bitch of a mother inside it, I thought to myself. Five minutes later, I heard cars pulling up and knocking on the door. I made my way over and opened the door to the police and ambulance service. I let them in, giving them my statement and then I got onto my bike and rode. I pulled out onto the highway and headed to Abby's. She was the only person I could stomach to see at that time. I pulled up to her house and shut off my bike before walking to the little cabin she stayed in at the back of her home.

"Ade? Are you okay?" she asked, opening the door when she saw me walking up.

I shook my head. "Mom's dead. She sliced herself up. I found her after my fight tonight."

She threw her hands up to her mouth in shock. "Come here." Pulling me in, she wrapped her hands around me.

I looked down to her, and she looked back up to me with complete sadness in her eyes. It touched something deep inside to see her hurt for me.

I wiped the tears away from her eyes. "Don't cry Abby, she's not worth it."

Abby had a rough life. She was raised in the system after her parents were murdered when she was four. It took someone one whole week to find her and when they did, she wreaked of death, because she was smothered in her parents' blood. They said that at night, she used to cuddle with them for comfort, not knowing the absolute horrific scene in front of her. Both parents were bludgeoned and stabbed to death. So after that, she was living in all sorts of fucked-up foster homes. That was until she was nine and got a family in Westbeach, who were equally as fucked-up. She ran away one night and my Aunt Shelly found her walking the streets in ripped clothes with dirty hair and skin. She and my Uncle Pincher took her in from then onwards. That was off the record, though, as far as the system knew, she was a runaway who raised herself.

She sniffed and took off my cut. "Come, you can have a shower. Clean you up."

She led me to her shower and began taking off my clothes.

"Ah, Abby? What are we doing?" I asked, looking down at her.

"Just, let me take care of you. Okay?" she whispered.

I thought her statement over for a second, standing still. I brought my eyes back to her and narrowed them slightly. She smiled at the hint of approval from me and took my clothes off before taking off her own. We both stepped into the shower, and I think, that was the first, and only time, that I'd ever had sex with a chick that had some actual feeling behind it. Not enough for it to mean anything, more than exactly what it was, but still *some* meaning behind it nonetheless. I spun her around so her back was against my front. I grasped her hair in my fist, pulling her head back before running my other hand over her tight torso and down to her pussy. She moaned out and threw her head backward. Pushing her head down roughly, I grasped her hips and lifted her onto my dick, slamming into her in hard deep thrusts until she was spilling herself all over my cock.

Present Day

I'm drinking in the bar at the clubhouse when Zane comes through. He pulls out a seat next to me, and orders a drink before looking over at me.

"Anything you want to tell me?" he asks, taking a sip of his beer.

I nod my head and tap on the bench. "I followed the high target (HT) to a warehouse, the same warehouse my dad took me to for my first fight to the death."

Zane looks to me, eyebrows scrunched together. "So you killed Bruce Peyton. Why? And I really hope you give me a better reason than your anger issues, brother. This has just started a war."

I clenched my jaws tightly together. "I'll handle it. Whoever they get to fill him, I'll handle him, as I will the next person and the next. Until I can think of something that will end their whole fucking organization."

Zane places his drink down and turns to me. "Brother, we'll handle it together. You, me, and

Blake? We were brothers before these cuts bonded us together. We got you." I smiled up at him and nodded.

Walking out of the clubhouse, and lighting my cigarette, I see Phoebe pull up in her Black 2015 Nissan GTR Godzilla. It has all black everything, black rims, black tints, and black lights. It's fucking immaculate, and so is Phoebe. She's been a car enthusiast since she could walk. It had driven Blake crazy when she started going to street races, not just attending them, but racing in them also.

"Hey Phoebs, looking for bridezilla?" I ask, blowing out a smoke ring.

She coughs and whips the smoke away from her face. "Ade, you need to ditch the smokes. How do you lift and smoke at the same time? I don't get it."

I laugh. "I lift iron Phoebs, and I don't fuck with cardio."

Her heels start clicking as she walks in, before whipping around to look at me. "Ade, do not fuck with Kalie more than you already have. Please. The last thing she needs is drama. Her ex still harasses her phone and I ju—"

I cut her off, as soon as she said the word "ex," I see red. "What do you mean, ex? I didn't know she had an ex?"

Phoebe's eyes narrow, as she crosses her arms in front of her and smirks. "Oh? You didn't think you were the only one, did you? Ade, the girl is tearing up the streets of Hollywood Hills. She's the latest Louis Vuitton handbag, and everyone wants their hands on it," I state before walking off to the bar.

I didn't realize I was fisting my hands together so tightly, till I feel my nails dig into my palm. Throwing down my smoke and stamping on it, I put on my helmet and ride out to see Drago. There's no way this fucker is living past this week.

CHAPTER 9

KALIE - ROSE

"Carter!" I scold down the phone line at my best friend's crassness.

"Oh, what? I'm just saying if you give him the nookie, it might change."

I roll my eyes while pulling bagels out of the toaster.

"He left last night, and he left a note with his number. I guess, I should text him?" I ask a little unsure.

"What are you eating?"

"A bagel, why?" I reply deadpan.

"Put the bagel down, Kalie. You have two weeks of not dancing, and we all know it goes straight to your ass."

I drop my knife to the bench. "You know what, Priscilla Queen of the Desert, just for that comment I'll be laying doubles down."

He gasps dramatically. "Kalie-Rose! I'm not a drag."

"Yet, girlfriend. You're not a drag—*yet*."

I take a big bite of my bagel, so he can hear the crunch and moan out in delight.

"All right, I've gotta go. I love you."

"Yeah, I love you too, bitch."

Laughing I hang up my phone. I love Carter, we can thoroughly cuss the shit out of each other, but he's like a brother to me and I love him dearly. I'm pouring myself a coffee when my phone rings again, I pick it up without looking mainly because I think it's Carter again.

"What's the matter? Forgot to tell me how big his cock was last night?" I say smiling down the phone.

"Kalie-Rose Reynolds! You watch that mouth." I throw my hand up to my mouth at the sound of my mother's voice. "Did he tell you, though? You know? How big it was?"

I scrunch up my face, dropping my bagel back onto my plate. My appetite is all but gone. "Mom, eew, no! I am not going there with you."

She laughs. "All right honey, how are you? I'm just checking in."

I pull my top off and my jeans. "Good. Vicky's the ultimate bridezilla, but it's all good."

I hear her whistle through the phone and mumble out ordering another drink.

"Mom? Are you sipping margaritas at ten in the morning?"

She giggles. "Oh honey, when you have kids and they move out of home, you will understand."

I huff my hair out of my face. "You have one kid, Mom, me. I didn't think I was that bad, not bad enough to drive you to drink at ten in the morning anyway."

She gulps down her drink. "That's not why I called sweetie. Your father and I want to see you. When can you come and see us?"

I take hold of my phone and put it onto speaker, throwing it onto the bed so I can get changed properly. "I'll try and make it over there soon. I promise. It's just so far."

"Kalie, we live in Vegas, not Chewbacca."

I stop what I'm doing and laugh. "Mom, Chewbacca is not a town."

"Yeah, yeah. Please come see us, darling?"

"I will Mom. I better go. I have a bride to please."

"Okay honey, I love you."

"I love you too, Mom."

Quickly brushing through my hair, platting it into a messy fishtail braid going down the side of my neck, I throw on a loose off-the-shoulder T-shirt and some denim short-shorts before heading down to my car. Popping open my door, I get in. Reaching into my bag, I pull out my sunnies and see my phone reminding me I need to text Ade. "Fuck! He probably...oh fuck it. I'll just text him." After slapping my forehead for talking to myself, I pull my phone out and text him.

Me: *Hey, it's Kalie.*

Throwing my phone back into my bag, I set off to Vicky and Blake's house. When I get there, I pull into the main gates and park my car outside their enormous house. *Seriously, are they all rich?* They must have their hands in all sorts of business. I'm making my way up to the door when Vicky swings it open, hair everywhere and mascara smudged over her face.

"You look like shit, Polly," I say, walking into her house. We like to call each other Polly, not sure why. It probably started from a bottle of alcohol.

"My dress, it's not going to be ready on time. I just know it."

I pat her on the back.

"Give me the number and let me make some calls, I'm sure you're just over-reacting."

I walk into the kitchen and sit on one of the bar stools, when Alaina, Phoebe, and another girl with dyed red hair and dark green eyes walks in. We are her only bridesmaids, Vicky doesn't have many friends. It has a lot to do with the fact that she can be hard to deal with but in the best way. I love her to bits.

"Abby this is Kalie. Kalie this is Abby." Vicky points between us.

"Hi, nice to meet you." I smile at her.

She narrows her eyes, without smiling back. "Wish I could say that the feeling was mutual," she retorts with a snarky tone.

I raise my eyebrows. "Oookay then..." I respond awkwardly.

I don't think too much about her hostility, I'll ask Vicky about it later.

"So, bridal party tomorrow night," I say with a smirk.

Alaina laughs. "Yeah, should be fun."

Phoebe looks to me through brown eyes and brushes her long white-blonde hair back behind her shoulder. She looks so similar to her brother. "Yeah, if Ade doesn't pull the caveman card on you for the one-hundredth time and drag your ass out of there."

Coughing awkwardly, I look over at Alaina. I know her and Ade are close, so I don't know if I'm comfortable talking about him in front of her. She must catch my look because she laughs.

"Oh, Kalie! No, you can say whatever you want about Ade. Just please, don't mention his hoe-wrecker."

I laugh and spit my drink out. "I'm sorry, what?"

She looks at me confused. "You know, it's what he calls his cock!"

I laugh aloud this time, clutching my stomach. "Well, that's interesting. You learn something new every day." I continue, "But no, we have an agreement…I think. He said he doesn't want me like that."

"I would believe him," Abby mumbles from beneath her glass.

I instantly know that whatever this girl's problem is, it has a lot to do with Ade.

Vicky laughs, walking to the cupboard getting some glasses down and pouring us wine.

"Girl, you're a fool if you think he doesn't want you. I've never seen Ade Nixon chase pussy before."

I look to Vicky with my mouth wide. "Vicky, he's not chasing me."

Alaina butts in, eating a handful of grapes. "No, she's right, babe. Ade is a very dark man. Emotionally shut off from the world, therefore, he cares for no one. Aside from his brothers, there's only one other girl he's ever cared about."

I didn't actually stop to think whether he might have a partner or a wife or anything.

I swallow a lump that's formed in my throat. "Do tell, I'm intrigued."

She laughs. "It's nothing like that. Ade is the epitome of unattainable. Women flock to his bed in hopes that they can finally tame the bad boy with no emotions. Hoping that maybe they are the one. Sadly, all they end up with is their heart in shambles along with their self-esteem. He's a prick and he walks all over women. Uses and abuses then discards them."

I drop my smile. "Even more reason to stay away from him, I guess."

She grabs onto my hand. "Mmm, honey, I don't think you have a choice. That's also not why I just said all that. Does he treat you like that?"

I shake my head and she nods. "I rest my case."

I tilt my head at her. "Who's the girl? That he cares about?"

She takes a drink and drags her eyes across the table. "That would be Abby here." Pointing to the red-haired bitch, smiling proudly at me. "She was raised with all of them. Although, I think her and Ade are a little deeper than her and the rest of the boys. They had a bond at a young age Zane said. Is that right?" she asks Abby.

Abby nods. "Yeah, you could say that." She smirks at me.

I raise my eyebrows. "Right, okay. Anyway, for the hen's party what are we thinking?"

Alaina stands, pouring another glass. "So, I was thinking, a stretch limo driving us around all night while we hit the town dressed as slutty as we can? You know, to support our ex-slutty friend on her final night of being single."

I giggle. "A bit lame isn't it? You guys are old ladies, and you," I say pointing over to Phoebe, "you have an over-the-top, over-protective, brother. This sounds like trouble."

Alaina nods her head. "Yes, but I'm in charge and I want this."

I sit back into my chair and drink the rest of my drink. This is so not going to go down well, not at all.

ADE NIXON

"Brother, have you heard what the girls are planning for tonight?" Blake asked Zane.

Snatching a bottle from the bar, I make my way over to them, pulling out a chair and swinging it around to sit on it backward. They all look at me awkwardly.

"What?" I ask, and Zane laughs.

"Can we talk about this without you losing your shit?"

I smile. "Very funny. I've already told Kalie, I won't be going near her."

This is true, I did tell her that, but I don't intend on following through with it. She's different, this much I know. I'm completely aware of how much she means to me. I fucking hate it. I hate everything about the fact that she brings out feelings in me, brings out that same humanity I buried a long time ago. But a man wants what a man wants, and what I want, is her.

"Yeah, I don't believe you," Blake states calmly.

I narrow my eyes at him. "Well, I don't give a fuck what you believe."

He laughs and drinks his bottle, throwing his hands up. "Wow, I don't want a repeat of the bar fight we got into."

I smile a full grin. "That's what I thought."

After going to see Drago, I found out who this ex-boyfriend is. He's an accountant at a firm in the heart of Beverly Hills. Rich, trust fund kid. Knowing who he is now if he steps out of line, I have all my ducks in a row and ready to be shot. That's good enough for me, for now.

I hear a door open and see Abby walk in—out of uniform. Moving from my seat I get up and hug her.

"Everything good?" I ask.

She sits uneasily as Felix walks in behind her. "Yeah, everything's good."

Looking between the two, I can feel the tension rolling off them.

"All right so when are you going to stop bullshitting and tell me what's really going on?"

She shakes her head. "It's fine Ade, drop it. I'm getting a drink," she says as she carries on over to the bar.

I walk over to Felix. "You going to tell me what's going on with her?"

He shrugs. "Don't know, brother."

Walking away from him, I make my way back to the bar to sit down with Abby, something's not sitting right.

She jumps up so fast when I grab onto her shoulder, her chair falls to the ground.

"Wow! Abby, it's me, Ade."

She begins shaking where she's standing. "Bear?"

I reach my hand out and pull her into me. "Yeah baby, it's me. Come here."

She starts to heave in my arms and I swing my head around at Felix.

"What the fuck happened to her?"

He shrugs. "I don't know."

"Like fuck you don't know."

Zane stands from his seat. "That's enough! Shut the fuck up, both of you."

He begins walking up to Abby, bringing his face down to her level. "Abby? What's happened?"

Abby is fucking strong, so seeing her like this has me on edge. This girl has been dragged through hell and back.

"Just having an episode. I'm sorry," she breathes out, pushing away from me.

"I have seen your episodes Abby...that was *not* an episode."

She shakes her head. "No, I'm fine. I've got to go and see the girls. They're planning the hen's night."

I narrow my eyes at her. "I don't fucking believe you, Abby. Stop fucking playing hero and let me help."

She glares at me and straightens her shoulders. "Maybe I don't want your fucking help this time, Ade. You can't save me all the time."

I blow out my breath and mumble, "Where the fuck is Ollie."

She looks to me, fire in her eyes. "Fuck Ollie."

"Whatevs Abby. Don't fucking say I didn't try."

She storms out of the bar with Felix hot on her tail. Why the fuck the old man is following her around for, I don't know.

It's not long after Abby's episode when I decided to head home. I take off my cap and put on my helmet, throwing my leg over my bike, kick start it and ride out of there leaving a trail of smoke behind me.

CHAPTER 10

KALIE - ROSE

"Okay Kalie, can we stop now," Phoebe moans from beside me.

"No, we're about to abuse our body enough tonight, we need to get some health in."

We slow to a walking pace as we make our way back to my hotel room.

"Fuck health. Give me a burger and fries over this shit, any day."

"Yeah, well, not all of us are fortunate enough to eat whatever we want and for it not to show."

We reach the hotel, pulling the doors open and make our way up to my room. When we're in the cart, Phoebe looks to me. "So, I talked to Ade."

I look up at her, eyes wide. "You did what?"

She nods. "He's a hard one, Kal. I've known him all my life, and out of all the boys, he's the most reckless and ruthless. I just don't know if he'd be good for you."

I shrug. "Well, I wasn't planning on going there again, so you can rest easy."

She stops at the door and adds, "If you did, though, I'd totally get it. What's not to love about him, aside from his complete disrespect for the female species, he's all things any women would want and need in a man...plus more. I had a crush on him when I was younger, big time. Until I realized, he wasn't interested. It took me three years to get over him," she laughs to herself.

I laugh along with her while walking into the bathroom, stopping and leaning against the doorframe. "Yeah, I still can't believe someone so...beautiful, exists. Every time I'm with him, I have this insatiable need to touch him, to make sure he's real." I shake my head, and then snap my mouth closed when I realize I just said all of that out loud.

She laughs and walks up to me. "That bad, huh? I get it." She waves her hand away, seeing my shock. "He's, well...he's Ade Nixon, and that's all anyone really needs to say. But Kalie? He's not a good man. All that's good is on the outside, he has a lot of demonic shit going on inside him. Be careful?

Okay?" She looks into my eyes, worry etched all over her.

I nod my head and gulp down, pushing off the doorframe. "Of course, Phoebs. As I said, I don't think it's like that anymore. At least, not with him anyway."

She rolls her eyes with a smile, picking up the sound dock remote from the coffee table. "Honey, it is *a lot* like that with him. I'd begin praying, you know why?" she asks with a raised eyebrow, pushing play and VinylShakerz *'One Night in Bangkok'* pulsates through the speakers. "Because he doesn't take no for an answer. And when he wants you...*and he does want you*...you won't have a say in the matter." She smirks and pumps it up louder as she begins shaking her ass around the living room. Ignoring the flutter of butterflies I'm getting from the probability of her being right, I shake my head and shut the bathroom door.

Turning the faucet on, I wait patiently for the water to heat up. She's right, he is no good for me, but since he's walked into my life, I can't get him out of my head. Every time my ex would kiss me, I'd be thinking of Ade. Horrible, I know, but I couldn't help it. Once the shower is hot, I step in and scrub my body, hair, and face. Tonight is going to be interesting. I hear the bathroom door open, then close.

"Phoebs, could you not have waited until I was finished?" I laugh.

"Yeah, it's not Phoebe," a low, sexy, voice growls from the other side of the curtain.

I gasp and wrap the shower curtain around me. "Ade? Get out!"

I hear him chuckle. "Yeah, not going to happen."

He pulls open the curtain and I squeal, trying to grasp it back away from him while trying to hide the most private parts of my body.

"Ade! Get the fuck out. I swear to God—"

His lips smash onto mine pushing me back against the wall. I try to push him away, but it makes no difference, the man is hard as rock—everywhere. He picks me up and pushes me against the wall harder, stepping into the shower fully clothed. I moan into his mouth, and he draws out a low growl. With the water running down us both, he pulls back briefly.

"What happened to, *'you're not going to sleep with me?'*" I ask, looking up at him. He removes his clothes in one quick motion, running his hands through his hair. The water is running off his beautifully inked body and his eyes are dark with need.

"I said that did I?" he asks, tilting his head to the side with a sexy smirk.

I gulp down and nod. "Yeah, you did."

He shrugs. "Never been one to follow rules."

He brushes my hair back, moving one leg inside mine and pushing his groin into me. I bite down on my bottom lip, trying to contain the explosive feeling between my legs. I look up at him, his eyes narrow before he places his other leg between mine, causing me to open wider for him. My breathing is ragged and if he doesn't fuck me right now, I'm going to rub myself all over him until I get my release.

He brings his hand to my chin and pushes it up to look at him.

"How many men have you been with since me?" he asks, searching my eyes.

I narrow my eyes at him and scowl. "What's that got to do with what we're doing right now?"

He raises his eyebrows, jaw ticking dangerously. "Answer the fucking question Kalie."

I huff out, dropping my eyes to the shower floor. "I have seen two guys since I met you." His jaw clenches tight and his lustful eyes have been replaced with anger. "But…" I raise my finger in the air when I see he's about to say something, "I haven't *been* with anyone since you," I whisper out the end of that sentence. I watch as his eyes set into understanding and then turn hungry again. He brings his lips down to mine and swipes his tongue across my bottom lip. When I open my eyes again, I'm greeted with a smirk.

I cock my head to the side. "Something funny?"

He shakes his head. "Yeah, actually."

I raise my eyebrows. "Oh? Do tell."

He laughs and nips my ear. "I think it's funny that this pussy here," he brings his hand down and cups my pussy in his hand, sliding a finger inside, "is *mine*," he growls into my ear. He extracts his finger and I moan out at the sudden loss of it. Lifting me back up, he slides his dick inside of me in one, tight, move. "Fuck," he groans and I moan out at the feeling of his thick, long, cock filling me.

Every...

Single...

Inch...

And there's at least nine.

The feeling is unreal. How I had gone this long without having this man inside of me, I have no idea. He pulls out of me, only to slam into me again, causing my body to push up against the wet wall. He brings his hand around my waist, getting a better grip, and the other on my neck. I throw my hands around his neck and push my lips to his, licking over his two rings and sucking on his pierced tongue.

Every thrust that he pushes into me, I feel his head hit my spot. And every time he pulls out, I feel the pressure of his extraction. The feeling is addictive, and I never want to stop. He brings his face down to my nipple, pulling it roughly into his mouth, the metal of his tongue ring sliding over it in rhythmic fashion. Sticking to his same torturous pace, he continues to fuck me with raw intensity and passion. Sweat dripping down my forehead and the fog filling the room only adds to my need. I grab onto his face, running my hands over his jaw and down his fully tattooed neck. I lean down and slide my tongue all over his jaw and down his neck, following my hands movements.

When I begin to feel that same familiar pull begin deep in my stomach, I clutch onto him tightly as my orgasm rips through me like a tidal wave of euphoria. I'm panting, trying to catch my breath when he places me back down to my feet. I drop to my knees quickly and push him deep into my throat. His hand grasps onto my hair and he throws his head back. Wrapping my lips around my teeth, I bite down a little, pushing him in deep. Well, the most that I can take of him anyway, which isn't that much—he's big, *everywhere*.

I wrap the base of his cock in my hand and begin to squeeze lightly while pumping and twisting him, following the motions of my mouth. I feel his balls tighten, so I rub them in my hand as his hot liquid pumps down the back of my throat. I swallow every bit of him and stand back to my feet. He looks at me with a smile, lightly kissing me.

Mumbling against my lips, "Should I ask why you know how to use this mouth of yours so well?" He raises his eyebrows at me, touching my swollen lips.

I shake my head. "Probably not," I say looking up at him and watch his mouth set into a hard line.

"Cut it out. You were my first," I point down to his dick, "you know, so quit it. You do and always will own that *big* part of me. And anyway, I wasn't expecting this to happen," I say surprisingly at him.

He smiles and pulls me up against him, kissing me briefly. "I was. I had no intention of staying away from you Kalie. When I saw you in the bar, I knew this was it for me. It was hard enough having to walk away from you that first time, I won't do it again." He stops briefly before continuing, "I will need the name or..." his face sets into a murderous glare, "names, of the men you have gone past kissing with. Nope, I'll need the ones you have kissed too. Actually, just anyone that's ever touched you will do."

I pull my head back and search his eyes, hoping to see some sort of joke behind his words, but came out with nothing. I turn the faucet to a scorching hot temperature and stand underneath it, letting the water run over me. I look up at him and see he's watching me intently. "Are you serious?" I ask, knowing damn well that will never happen.

He stalks over to me until his chest is flush up against mine. He wraps his hand around my chin and jerks my face to meet his. "Kalie, I haven't had a girlfriend…ever. I don't know the rules of how this is supposed to go, but as I said before, I don't abide by rules anyway. I make my own and people follow those." His hand doesn't move from my chin, but his thumb glides over my bottom lip. He watches the movement carefully before continuing, "I'm going to fuck up eventually. I don't lose my shit, I know exactly what I'm doing when I do it. And trust me, if I ever see, or hear, of anyone touching, or have touched this…" He runs his hands down the front of my body and around to my ass. The movement causes a shiver to break over me. That shiver is need mixed with fear. "I *will* kill them," he states matter-of-factly. I see the look in his eyes, and I know with one hundred percent certainty that this man is serious.

"What are you saying?" I ask, searching his eyes for clues.

"I'm saying, *you…are…mine.*" He accentuates every word.

"You would kill someone if they had touched me?" I gulp down.

"I will kill someone if they so much as look at you too long."

"You're crazy," I say with a chuckle. I'm trying to lighten myself up.

He nods his head. "When it comes to you? I'm fucking deranged, baby. Don't mess with that."

Swallowing down my fear I say, "You're a little intense, anyone ever told you that?"

He doesn't reply, so I squeeze some soap into my hand and begin rubbing it all over me, forming suds.

"It's been hard for me too, you know. I've had two boyfriends since met you—"

He clamps his hand down onto my mouth, narrows his eyes, and pushes himself up against me. "Shut the fuck up, Kalie. Don't test my limits, because I have *none*. I'm a ticking time bomb waiting to explode when it comes to you. Choose your next words wisely."

Glaring at him, I whack his hand off my mouth, giving him a scowl. "As I was saying, before I was so rudely interrupted. Both of them cheated on me because I wouldn't sleep with them."

I rub more soap over my legs, and then him. "I couldn't, Ade. You ruined me after that night. When you took my virginity, you took a piece of me. Every time another man touched me, or kissed me, all I wanted was to be in your arms again. I felt sick to my stomach, it never felt right."

He brushes a stray strand of hair out of my face and smiles. "Ditto baby. I just tried a little harder than you did."

I smack him in the arm and smile. "Eew, I don't want to know."

He laughs, pulling me into his arms, where I melt. "All that doesn't matter, it's just you and me now."

CHAPTER 11

Pulling my baby doll dress off the hanger, I squeeze into it. Ade looks over to me as I'm adjusting my boobs into the dress and he drops his cut back on the bed, along with his mouth.

"There is no fucking way you're wearing that. Take it off. *Now.*"

I laugh. "Don't be stupid, Ade. It's dress up. We have to dress as skanks, and it was your precious Alaina's idea. So have words with her."

He walks over to me and grabs onto my ass, pulling me into him.

I look up and tilt my head. "What does all this mean? Are we monogamous?" I have to ask.

He picks me up and slams me against the wall while dropping little kisses on my lips. "This means that you are mine. So as of now, yes," he murmurs, pulling my bottom lip into his.

I wrap my hands around his neck and look deep into his eyes. "Why me?"

He brings his hands back down, cupping my pussy. "I don't fucking know. I've been asking myself the same question for the past two years." Wrapping his fingers around my panties, he pulls them down and drops to his knees in front of me, turning his cap backward.

"Ade, I don't have time for this" I attempt to say more, but words are lost on me when his hot mouth covers my pussy. I feel his pierced tongue slide over my clit slowly before two fingers are sliding inside me. I grab onto his flat cap and pull it off, gripping his hair with my hands. He lifts one of my legs off the ground and places it over his shoulder. His pace is torturous; he's an expert at this obviously. Trying not to think too much into that, I moan out and bite my bottom lip. His tongue flicks over me repeatedly as he works me up. Bringing his arm up, he pushes it against my lower belly, using his thumb to circle my clit. He slips his tongue inside me and I throw my head back, smashing it against the wall. I'm panting and grinding up against his face. Looking down on him, just as his eyes meet mine, my orgasm rips through my body in gushing waves, causing my legs to give way. I almost drop to the floor, but instead, dropping into Ade's arms.

"You are mine, Kalie. Don't take that shit lightly. Get changed." He smacks my ass while he walks out of the room.

Well, if that's how he claims his women, consider me claimed. I smile to myself and run my fingers over my lips as butterflies erupt inside my belly.

I think about protesting about the dress issue but decided on a better idea. I shove on a more placid dress and put my skimpy one into my bag. Walking out to the living room dressed in a short, but not too short dress, which does not cling to my body at all, he looks up at me.

"Much better, baby," Ade says coming up and kissing me on the forehead.

I fake smile and walk to the kitchen to pull out some vodka. I may be nice, but I'll never let a man tell me what clothes I should wear, whether that's Ade Nixon or not. I bring the bottle into the living room area where Phoebe is sitting on the couch with her eyebrows raised. Ever the over opinionated beauty that she is.

"Spit it out, Phoebs," I say, twisting the bottle open.

She looks to Ade then back at me. "So hang on, you fucked him again?" she bursts out.

Ade throws his arms over the couch and laughs. "None of your fucking business, Phoebe."

She stands and puts her hands on her hips. "Ade, she's my best fucking friend. This is absolutely my business. *Fuck*."

He shakes his head, spreading his legs out in front of him and I have to bite down on my lip to stop me from moaning out loud. *I need therapy,* I think.

"What's the fucking issue, Phoebe?"

She laughs and begins to pace walk. "My problem, Mr. Nixon. Is that you're a man-whore, who cannot keep it in his pants for more than a week. And you're going to hurt my best friend because she doesn't fucking roll like that! She's not cut out for all this shit," she yells throwing her hands in the air.

Ade gets up and makes his way to her. Swallowing my first glass of vodka, I wonder whether I need to tell him to stand down.

"*One.* Just because you're Blake's sister, and I've known you all of my life, does not give you the right to raise your voice at me. *And two*," he responds smirking. "She is not one of my whores. She's mine Phoebe, always has been."

She pauses her walking and looks between the two of us. "Wait, so you're together?"

I look to Ade and take another big gulp of the clear goodness. Straight from the bottle this time, there's no need for a shot glass—we're way past that.

He nods his head at her then looks back at me. "Yeah, and as of now, it is official."

We're getting into the huge stretch limo when my phone vibrates. Leaving it for now I concentrate on getting out of this nana dress I'm in.

"Oh, my fucking God, Kalie. What the fuck are you wearing?" Vicky asks with disgust.

"Shut up," I snap at her. "Ade wouldn't let me out of the house in what I wanted to wear, so I had to pack it into my handbag. Ta-da," I say in a magician's voice. Let's face it I may be slightly intoxicated. Whipping out the short, skimpy dress from my bag, there's nothing much to it. It's tight, white, and strapless. Under the boobs are two straps that run across each other, showing half my mid-section and rib cage. Actually it's pretty fucking scandalous. I paired it with red pumps and I was done. After shuffling around and squeezing into it, everyone stops and looks to me.

Alaina shakes her head, lifting up her glass. "Fuck. I am in so much shit for this."

Vicky interrupts Alaina's worries, pouring a drink into a glass and handing it to me. "So, you and Ade? Are you sleeping together again?"

I laugh and take a mouthful of my drink. I need to be more intoxicated if I'm going to get through tonight. I start to answer her when Phoebe steps in for me.

"They are not just sleeping together. He's claimed her. Officially."

Alaina gasps and whips her head around to me. "No freaking way! Are you serious?" She claps her hands with excitement.

Vicky looks shocked, but only a little. "You attained the unattainable," she states, looking at me with a proud smile.

I laugh nervously. "Let's not get carried away. It's early days yet, and anyway, if he ever finds out about me dressing like this, I will be buried in his backyard."

Alaina scoffs. "Actually he would bury you in, um...never mind. Not important."

I widen my eyes at her and Vicky turns to where Alaina is sitting. "He tells you? You know, about everything in the club?"

Alaina peeks over her glass with innocence. "Who? Ade? Fuck no."

Vicky shakes her head. "No, Zane?"

Alaina looks to her. "Yeah, of course. Has Blake not given you the two options?"

Vicky nods her head. "Yeah, but I wasn't sure which one you took."

Alaina laughs. "Well, you have four sleeps to figure that out."

"What's this about?" I ask. I have no idea what goes on in their world, but I'm very aware that they live a little differently. They are outlaws after all.

"When you're an old lady, you get two options and you have to pick one before your wedding night. Option one...you want to know everything that goes on, or option two...you want to know nothing," Alaina says a little too calmly. Making me question her level of sanity, just a bit.

"I don't get it. Know what?" I ask, looking between both Alaina and Vicky.

"You know," Alaina, says pouring more alcohol into her glass.

"Where they hide the bodies." She winks at me.

My face pales. "Right. Shit. So he wasn't kidding then."

Vicky narrows her eyes at Alaina and me, pauses what she's pouring into her glass. "What did he say?" Alaina asks.

"Oh you know, that he will kill anyone and everyone who has and will touch me."

Alaina relaxes and laughs. "Yeah, I wouldn't play with that."

I'm still trying to swallow the questions in my head when we pull up to the bar.

Who the fuck is Ade Nixon? And what exactly does his position entail?

We pull into a car park at some flashy nightclub and get out. By now, we're all very drunk, so drunk, I'm almost certain we will not be able to get in. We pass through the bouncers anyway and make out way inside the club. As soon as we walk in Dawin *'Desert'* starts playing over the speakers. I squeal and pull everyone to the dance floor.

After we down a few more drinks, I feel a body push up against me with his groin flush up against my ass. I turn around and see the sweaty tween smiling.

I push at his chest. "Yeah, can you not?"

He wraps his hands around my waist and pulls me into him.

I push him again. "Seriously, fuck off!" I push away from him and make my way to the bar. Pulling out a seat and ordering a rum and coke. I fucking hate pushy guys. Vicky sees me sitting and waves me over to her, so I grab my drink and walk to them.

"Sorry, he was annoying."

Vicky shakes her head. "Don't apologize. I was just about to start sharpening the knives."

I laugh and sip on my drink. Alaina turns around. "Right, next trip. Let's bounce," she says as she begins to pull us out of the bar. We're all laughing when we jump back into the limo and make our way to the next destination the queen has on her list.

ADE NIXON

"Can't say I'm surprised," Zane says in between his drinks.

"Me either," Blake adds.

I laugh. "Oh really? None of you fuckers were going to let me know about these thoughts?"

They both laugh. "So, you're going to make her your old lady?" Blake asks.

I shrug. "If there were ever to be a girl that could tame me, it'd be her."

Blake chuckles. "Brother, do not go down that road. Trust me."

I nod my head in understanding because I do trust him. He and Vicky fucked around a lot. "I trust you, but I'm not fighting my feelings for her. I know I care about her a little too much, and I know she had an impact on me all those years ago. But that doesn't mean I'm ready to cut my balls off and hand them to her. Fuck that."

They both start laughing when Zane stands, throwing bills on the table.

"Where are we going now?" Harvey asks while getting a lap dance from one of the strippers.

"To check on something."

KALIE - ROSE

We're dancing to Ludacris *'What's Your Fantasy'* when I feel another body push up behind me, only this one feels like a big rock wall.

I whip around, ready to start swinging. "Yeah, fuck—" I stop mid-speech when I see it's Ade. He wraps his arms around my waist, pulling me into him.

"Is there's a reason why you're skittish with people touching you?" he asks, tilting his head.

"You're very observant." I narrow my eyes at him bravely, and then I remember his threats from earlier. Turning bright red, I realize I'm standing in the first dress I pulled on.

Oh, fuck.

He shrugs. "I have to be. Now answer the question?"

Wrapping my arms around his neck I pull him back down to me. "There was a guy at the other bar that tried to grind on me. Told him to fuck off, though." He narrows his eyes, pulling me into him forcefully before picking me up. I wrap my legs around his waist while he carries me out of there. At least I'm not over his shoulders. He brings his lips up to mine and smirks before sliding his tongue over them slowly.

"Maybe, it's because you wore this?" He pinches at my dress and instantly I go red.

"I...um. Peer pressure," I say coyly.

"Peer pressure?" he asks, dropping his eyes into an evil glare.

There's that look again.

I'll need new panties.

"Mm-hmm." I smile and bite down on his lip.

"You're fucking trouble, you know that. But you're *my* trouble."

He places me down to the floor, grasping onto my hand. "We are leaving. If I have to watch one more guy look at you in that dress, I'm going to go *Rampage Jackson* on them."

I'm certain he's just as scary, if not more than, *Rampage Jackson*. We're almost out the door when I feel my phone vibrate again in my clutch.

"Shit, I need to get this." Opening my clutch, I rush out the door to answer my phone without the loud music blaring in the background.

"Hello," I answer, watching Ade saunter to me slowly.

"Kalie? It's Sarah. Carter's mom."

"Oh. Hey, Sarah. Everything okay?"

"Carter's been in a serious accident. He's in the hospital right now."

I throw my hand up to my mouth in shock, my stomach rolling over. "What! What happened?"

"I don't know love. I can discuss the details with you when you get here."

I nod my head and look to Ade as a single tear drops from my eye. Wiping it away quickly I tell her, "I'll be there in a few hours."

Hanging up my phone, Ade's face slackened, his brow furrowed and he bit his lower lip in concern. "Who was that?"

"It was my best friend Carter's mom. He's been in a serious accident, and I have to leave. Now."

"The wedding is on Sunday," he murmurs.

"I know. I'll be back. I just have to go and see what's happening. I'll come back tomorrow night."

"I'm coming with you," he says, pulling me to him.

"You don't have to do that," I reply, hugging his huge body.

"I want to, we can take my car. You can text Vicky when we're on the road."

I nod my head in understanding and look up to him. He brushes my hair out of my face and kisses me softly on the lips. My feelings for him are growing too fast for me to handle, and I really hope I don't get hurt.

CHAPTER 12

After going back to my hotel room and quickly changing, we get on the road, heading back to Hollywood. Feeling sick, I hope he's okay. Ade's hand grasps onto my thigh.

"It's going to be okay, babe."

Smiling at him and looking out the window, I watch the trees passing the window. "I hope so. Carter's my best friend and I love him, but I know he can get rowdy."

"Is he straight?" Ade asks, looking at me sideways.

"No Ade, he's as gay as they come."

He nods his head in understanding, turning his attention back to the road. "So you dance in Hollywood? Phoebe says you're quite the girl here."

I raise my eyebrows. "Yeah, I guess I am. I'm pretty good at what I do. I think that came from the endless ballet glasses my mom pushed me into from as soon as I could walk. I hated it, ballet sucked, but I was good…really good. One day, I was dancing along to Timberland *'Bounce,'* you know, after watching *Step Up 2*, I wanted to learn the whole dance, and I did. However, my mom walked in on me in my dance studio that she'd had built into our home. She was disgusted with me and converted my dancing studio into another drinking slash living room for her and her friends as punishment." I look to Ade and see him watching me every two seconds while keeping his eyes on the road.

"Your mom sounds like a bitch."

I laugh. "She was. That was mainly because she was constantly trying to keep up with her pathetic Stepford wife friends, and the church. My parents were Mormon, they are not anymore. They're entirely different people now. Not like that at all. I love to dance, it's a passion of mine and I think something incredibly beautiful happens when your passion turns into your work. However, I also would love it to be just a hobby. I don't want to be shaking my ass for these music videos for all my life." I open the glove box and pull out a bag of pretzels that Ade put in there before we left.

"What is it that you want to do?" he asks softly.

"I've always wanted to be a criminal defense lawyer."

He laughs and rubs a hand over his mouth before he stops abruptly when he sees my eyes drop. "Sorry baby, I wasn't laughing because I don't think you can do it. I was laughing because how ironic that would be if you were a lawyer, and being with me."

I smile and crunch down on a pretzel. "Yeah I guess. It's just a dream anyway."

"Wake up baby," I hear Ade's voice through my sleep.

"Shit, did I fall asleep?" I stretch out my arms.

"Yeah, come on, we're here."

Unbuckling my belt, I open my door. Ade walks around to my side and grabs onto my hand while we walk into the hospital hand-in-hand. It feels natural, everything with him does. It feels as though we've been together for years. When we reach the reception area, I notice an elderly woman typing away at her keyboard behind her desk.

"I'm here to see Carter Benson," I say, tapping the counter out of nerves.

"Are you family?" she asks.

"Yes. Yes, I'm family," I say without hesitation.

"He's in the ER, follow the red arrows."

"Thanks."

We begin following the red arrows until they lead us to a set of large doors. Pushing them open, we make my way in to where Sarah and Rob, Carter's parents are sitting. I drop Ade's hand and pull them both in for a hug.

"This is my boyfriend, Ade," I introduce casually pointing to him standing beside me.

It's not until I see the smile on his face that I realize what I've just referred to him as. I don't know why the man is surprised, it's not as if he gave me a choice in the matter.

"Nice to meet you, Ade," both Sarah and Rob say in unison. They are amazing parents, never judging anyone. So meeting a man with an MC patch is no issue for them.

"What happened?" I ask them both while taking a seat.

"The police are saying that someone ran him off the road."

I look to them both the color draining from my face in shock. "What do you mean *ran him off the road*?"

"There's evidence at the crash site that shows there was another vehicle involved. The police are in the process of gathering CTV footage."

"Oh my God," I gasp staring wide-eyed. "Why would anyone want to hurt, Carter?" I shake my head.

Ade sits down next to me and pulls me under his arm, laying a kiss on my head. "It's going to be okay, baby. I'll handle it."

A couple of hours later, two police officers walk in with a doctor. We all stand and make our way to them.

The officers look between Ade and me. "Are you okay with them hearing this?"

Sarah nods. "Kalie is family."

"We have the footage we were looking for, and just as suspected someone ran him off the road," one of the officers says to Sarah.

I look up to the police officers confusion written all over my face. "Intentionally? Carter has no enemies *at all*."

He smiles. "It appears that he doesn't right now, but—"

Tainted Love

"No, he has no enemies. I live with him. Sure he has his cat fights, but no one that would want to harm him—"

The doctor interrupts. "He would like to see you all now, said something about a nookie?"

I laugh and hook my hand around Ade's elbow. "You're in for a treat."

Walking down the corridor until I see his name on one of the tags, Sarah and Rob follow closely behind me. When I see the door, I push it open and notice Carter sitting up in his bed with a bandage wrapped firmly around his head.

"Oh my God!" I run to his bedside. Ade hangs back, closing the door behind all of us.

"Hey baby G, I'm fine. Mom! Vicky is going to kill me if Kalie doesn't show for the wedding!" he scolds his mother.

Ade walks around the curtain and Carter gasps. "Sweet baby Jesus. I would stay celibate for two years for that too," Carter says loudly, eyeing Ade from head to toe. Ade looks to him eyes wide. I smack Carter on the shoulder, saving him before Ade decides to go all *Jack the Ripper* on his ass. Although, something tells me, that because he knows how much Carter means to me, he will tolerate him. I hope.

"Stop! Ade, this is Carter. Carter…Ade."

I sit down on a seat at the end of the bed so his mom and dad can have a moment with him. Ade walks over to me, picks me up out of my seat, sits in it and then places me on his lap.

He kisses my neck and whispers, "Boyfriend, huh?"

"Well, after all that begging from you, I thought I better, at least, put a label on us."

He smiles a broad smile, squeezing my inner thigh. "Touché babe." The gesture setting all my hormones into overdrive. I look to him behind me and smile. Leaning in, he kisses my nose. I feel like locking him up for months just to have my wicked way with him.

Seriously, I think I need to do that. I make a mental note of that fact.

Basically, I just want to have sex with him nonstop while loving the shit out of him. Loving is in the eventual category, I think. *Shit.* When I snap out of our playfulness and look up to Carter, I can see him smiling at us.

"What!" I snap at him with a grin.

"You gave him the nookie. See, I done told you."

Rolling my eyes before setting my face back into a serious look. "Carter, do you remember much from that night?"

He looks uneasy, all playfulness gone. He sits up on his bed and looks at his mom and dad.

"Can you guys go home and get me some clothes, please? I have none here, and I'm not wearing these the whole time I'm in this hole."

His parents look at him worriedly before he adds, "Its fine, Mom. I just want to catch up with Kalie." They both nod, giving him a kiss on the cheek and then leaving.

Once they've left the room, I look to Carter. "So?"

He shakes his head. "I don't remember much, but I do remember a van. It was white and had men in balaclavas inside it. When they were trying to push me off the road, I wouldn't budge, until one of them wound their window down and flashed a gun at me. I freaked the fuck out and swerved off the road, hitting a tree."

Looking to Ade who has his eyebrows drawn in together he says, "You didn't see anyone else? Remember anything distinctive about the van?" Ade asks with his arm draped around me as he rubs circles on my arm causing goose bumps to rise on the skin.

Carter shakes his head. "I didn't see anyone else. The only other thing I can think of regarding the van is that it had chrome mag wheels."

Ade nods his head looks at me and smiles. "That's enough information, I can get the rest."

He taps my leg. "Hop up for a sec, baby."

I jump up off his leg while he pulls out his phone. Looking to Carter I ask, "You're okay, though? Aside from your head?"

Ade pulls me back down onto his lap forcefully while I'm talking, causing me to yelp in surprise.

"Yeah, I'll be fine, baby G."

"Drago? Need you to run through some CCTV footage, I'll be home tonight," Ade says authoritatively over the phone. I glance at my watch and see it's close to four o'clock in the morning. I look down at him from his lap, studying his eyes, and he smiles and winks at me before looking at Carter. "Where was the accident?" Ade asks Carter, who tells him the location, which Ade then relays to the man down the phone line before he ends the call.

He grabs onto my hand and kisses my knuckles. "I'll have some more info tonight."

I swallow down my worry and look back at Carter. "We better go, no doubt Vicky will be freaking out because I didn't get time to tell her we were leaving."

Carter nods his head. "Then yes, you better."

"I just need to stop at home and pick up a few more things. Do you need anything else from home?" I ask Carter, but he shakes his head. "All right then," I say walking up to him and giving him a quick kiss on the head. "Stay safe, please!"

He brushes my worry away. "I'm always safe."

I pull open the passenger seat door and slide in. Ade puts his belt on and roars the car to life before putting it in reverse.

"Who's Drago?" I ask out of curiosity.

"He's our computer nerd. He'll sort out anything we need to know about that van," he replies, putting it into first gear and pulling out of the hospital.

"Are you hungry?" he asks looking over his arm.

"Starving."

We pull up to an in-and-out burger place. Ade orders the whole burger joint, and I fold my arms in disbelief.

"I'm not going to eat that much." He laughs before pulling out of the drive through.

"Take a left up here, it takes you onto the boardwalk," I say grabbing the chips out of the bag. It's a habit I have, it's as though they call to me begging me to eat them. We pull up to the carpark and I turn in my seat, putting one chip after the other in my mouth.

"You wanna eat here or out there." I point toward the beach.

He laughs, rubbing his fingers over his mouth. "Come on my little chip eater," he says laughing and picking up the bag of fast food.

Sliding out of the car I follow him to the beach. It's beautiful here, so serene and peaceful. He stops walking and nudges his head, so I pick up my pace and grab onto his hand. Once we've sat down, Ade lies on his back, propping himself up on one elbow. I pull my burger out and moan as I take the first bite from it. He laughs putting a chip into his mouth.

"That good, huh?" he asks, swiping the sauce from my lips with his thumb before sucking it off.

I nod. "Really, really, good. Good enough to not want to go for a run just for eating it."

He shakes his head and kisses my hand. "You're pretty fucking special, you know that?"

I swallow the bite I'd taken and laugh. "Good special, I hope."

His laughter dies out and he just smiles at me. "Real good, darling."

"So," I say, wiping my hands with the provided napkin. "You have no brothers or sisters?" I ask.

"Nah none. My parents were as fucked-up as they come. My dad more so than my mom," he replies, looking out to the ocean.

"Your mom? She passed away when you were young?"

He doesn't look to me, just keeps his eyes locked on the ocean. "Yeah, she killed herself when I was fifteen. Came home after a fight and found her sliced up on the kitchen floor. Lifeless."

My eyes widen in shock. I'm speechless. No one should have to find their mother dead, let alone a fifteen-year-old boy discovering such a graphic scene.

"I'm sorry," I mutter because I have no idea what else to say.

He pulls his eyes away from the ocean to look at me. "Don't be sorry, I got over it pretty quickly."

I raise my eyebrows out of shock at his choice of words. How would one get over that, let alone get over it so quickly? I don't know what else to do, so I move into his arm and lay down with him. He looks down at me and smiles before pulling me under his arm and rolling on top of me.

"Ade…" I say in warning. He tilts his head to the side, smirks and places one of his legs inside mine.

"Kalie…" he mimics.

"Kalie-Rose, if you want to be formal."

His eyes narrow and he sucks in a breath. "Kalie-Rose is your full name?"

I smile. "Kalie-Rose Reynolds is my full name. But yeah, Kalie-Rose is my full first name."

His eyes search mine and he plants a soft kiss on my lips. "How did I get someone so fucking perfect?"

"Seriously, people will start staring soon," I say, slowly turning bright red at his movements. His face holds that same smirk while he pulls on his other leg.

My eyes widen again. "You cannot—"

He grinds his hips into me in a circular motion. I moan out and bite my lower lip. He brings his head down to my neck and bites down.

"I'll do what I want, baby." Running his tongue all the way over my neck and up to my ear. I'm lost in my own little world of Ade and Kalie when it all stops and he gets off me. I frown and prop myself up on my elbows.

"No fair!" I pout, and he laughs, gripping onto my hands and pulling me up.

"We need to get back to this wedding before shit blows up." He pulls me in for a kiss. When he lets me go, I pick up our rubbish and follow him back to the car.

CHAPTER 13

On our way to my apartment, we talk as though we've known each other for years. Everything is so easy with him. However, I can't help but feel it's a little too easy, like the calm before the storm. No one gets this much of a good thing without a little crazy. The car shuts off and I jump out.

"I'm pretty sure you're too big to even fit in my apartment door, but let's try."

He laughs while slamming his door closed. "You want me to stop shredding?"

I grab onto his humongous arms, my little hands can't even wrap around half of his bicep. I shake my head and turn red. "Nope, definitely a no to that one."

We begin walking into my apartment. Dropping my keys onto the bench I walk up into my room. "I won't be long, just need to get a few things."

I start to gather up my shampoo and conditioner when I feel him walk into my room. He looks around and for the first time ever, I feel self-conscious about what my room looks like. It's all very casual and plain. My wooden bed sits in the middle of the room with bedside drawers on either side. There's a long boy chest opposite the bed that has a large flat screen television on it, because, well, I love *Netflix* in bed. He walks up to my bedside table and picks up a photo. It's a picture of me, Carter and Dominic. Swallowing hard I look up to find him staring at me, silently questioning the photo.

"Friends Ade. He's just a friend."

He puts the picture back down and moves to me.

"Friends, hmm? Did he, or did he not, make a move on you?" he asks.

"He was confused," I reply nervously, looking around the room.

Ade wraps his hands around my neck and pulls me into him. I feel the bulge in his pants pushing up against my stomach, and it turns me on. He brings his lips down to my ear, running over the edges carefully, making my eyes close and a moan slip out.

"Let's try that again pumpkin, and it would be in your best interests to be honest with me. Did he…"

he licks around my earlobe, "or did he not..." running his hand down, cupping my ass and pulling me into him, "make a move on you?" he whispers into my ear, rubbing me roughly up against his dick.

I moan out and tilt my head back. "Yes, yes he did," I whisper out, lost in my own little world. He hisses, picking me up and throwing me onto my bed. He removes his cut, T-shirt, and unbuttons his jeans, leaving them open and loose before crawling up the bed to me. I swallow and slide down the bed. He places both his fists on either side of my head, moving on top of me and widening my legs with his. He grinds his hips into me in a circular motion, bringing his mouth down to mine and licking me from my collarbone to my lips.

He just licked me.

It felt predatory, possessive and proprietorial. It felt like a statement, and I would not want to be the person standing between Ade Nixon and what he wants. He unthreads his belt from his jeans and wraps it around my wrists. I look up to him studying his perfect features.

"What are you doing?" I ask nervously.

He laughs. "Teaching you a lesson. Always be honest with me Kalie. I will always be honest with you, even if I know it would hurt you."

He pulls my hands over my head and ties the belt to my headboard.

"Oh shit," I whisper out in a hushed tone.

"*Oh shit,* is right."

He lifts my top up, rolling it over my eyes, using it as a blindfold before taking charge of my mouth, and caressing my tongue slowly with his. This kiss alone has my pussy wet with need. Without breaking our kiss, he runs his hands down my stomach and over my jeans, unbuttoning them and pulling them down past my ankles. I can't see anything and I can't feel anything with my hands, but the need to touch him becomes stronger with every brush of his hands on my body. He pulls down my panties before unclipping my bra, squeezing my nipple briefly and bringing his mouth down over it. I arch my back off the bed, panting shamelessly.

"Ade?"

"Shhh baby, no talking, or I'll gag you."

I snap my mouth shut quickly. There's no way I'm doing the gag thing. Nope. Not a chance.

He slowly licks a trail down my stomach and over my inner thighs, licking that sweet spot where your thigh and pussy meet. I feel a hard suction in the same spot then I hear him chuckle. Feeling his body move off me, I begin turning my head from side to side, wondering where he went.

Before I can speak, his warm mouth closes over my pussy, licking it from bottom to top before beginning a torturous pace. A pattern of lick and suck. I moan out in pleasure before a finger slides inside me, pushing up on my g-spot. I begin to grind on his face and I feel my body reach the peak of that glorious mountain we all love to climb, all for me to go rolling and tumbling down when his mouth unlatches from its duty.

"Fuck!" I yell.

Ade chuckles, running his hands softly over my body again.

"Hmmm…" He grips onto my hips, flips me on all fours, pulls his jeans all the way down, smacks my ass and pushes into me. I scream out at the sudden movement, throwing my head back. He grips onto my hair with one hand, and wraps his other around my waist, pushing down on the arch of my back. I moan out again while he pounds into me, every thrust hitting my spot. I don't know if all men can hit it that perfectly, and constantly, but Ade can and it is freaking euphoric.

Sweat is dripping from my forehead as both of our bodies are slapping into each other at rough and raw speeds. It's not long before I feel myself tighten up around his dick, so tight that I don't want to let go. One more thrust after that, I can't contain it anymore and let myself go. I feel his cock pulse inside me with his release almost instantly behind mine. The feeling of pure pleasure overwhelms me and takes over my entire body, causing my legs to shake so much they collapse out from under me.

I feel a slap on my ass before being picked up and flipped onto my back like a ragdoll. He pulls my top down and unbuckles the belt before pulling up his jeans. I look up to him and smile, rubbing my wrists.

"I'll have wet dreams about that no doubt," I mumble to myself.

"What?" he asks, smiling at me.

I shake my head. "I used to dream about that one night years ago. Every time I did, I would wake up with wet panties," I say honestly. His face sets in stone before a wide grin pulls across his face.

"That is the hottest shit ever. But I'm pissed off that I didn't take care of you all those times. That stops now," he states pulling his top and cut back on.

Getting off the bed I walk into my closet, pulling out some more clothes to take with me. I haven't really thought about what we'll do after this wedding, I live four hours away from Westbeach. That's a bit far for a possessive, controlling man like Ade Nixon. We can cover all that after the wedding I guess, right now, I just want to enjoy what we have. Pulling on my jeans after getting into a clean set of bra and undies, I can tell being around Ade is going to be costly with all the panties I'll need to change into throughout the day.

Maybe I should bill him for that?

"You ready?" he asks.

I nod my head. "Yeah, let's go."

He pulls on my hand, tucking me under his shoulder as we begin walking down to his car. The past twenty-four hours have been fantastic. I've loved being away from everything with just him and me, even if it was under shit circumstances. Pulling out my phone and text messaging Vicky, I let her know we're on our way back. No doubt, she'll be panicking. I intentionally haven't picked up her calls over the past day. I shove my phone back into my pocket.

She's going to be mad as fuck.

We set off on the highway, heading back toward reality.

The next morning, I wake up and stretch my arms out. It's wedding day! I clap my hands and jump off the bed, trying not to wake Ade, who's sleeping peacefully next to me. I pull on his SS T-shirt, which hangs to my knees and stare at him for a few seconds. Admiring him like a stalker, before going into the kitchen and preparing the batter for pancakes. I plug my iPod into the hotel dock and turn on 2Pac *'Thugs Get Lonely Too,'* I need a bit of gangster in my life this morning.

Beginning to dance around the kitchen, I'm in my zone. I love dancing, it heals everything, not that I need healing right now—I need Ade Nixon rehab. Looking up after pouring some batter into the pan I see Ade leaning against the doorframe, smirking with his arms crossed in front of his bare chest. His hair is all messy, standing around his face and his piercing blue eyes are peering into me as if they can see into the depths of my soul. My tummy flips upside down and I try my best to hide my sudden excitement at seeing him standing there watching me dance. I turn the music down a bit.

"Hey! Pancakes?" I ask him, holding up a pancake on a spatula.

He laughs, walking over to the bar stool and pulling it out.

"I'll eat anything you want me to eat just to watch you shake your ass like that again."

"Hmmm, maybe you don't need to eat anything to see me shake my ass. Maybe I'll just do it for free, alone, locked in a room, for months," I say smiling at him innocently.

He raises his eyebrows in surprise before leaning over the kitchen bench and pulling my face in, kissing me long and hard. "Maybe I'll just eat your sweet pussy all day and you can dance your little ass all over my face." I gulp down in shock and he laughs.

"You're fucking perfect, I don't deserve you," he states, running his thumb over my bottom lip.

I lean my head into his grasp and look up to him. "You deserve more than you realize Ade, and I will happily prove that to you for as long as you need."

His eyes turn soft, a gentle smile arriving at his lips. "You're too much sweet, Kalie-Rose. Way too much." My name rolls off his tongue and heads straight to my core. I'm doomed with this man, everything he does affects me. He sits back on his stool and leans into it. I continue stacking up the pancakes before placing them in on the bench. Moving around the corner I sit on the stool next to him. Picking up a stack and pouring maple syrup all over them—a little excessively—
but that's how I like it. Scattering some bacon, bananas, and strawberries before digging my fork into them. I can see Ade look at me out of the corner of my eye and I turn my head to him.

"What?" I ask around a mouthful of pancake.

He laughs, wiping some maple syrup off my chin and sucking it off his finger.

"I love how you eat whatever you want without counting calories. I fucking hate bitches like that. Eat a fucking pizza and shut the fuck up about your weight. We don't even notice the things most girls complain about on their body, they probably waste half their life stressing over bullshit things we as males do not give a fuck about," he mumbles while eating his pancake. I put another big piece into my mouth.

"Well, rest assured, you will not have to worry about me complaining about what I eat. As long as I get exercise in six days a week, I'm happy to eat pizzas with you," I say smiling at him.

He laughs and kisses me on the lips, despite the fact that both of us have food in our mouth. "Like I said…perfect."

After breakfast, we go our separate ways. He needs to meet the boys and I need to meet the girls and the wrath of Vicky.

CHAPTER 14

"Vicky! You look beautiful," I say pulling her into me as I walk through her hotel room door.

"Is Carter okay? I'm still gutted he couldn't come," she pouts.

"He's all right, a little shaken up, but I think Ade is looking into it."

"How are you two?" she asks, wiggling her eyebrows.

"Please, don't ever do that eyebrow thing again. You and Alaina creep me out. We're good," I say smiling. "Really, *really* good. I really like him, Vick," I confess to her shyly.

"He *really* likes you too, babe. Relax and help me with my dress," she says, pulling at her gorgeous gown.

"You look so beautiful, Vicky. Holy shit," I say with complete honesty.

Her dress has thick straps. Pulling tight around her waist and mid area, before it flows freely down to her feet. She looks amazing.

"Thank you, Polly. No more sweet talk or you girls will make me cry."

Blake is going to demolish her. That much I'm sure of.

Alaina, Phoebe, Abby and I are all in pastel blue strapless dresses. They sit mid-thigh and are a little on the tight side, typical Vicky. I'm a bit nervous about today, now that Ade knows about Dominic and me. It has me a little on edge.

Vicky's mom walks in, tears in her eyes. "Dad is waiting for you, precious," she says as she wipes the tears from under her eyes. We all gather up our belongings and make out way down the corridor, into the cart, and down the hallway. We are waiting for the limo to come around outside when Abby looks over to me.

Here we go.

"You do know that Ade isn't that serious about you. He has no feelings. How could he feel for you."

My eyes widen. She hasn't said much to me since I met her, only the odd stabs of hostility but nothing just between the two of us, and it makes me a little uncomfortable. I had noticed the glances she gives me as well, but I always brush them and her off.

I shrug. "He seems to have feelings when his dick's inside me. More than once," I add. I have a feeling that maybe she and Ade have slept together, with all the hostility and how everyone insinuates that, *'they were always something more,'* made me notice it.

Vicky looks at me and laughs. "All right girls, enough."

Looking straight ahead and wrapping my arms around myself. This is going to make things a little more complicated. I know how much she means to Ade. Somehow, I just don't see her making this easy for me. The limo pulls up and I watch as everyone gets in, me after the last person. I slump back into the seat and pour a wine. Vicky looks over to me, seeing my discomfort. She knows that I don't do well with confrontation. I'm just not like that. She pats my leg and winks to me before shooting a glance at Abby, and I wouldn't want to be on the receiving end of that glance. Alaina looks at me then looks to Abby. There's apparent tension in the air.

"Abby, I love you, but you need to lay off," Alaina says being her blunt self.

I shake my head. "Don't worry about it, she's wrong anyway."

Abby laughs, taking a sip of her drink. "Wrong? I am right. I've known Ade since I was ten. I know him better than he knows himself. Trust me when I say, you are just a convenience. He wouldn't know commitment if it smacked him in the face."

Wincing at her words I turn my head to my window, watching the passing trees.

"Alaina may feel like that about you Abby, but I don't. The way Alaina feels about you doesn't even scratch the surface of how much I care about Kalie. So make no mistake when I say, I'll fanny kick you out of this car so fast you won't know what hit you. Oh, and by the way…" she says, pausing to sip some more of her drink, "you're only a bridesmaid because I felt it was the right thing to do, for Blake. Learn your role," Vick warns.

Abby throws her hands up in defeat. "Hey, just say'n. I'm not here to fight."

Could have fooled me.

We pull up to where the ceremony will be held and it looks beautiful. It's all in an open garden area with the altar sitting in direct view of the carpark. I glance behind us and see Vicky's dad following us in his Camaro before getting out and waiting for Vicky. I look to the crowd and see everyone sitting there waiting for us, with the boys at the altar looking freaking edible. When I see Ade, I feel my heart freeze and my pulse picks up. A bright red blush wraps around my face. Alaina stands out of the car first, followed by me, Phoebe, and lastly Abby.

We begin walking down the aisle and look up at Ade to see his eyes fixated on me with a half grin on his face, which makes me blush again before looking to the ground. When I look up again, I find him smiling at Abby. My smile drops and he must notice because now his eyes show anger and his head is cocked. Once we reach the altar, we watch as Vicky and her dad walk down to meet us. She's the most beautiful bride I've ever seen. Glancing over at Blake, I see the love and adoration in his eyes for his bride to be, and it gives me hope. These two had a crazy, dysfunctional relationship. But looking at them now they're in complete awe of each other. Feeling as though I'm interfering in a private moment, I smile and look up to Ade, who still has a grumpy look on his face. The sexiest grumpy face I've ever seen.

After a whole round of *I do's* and a scream of cheers, Vicky Abrahams is now Vicky Rendon. Dominic comes over to me, picks me up, and swings me around. That's until I feel equally big arms wrap around my waist, pulling me back down.

"Fuck off," Ade growls, pulling me behind him.

Dominic looks up at him and narrows his eyes. "Ade? Yeah, chill. This is PG for Kalie and me." He winks at me.

A slight laugh sits in my throat until I look back at Ade who looks murderous.

Abby steps up to him, placing her arm on his chest. "Come on, Ade. Let her catch up with her friend. We need to head to the reception." I look down to her grip and bring my eyes back up to Ade, who then pulls me into him smashing his lips onto mine and opening my mouth with his tongue as he dominates me right here out in the open.

"I'll be right, there." He points to the road and swings his eyes back to Dominic. "You so much as touch her, I won't be responsible for what happens to your face," he states and then walks off with Abby latched onto his arm. *Fucking prick.* My stomach feels as though it's been ripped out and stood on by a hypocrite, because it has. I swallow down my insecurities and look back at Dominic.

"I'm sorry about that."

He shakes his head. "Don't worry about it. I was expecting that to happen."

He pulls me under my arm and we begin walking back down the aisle, toward the road.

"You have a ride? To the reception?"

I shake my head. "No, I was too busy with yours and Ade's pissing contest. I've missed the girls I think." He points up to Abby and Ade, who are a bit in front of us.

"Who's the redhead?"

I raise my eyebrows. "Um…she was raised with Ade, Zane, and Blake. She doesn't like me very much."

He laughs. "You don't say. I saw the evils she was eyeing you with."

We're standing in the same spot where the limo had pulled up when I hear gunshots ring out. I duck instinctively and Dom shields my body from the shots. There's no car for us to hide behind, though, so we're basically sitting ducks.

"Kalie!" Ade yells, running over to me.

Everything happens in slow-motion. I look up and begin to run to him to meet him half way when a white van screeches to a halt in front of me. A man jumps out, wearing a black balaclava. He grabs onto me, throwing me into the van, and causing me to hit my head on the metal floor. The last thing I feel is something heavy hit the front of my face before darkness descends over me.

ADE NIXON

I pull my gun out and start shooting at the van, only to drop it in defeat when I watch it disappear around the corner.

"Fuck!" I roar from where I'm standing, falling to my knees.

I feel manic and out of control. I want to murder someone and I need to now.

"Ade? We need to get out of here," Abby softly says from behind me.

"Fuck off. If I were with her Abby, instead of *you*, this would not be happening."

"It wasn't my fault, Ade! If she had not been such a cock tease and stuck with you, then she'd still be here."

I get up and walk up to her, shoving her in the chest. I've never laid my hands on a woman before—outside of the bedroom—but I will fuck her up right now.

"Keep her fucking name out of your dirty little fucking mouth."

Dominic's still trying to chase the van up the road before he stops. *"Fuuuccckkk!"* he roars as he drops to his knees and pulls on his hair.

Walking up to him, I grab his collar and punch him square in the jaw. I get on top of him, and let loose, blow after blow. The next thing I feel is someone, no there's more than one lifting me off him. Looking beside me I see it's my brothers. It took all of them to lift me off, but Zane pushes me back.

"Stop brother. *Stop.*"

I shake my head. "Fuck no! Stop? What the fuck are you talking about? Stop!" I'm about to reign in on Dominic again, only to be pulled back.

I walk up to Zane, eye to eye. "Brother, I love you, but if you don't get the fuck out of my goddamn way, I will happily go through you to get to him, without hesitation."

He pushes me back. "I know you're fucking hurt, I've been there! But this is not the way around it."

My heaving dies down and I look down to Dominic. "This is not fucking over."

Vicky comes running over to us screaming with tears pouring down her face and make-up smudged. "ZANE! Alaina, Alaina, they took her. They fucking took her, too." Vicky's face is bleeding. Her white wedding gown has blood all down the front. I look to Zane and watch as his absolute psychopathic mood kicks in.

"I'm so sorry, Zane. I tried...I attempted to kick one of them and I think I got him, but then he punched me in the face and took her."

Zane begins walking in circles, pulling at his hair before he lets out an almighty roar. *"Fuuuccckkk!"*

The whole world starts to close in and panic sets in. I feel lethal, absolutely *Jason X* lethal. I want to rip my fucking heart out just to stop it from hurting. Physical pain I can take, but this shit? This shit is fucking excruciating. It's why I turned off my humanity so many years ago. It's why I never wanted to have someone this close to me. I'd fucking wipe out the entire human race just to have my girl back in my arms again. I'm paralyzed. I can't even move my legs. They're mounted to this pavement. I look to Zane, who's looking at me with an equally ruthless stare.

"We raise hell, brother," I say calmly.

CHAPTER 15

We're all sitting around the table in the bar back at the clubhouse, and when I look up at Zane, we share the exact same look. It's the look of loss mixed with psycho.

"We don't need a plan. The only plan we need is death," I state.

Zane looks to me with a deadpan look. He usually has all the brains, he's smart and likes to do things cleanly.

"Done," he replies in a deathly shallow tone. Blake sits forward on his elbows.

"Our enemy list has gotten mighty long over the past two years."

I shake my head and rub my hands over my face. "This is deeper than that. This is Bruce Peyton, and if it is we need to get moving a lot fucking quicker than usual."

Zane nods his head. "We go on lockdown. Families are to come in, now."

Everyone stands from their seats and begin making their way out, leaving Zane, Blake, Ollie, Chad, and me in the room. Ollie and Chad have been pulled in a little tighter with us over the past couple years. We are a brotherhood, but there are still ranks.

I exhale, throwing off my cap and pulling at my hair. "Fuck, I can't help but think this is my entire fucking fault."

Zane sits forward. "Don't do that, brother. Don't you fucking do that? Bring out *'The Executioner.'* Use that rage one last time."

"No offense Z, but you're handling this a lot better than I am."

Zane sits back in his seat, his eyes look lost and disconnected. "On the outside it might appear that way. But on the inside...I feel like all my organs have been ripped out. I promised her, Ade. I fucking promised her when I got her back the last time that I'd never let anyone ever come near her again. I've fucking disappointed her, and if I think too much into that, I will shut down so bad that I will be useless in getting her back. I'm putting all my energy into getting her back. That's why it may look like I'm handling it better, and that's why I am president."

His eyes are glassed over in pain, but I've known him long enough to see when he's hurting more than what he is used to, and this is one of those times. I nod and cock my head backward, leaning into my seat.

I look over to Blake and see him nod his head. "Needs to be done, brother."

I raise my eyebrows. "Done."

Pulling my phone out of my pocket, I dial the only man that will ever be able to locate the girls.

"Drago makes the panties drop low. What's up."

I shake my head. "Not in the mood. We need your help."

After explaining the minor details over the phone, we jump on our bikes and ride out to Drago's office, which is his home. He's everything you'd expect in a nerd, but he has been working with us since Zane took over. He went to school with us, and we would always beat up the bullies who picked on him. Since then, he always felt like he owed us. He's a fucking good little dude. We pull up to his long driveway where he lives in a cabin in the middle of the woods. Turning off our bikes and making our way up the front steps, he swings opens his door. And under those glasses, he looks worried. He loves Alaina. Let's face it everyone loves the bossy bitch.

"I'm so sorry," he says looking at both Zane and me.

Nodding I make my way into his house, heading straight for his office. Opening the double doors I see nothing has changed since the last time I was here. It's about the same size as Phoebe's garage—Phoebe has a fucking garage built for a man, filled with all sorts of cars you could only dream of—all with computers and tech shit still scattered around the room. It looks like I just stepped into a scene from *The Matrix*. I sit down on one of the seats as everyone else makes their way in.

"Got anything?" I ask him.

He pulls his glasses up and nods his head. "Yes, I believe I do. However, it's not good. So Ade? Leave your gun outside."

Ollie chuckles. "His gun is the least of your worries."

Drago pauses for a second before taking a seat in his big chair and starts typing on his keyboard. "So as I said, you're not going to like this," he says as he continues typing.

I lean over to him. "Drago, hurry the fuck up and spit it out."

"You see this?" he points to the screen, "This is where I followed them, using all the CCTV cameras across the city. It takes us to an airport."

I lean back on my chair. "What the fuck do you mean, an airport?"

He puts his hand up, pausing my talking. "That's not all. I traced the jet they took and it belongs to a Kazimir Lyov."

Sucking in my breath at the mention of that name and yelling, *"Fuck!"* I smash my fist on the table.

Zane looks at me sideways. "What is it, brother?"

Drago pulls his glasses off and squeezes his fingers over the bridge of his nose. "Kazimir Lyov is a Russian name, right?" The stress evident in his tone.

"Don't tell me he's a part of the Russian Mafia," Ollie adds with disbelief in his tone.

I bring my fist up to my mouth, running my index finger over my lip. "Kazimir Lyov *is* the Russian Mafia."

Zane circles his steps, coming next to me.

"What do you mean *'is the Russian mafia'*? And what the fuck would he want with us?"

I clench my jaw together. "When I was younger, my dad would take me to these fights."

Zane nods his head. "Yeah, the fights we went to."

I shake my head. "Nah, not those ones. They were child's play. I'm talking death matches."

Zane's arms cross in front of him. "So that one fight he took you to at the warehouse, wasn't the only time?"

I shake my head before continuing, "The first life I took was when I was thirteen. It was the first time he took me to Bruce Peyton. I had no idea what the fuck was going on, but I did it. Killed him in under a minute, made a lot of men filthy rich."

Ollie and Chad sit on the floor. Zane and Blake knew some of this story, but nothing past it.

"This carried on until I was fifteen, then I was done. I walked out of there, told my dad to get fucked...for real this time...right before he died. Anyway, the underground fighting was just the surface of what kind of operation they were running. I'm talking, trafficking, child slavery, drugs, everything. They would train up orphan boys from a young age and throw them in the ring once they hit thirteen, sometimes even younger. They'd gamble on these young boys in hopes that they would find one, like me, that they could put a lot of money on. It was a money pot, and eventually the Russians wanted in. No one has ever met Kazimir Lyov aside from his bitch boys. He's the ghost who's been running all major underground operations for over thirty years. Some say he lives a double life, some say he works for the CIA. It's all shit talk obviously—the CIA bit.

But that's not even the part that fucks me up the most." I swallow down the bile that I can feel in my throat. "Kazimir Lyov's specialty is trafficking women." Zane hisses and I throw my head into my hands.

"Fuck brother," I say into my hands.

"Kazimir Lyov's location is off radar. No one has ever been able to find him. He lives in the fucking Bermuda Triangle."

A week passes—*a fucking week*. We have nothing. I have nothing. Pulling myself out of one of the beds in the clubhouse, my head pounds from a hangover. I'm rubbing my hands over my face when the bathroom door opens and out strolls Gretchen in one of my SS T-shirts, looking smug as fuck.

I shoot up off the bed. "What the fuck!"

She rolls her eyes, walking back to the bed. "Don't play dumb, Ade. You fucked me as good last night as you've done every other time."

I walk over to her, wrap my hand around her hair and yank her head into me.

"What the fuck did you just say?" I whisper into her ear.

She taps on my hand. "Ade, a little rough, seriously. Even for me."

"*What. The. Fuck. Did. You. Just. Say*?" I whisper again into her ear, venom dripping from my stuttering tone.

She scrunches up her face. "We had sex, like all the other times. Seriously—"

I grip onto her head and put it in a lock hold. Grasping onto her temples, I snap her neck in one swift, perfect, twist. Making her lifeless, disgusting, body drop to the ground. I spit on her, throw on my T-shirt and my cut over the top, before walking out of the room.

Once I hit the bottom step of the stairs that leads to the bar, I light up a cigarette and nudge my head to one of the prospects. "Clean out the whore in bedroom three," I tell him while continuing to make my way over to the table where Zane is sitting. I pull out a seat and order over Ashley to bring me a drink.

"I can't fucking do this for much longer," Zane says, putting his hands around the back of his neck.

His beard has grown out and he has wrinkles lining around his eyes. I swallow my drink, swallowing down the emotion that's a second away from rising up my throat.

"I can't think about it. If I do, I'll explode," I reply calmly.

"I get that, brother. We need to find them now. I'm not going to wait around on Drago for much longer." His phone starts ringing from his pocket, and he places his bottle on the bench, swiping it unlocked and answering it. "What," he snaps. "Yeah? All right. We'll be there soon." Shutting off his phone and standing from his seat. "Come on, Drago has some info for us."

About fucking time.

KALIE - ROSE

I attempt to open my eyes, but they refuse to open. All I feel is the pounding in my head.

Boom, boom. Where is that sound coming from? Where am I?

I try to open my eyes again, this time succeeding. Everything is black.

"What the fuck," I mumble.

I think over my jumbled thoughts, trying to think of the last thing I remember.

"Vicky's wedding," I whisper.

"Kal? Kal, is that you?"

"Alaina?" I gasp in shock.

"It's me, babe," she quietly replies, her voice hoarse and dry.

I attempt to move off the bed, but I feel like an anchor weighs me down. Using all my strength, I push myself up and stand off the bed, only to fall to the ground when my legs give way.

"Fuck!" I scream out in frustration.

"Shhh Kal, if they hear you they'll come back."

I begin crawling across the cold hard concrete floor. "Alaina? How long have we been here?"

"I don't know. You've been out for a few days. I lost count. I'd say a week, maybe more."

I pause my shuffling. "How have I been asleep for a week?"

"They've been drugging us with something. More you than I. They found me fascinating, being Zane's old lady."

Continuing my shuffling, I keep my hands feeling around in front of me. Feeling cold chains, I follow them up until they lead me to one of Alaina's hands. They are cold and stiff, she feels like death. I keep feeling around her until she winces.

"What did they do to you, Lain? Who are they?"

She pulls her arm out of my grasp. "It's going to be okay, we just have to be strong until the boys arrive."

The metal door swings open and a dark shadow looms. I swallow down and look at Alaina. Now there's light shining through the doorway, I can see her.

I wish I didn't.

I wish I never looked her way.

My stomach coils over, as little more than bile spews out of my mouth.

CHAPTER 16

The shadow makes his way in toward us and I swallow down, putting my body in front of Alaina. He laughs so hard that his fat stomach jiggles right in front of me.

"Oh, how cute. You think you can save her?"

"What do you want?" I ask my voice shaky.

"I want nothing but your sweet cunts, which I have enjoyed very much by the way." He laughs. I heave and throw my hand over my mouth again instantly feeling violated. *Surely I'd I know if he had done anything to me?* I look to Alaina, her body naked, bruised and bloody. Her once white pearly perfect hair is now bright red and matted in blood. She has bruises and dirt covering her entire body. A tear drops from my eye.

"Alaina." I take hold of her hand. I've seen her and Vicky do the motion so much. My heart breaks for her. I'm a mess, but I'm not bleeding all over the place, bruised and naked. They have really worked a number on her and it makes me sick to my stomach. I need to take as much heat off her as I can. A fat hand wraps around my arm, picking me up.

"We can continue our playtime later, sweet thang. We need to send a video first."

Looking back at Alaina while I'm walking out, the last thing I see is two more men walk into our room, zipping down their zippers of their jeans.

I scream. "No! No! Don't you fucking touch her!"

Trying to push out of the fat hands that are grasping me so tightly, I think my arms might snap. The men stop their laughing and make their way to me. Instantly I quiet, and the fat man laughs, letting go of me. One of the men opens his mouth, revealing a strong Russian accent. *Interesting.* I took Russian in school. I was fascinated by their culture, not so much anymore.

He wraps his hand around my throat and pushes me up against the wall so hard I heard a slight crack come from the back of my head. He gets in-between my legs, lifting my dress up and ripping off my panties.

He sniffs them and laughs. "Still feel like being a hero, bitch? I can make you wish your mother had swallowed you."

I gulp down as he eyes my body up and down before looking back to the fat man.

"Is this Aiden's woman?"

My eyes go wide at the mention of Ade's real name.

"Sure is. Kazimir doesn't want anyone touching her, though. She's going up on the podium."

The young man in front of me laughs. "Oh, boss man always likes taking the fun out of everything."

He then slides his hand down and under my dress again, sliding his fingers over my pussy before cupping me and shoving what feels like his whole fist inside me. I scream out in pain while he starts pumping his fingers into me in a rough, raw, and dry motion. I dry reach, with tears streaming down my face. The fat man looks worried from what I can see through the blurry vision my tears are causing.

The young man brings his other hand up to my neck, squeezing it to hold me in place. I can't breathe. He's actually going to kill me, and at this moment, I couldn't care less. There would be no coming back from this. I've lost all hope in myself. His fingers are going harder and I feel his pants pull down and the nakedness of his thigh against mine. I panic again, slipping in and out of consciousness. This is it, this is how I die, being digitally raped up against a wall. My mind drifts out, my breathing stops and I shut myself down.

ADE NIXON

We walk up the stairs to Drago's and open his door, making our way back into *The Matrix* room. Zane, me, Blake, Ollie and Chad all walk in, closing the door behind us.

"What is it Drago?" I ask, moving over to the seat next to him.

"Something just doesn't add up," he replies, typing away on his keyboard.

"You say you've never met Kazimir Lyov?" he asks, spinning his chair around to us. I notice he looks like he's had a rough week as well, the lack of sleep evident in his eyes.

"That's right, I've only ever heard of him. There is only a handful of people who've seen him in the flesh."

Chad makes his way over to where I am. "So he's started this shit storm because you took out Bruce Peyton? It sounds like there may be more to it than that."

I shake my head. "Nah, that would do it. Bruce wasn't the only man I took out. I took out his right-hand man also. That's their entire line into the underground ring."

Chad shakes his head, "I have a bad feeling about this, and I feel as though there's a lot more than what we are seeing."

I stand from my seat and lean over Drago. "Anything else?"

Drago nods his head. "You said that no one has ever found him? Well, no one is Drago." He spins his chair back around to face the computer, and I spin him around to face me again.

"What do you mean by that?"

He looks up at me uneasily. "Ade, you're a very scary man. So can you *not* stare at me like that." I look over to Blake and he rolls his eyes, coming over to Drago's rescue.

"Sit down, brother," Blake says.

I can't, I can feel myself slowly becoming more and more out of control. I've been calm up until this point, calm on the outside but livered in the inside. I can feel her slipping away from me, and I swear to fucking God the thought of anyone laying a finger on her slices my dark soul into two.

"I have an address," Drago states casually and I pause my evil thoughts.

"I'm sorry, what?" I ask, tilting my head at him.

He nods his head casually. "I hacked the RMS system that they use, and I've got an address. It didn't take me long either," he adds at the end smiling a cocky smile.

"Yeah, just a week," Blake mumbles under his breath sarcastically.

"Blake, these things take time. I'm not a magician," Drago replies defensively.

Zane looks over to me before looking back to Drago.

"Fuck, you're a smart little shit," I say to him with a small smile.

"I am. So the good news is, I have an address where they *may* be holding her. I can't say if that is where they are, but I have an address and that's a start. The bad news? This is the Russian Mafia you're going up against here. This is big time shit, and you *will* need an army."

Nodding my head, I look to Zane. "He's right. This isn't New Zealand. This is the Russian Mafia. We need to do this smart."

When we walk back into the clubhouse, I see Phoebe and Vicky sitting there worried. They've been taking it rough the past week and I get it, I fucking get it. Those are the two most important girls in my life right now, and it's taking all my fucking strength to not completely lose my shit and go on a massacre to fill the empty hole in my fucking heart. Killing is not a task for me, it's a mood, and no one here wants me in *that* mood—at least, not right now. Phoebe sees me and gets out of her seat.

"This is *your* fault, Ade! I fucking told you to stay the fuck away from her," Phoebe screams from where she's standing.

Blake puts his body between us. "Phoebs, sit the fuck down."

"Call her and Vicky into the boardroom too, they need to know what's going on," I mumble to Zane. He nods his head in agreement and I pull a bottle of whiskey from the top shelf of the bar before following everyone in. I pull out my chair that sits to the left of Zane while Blake sits on his right. I'm Vice President, yes, but Blake is also his other half. Once everyone is in the room, Ollie closes the door to the crowd of families on the other side.

"We have information on Alaina and Kalie," Zane whispers out hoarsely.

After Zane explains everything that we've found out, which leaves Vicky and Phoebe in tears. Everyone apart from Zane, Blake, Ollie, Chad, Vicky, Phoebe and me leave the room. I'm halfway through my bottle when I look over to Phoebe. She smiles softly at me, which is surprising considering the girl wanted to rip my head off thirty minutes ago. Zane and Blake depart with Vicky in tears, leaving Phoebe and me in there alone.

"So you know who this man is?" she asks quietly.

I nod my head. "Yeah, I do."

She swallows and pulls out a seat next to me, taking hold of my hand. "Ade, I need to help, please."

I pull my hand out of her grasp. "Fuck no, Phoebe. Are you fucking crazy!"

"Yes, Ade, I'm very fucking crazy! Kalie is my best friend. I *am* helping."

Shaking my head, I take another long skull of my drink. "I can slip in undercover. Abby can help me."

I look at her in disbelief. "You've gone off the fucking rails if you think Blake will be down with that. And as much as you are a pain in my fucking ass, I still care about you. So the answer is no, Phoebe." I stand from the table, swing open the doors and sit on one of the sofas by the pool tables. Fucking Phoebe and her crazy ass attitude. If it were anyone else, I'd happily pawn them off. As much as no one even comes close to how much Kalie means to me, I can't do that to Blake.

Slowly I feel myself begin to tip over the edge again. Feeling out of control, I have energy that needs burning. When I can't fuck someone, I'll kill them. I walk to the back of the room and push open the fire exit. We don't have a plan as of yet, but we will. I need to talk to Abby though as I took it all out on her. She picks up her phone on the third ring.

"Ade? Are you okay?"

I sigh down the phone and lean my head against the wall. "I'm really fucking not. I'm one stupid comment away from losing my shit and slicing everyone apart," I reply.

Hearing a door close through the phone before she starts talking again. "What do you know?"

"We know that they're in Russia."

"Russia?"

"Yeah, with Kazimir Lyov."

She gasps. "Kazimir Lyov?"

"Yeah."

"As in the Russian fucking mafia?" she whispers out in an angry tone.

"The one and only."

"Holy fucking shit, Ade."

I look down at my phone in my hand. "Wait, why the fuck are you not here?"

"I can't, I have work, you know as Chief of Police. I can't exactly tell them that my family is on lockdown because two of their girls have been taken by the Russian Mafia."

"Good point."

"I'm coming now, though. Tell bum boys to let my Chrysler in."

I hang up the phone and walk back into the clubhouse, letting Travis know to let her in.

CHAPTER 17

An hour passes and I notice Abby still isn't here. Which is strange, she's never late to anything. I take my phone out of my pocket and dial in her number, only for it to go straight to voicemail. Blake pulls up a seat next to me.

"Don't look at me like that Blake. I'm not going to turn ripper on everyone...yet. I just need her home. I need them both home."

He throws his arms up in surrender. "I wouldn't blame you if you did."

I pull my phone out again, checking for messages.

"You waiting on someone?" he asks, pointing down at my phone.

"Abby. She was supposed to be here over an hour ago."

Looking around the room before landing my eyes on the boardroom. I slide my seat back and walk into the boardroom, swinging the doors open and seeing it empty. Blake walks up behind me.

"Looking for something?"

Walking back out I slam the door shut loudly, before swinging around to face everyone in the bar.

"Where the *fuck* is Phoebe!" I yell, glancing around the room.

Everyone looks at each other before shrugging. Blake stands in front of me. "What do you mean *'where the fuck is Phoebe?'*?"

I pull at my hair and look at him. "She was tossing some shit off me earlier in the boardroom. Talking about how she needs to help, how she *can* help with Abby. I told her to fuck off, that it isn't going to happen. Now she's not here and neither is Abby."

"She fucking... *Fuck!* She fucking would." I begin to make my way out of the clubhouse.

"Where you going?" Blake yells from behind me.

"There's only one person who'd tell them where the girls are."

Right as I reach the door, I hear Zane's voice break the silence. "Ade. Come here brother," his voice a horse, a loud whisper. The foreign tone pulls me back to him.

Turning around I see him holding up his phone with a video playing. I blink my eyes a few times, trying to adjust them, but wind up walking to him and snatching the phone out of his hands.

What I see on that screen turns me *murderous*.

KALIE - ROSE

"Ade, If you get this video, Alaina is messed up she's not good they have been do—" A fist comes flying to my face at a rapid speed, hitting me so hard that I fly off the seat and I scream out in agony.

"Shut the fuck up!" The fat man squeezes onto my cheeks and spits on my face.

"Get the fuck up there and do it again."

"Should we leave that part on?" I hear someone ask from behind the camera.

"Yeah, leave everything. Make him see how fucking serious we are."

He pulls me up and throws me back into my seat. Now with a busted eye that's pissing out blood, I begin to sob. Looking like death and feel worse than shit, but all I care about is Alaina.

"Again bitch, and if you fuck up this time Jason's fingers won't be the only things that are shoved up your cunt!"

I dry reach and spit to the ground as the memories of what happened come back to me full force. Looking up at the camera with my hair sticking to my face, blood is pouring down past my eyes and cheeks as tears begin to stream down my face.

"I have forty-eight hours left until Kazimir is going to send me away with the highest bidder. You have forty-eight hours to come up two million in cash and a— A...*no!* No, I will not say that. *No!*" I scream. Fat man takes hold of my neck, squeezing with such force I feel as though my eyeballs are going to burst out of my sockets. He looks to the camera and winks while I'm choking. He begins to run his hands down the front of my dress, under my bra and squeezing my nipple so hard I feel it draw blood. I scream out in agony, making him let go and smash me across the face again which causes me to fall off my chair and splits my eye open even more. He looks at the camera with a smile.

"Sorry you had to witness all that boys," he says then lights up a cigarette.

"She's a feisty little one that one. Aidan, you still know how to pick them. I must say, Alaina's tight little pussy is just as good, though." He laughs while he blows out a cloud of smoke. "As the bitch said, two mill in cash in forty-eight hours. And Aidan...someone will meet you at the container port in Westbeach."

He shuts off the camera and turns to me. Pulling me back up and dragging me out of the room. I look around as much as I can but don't notice anything out of the ordinary. Am I still even in Westbeach? I don't think so. We reach the door of the room where they've been keeping us, and he swings it open before pushing me in. The smell of death hits me and I instantly feel sick.

"Alaina?" I yell out in panic. Everything is dark again, back to not being able to see.

"Alaina, goddammit. Answer me, please?"

I hear a wheezy cough and run to where the sound came from. I kneel down and feel around to find her face. She's lying flat on her back. I pick up her head and stroke off the hair that's on her face, ignoring the wetness I feel under my hand.

I begin to cry. "Please stay with me Lain, please."

I kiss her head and lay down with her just listening to her struggling breath. I begin to sing Metallica's *'Nothing Else Matters'* with tears streaming down my face, knowing this was her wedding song.

I wipe the tears from my face as I end the song and caress her cheek.

"Alaina?" I whisper.

"I'm here, Kal," she croaks out quietly.

Thank fucking God.

"That was so beautiful, Kal. Thank you."

"Shhh, don't talk. Just stay with me, please. Hang in there." As we both drift off to sleep.

Opening my eyes, I feel to where Alaina was lying and it's now empty.

"Alaina?" I yell frantically.

With no answer back, panic begins to set in again. I bring my knees up to myself and hug into them, laying my head on my knees as I start to rock.

"Please, please Lord let her be okay. Please," I pray, as tears begin to pour out of my eyes yet again.

I stay like this for who knows how long. Since I've been here, I have lost track of time. There's no concept of time here, similar to hell I guess. The door swings open with another shadow standing in the doorway. I stand instantly.

"Where is Alaina?"

The voice laughs at me, tilting his head. "Nice to finally meet you, Kalie. Do you know who I am?" the voice asks softly.

"I have no idea who you are. Where is Alaina?" I attempt to ask again.

"I'm Kazimir Lyov, and I'm your father-in-law."

ADE NIXON

"Fuck!" I scream out, throwing my bottle to the bar causing it to smash and all the alcohol to run out over the ground.

I look to Zane and he's hyperventilating. If someone unleashed both Zane and I out in a war, we could take out an entire army. I drop to the floor and pull my hands to my face.

"They fucking touched her. *They fucking touched her!*" I roar.

"She was mine. Just mine. So pure and so innocent and *they fucking touched her!*" I rip my T-shirt off and cover my face with it trying to control my breathing and pull myself back under control. My chest heaves as the feeling of pure anger takes control of me. I'm lost in the darkness of complete and utter rage. "They fucking touched my girl," I whisper in disbelief.

Zane begins walking out the door with no emotion evident on his face. "Everyone with a cut on, get the fuck in the van. *Now*," he yells as he continues to storm out the door.

I sit there motionless. Blake pulls me up by my arms, swinging an arm around my waist as he throws my arm around his neck.

"Yo, Ollie, need some help here," he says, trying to hold me up.

Ollie comes to the other side and throws my other arm over his shoulder while they walk me out to the van.

I need to kill something. Now.

When we hit Drago's gravel road, I see all his lights out. As the van has almost pulled to a stop, I swing open my door and walk up to his door, kicking it down.

"Drago!" I yell out, looking into the rooms.

When I reach the kitchen, I see a note on the bench.

Please don't kill me. We have a plan.

I scrunch up the piece of paper and throw it on the bench. Gripping onto the kitchen counter until my knuckles are white I yell, *"Fuck!"*

Zane walks in and picks up the paper. "Dumb motherfucker!"

Pushing off the bench I make my way into the computer room, kicking the door down and turning on all the computers, which are all locked. *Of course, they are*. I pick up one of the computers and throw it across the room.

"*What the fuck is he thinking?* He has Abby and Phoebe as well," Blake yells from behind me. I storm back outside and sit down on the step. Shaking my head when I feel Zane's presence behind me.

"He's not going to let them go, Zane. I've never met the man before, but I have heard of him. *A lot.*"

Zane sits next to me. "We fly to Russia," he states categorically as he hands me a bottle of whiskey.

I take a long pull. "We fly to Russia," I reiterate.

CHAPTER 18

The next morning the sun assaults my eyes. I look around slowly and notice I'd fallen asleep on the porch. Sitting forward I squeeze my eyes shut.

Zane walks out of the house, the front door slamming behind him. "Joseph is pulling a team together. We will take his jet, it's already here."

I nod and my phone starts ringing in my pocket. I fish it out and swipe it unlocked.

"What."

"Ade. It's Sandra. I heard about your girl. What can I do to help?"

Narrowing my eyes, I look to Zane and for the first time since my girl was taken, I smile.

"Thanks, Sandra. We have the jet. Could do with a couple of men and some extra weapons."

"Done. Now I need something."

I nod my head. "I thought you might."

"I need Kazimir Lyov. *Alive.*"

"Why?"

"Don't ask questions Aidan. Just do it."

I shrug my shoulders and hang up my phone

"That was Sandra Fisick."

I see Zane's eyes light up. "Fucking perfect."

Sandra Fisick is the Director of the CIA. There's times when she might need me. But that's not the only reason, she was close to my mom when they were younger, too. She watched me grow.

"Ready?"

"Born ready."

KALIE - ROSE

"I don't have a father-in-law," I say deadpan.

He laughs. "Well, I guess you don't."

"You're Ade's dad? I thought he was dead."

"Mmm, well, there's a lot you don't know."

"I don't doubt that," I say with a flat tone. "Where is Alaina?"

He walks in with two other men behind him. With a click of his fingers, both men come to either side of me, picking me up as they begin carrying me out.

"This isn't necessary. I can walk, I don't care anymore." I slump my feet down to the floor. I've lost all will and hope to live, and at this point, I don't care. I feel like who I am now, is not the same woman anymore. I feel dirty, violated, and corrupted, in the most disgusting way.

I hate Ade Nixon.

"Don't be like that, sweet cunt." The man runs his hands up my dress, slipping a finger inside me roughly. I look dead out in front of me, nothing showing in my eyes. My soul has been broken and my light has turned dark. This last week has *not* been like living in a nightmare because in this nightmare, you're awake. There's no waking up from this, there is no waking up from the feeling I feel inside me. This is my reality, not my bad dream. I've been living in a house secluded with pedophiles, rapists, and pig-headed men who think women are here for their pleasure only. When this is over, and if I come out of this alive, I know I'll never be the same again. There will be no coming back from this. I've been poked, prodded, touched and manhandled in ways that a woman should ever have to feel. I've gone from being a virgin to dirt in record time and then losing any purity that I ever thought I had.

"Where's Alaina?" I repeat in the same flat tone.

The man is still pumping his dirty, fat finger inside me.

Kazimir laughs from where he's standing. "Don't you worry your sweet self about little Alaina. She's being well taken care of."

The man pulls his finger out of me and forces them down inside my mouth, making me scrunch up my face in disgust. He pulls his fingers out and I look at him.

"Are you done?" I ask in the same bored tone.

He laughs so hard his fat belly jiggles. "She's getting the hang of this boss. Let me put my dick inside it."

Kazimir narrows his eyes, lighting a cigar. "Not yet. I need something intact to make my boy come with me. If he doesn't, I'll tie him up and make him watch me fuck that sweet cunt until next week."

I swallow down the very possibility that this could happen. Ade and I haven't been able to establish enough of a solid relationship for me to feel secure, in the fact, that he'd throw down his own life to save me. Sure, he plays caveman with me, but playing caveman and playing dead man are two completely different things. And that talk with Abby about him not having any emotions, doesn't help.

Standing there completely motionless until I feel a push from behind me, we carry on walking down the hallway until we arrive at another room. I haven't seen one window the whole time I've been here. The floor feels as though it's small pebbles under my feet, leading me to believe that we're on a boat. The walls and doors are metal. I have no clue where the fuck I've been for the past week. We walk into an enclosed room, where there's a light in the middle, hanging from the ceiling and a chair sitting underneath it. Kazimir points to the chair, shutting the door with just him and me inside. I walk to the chair and sit down. He kneels in front of me and tilts his head.

"Do you know why this has happened?"

I shake my head. "No."

"I need my son on my team. I heard that there were only two little girls that he favors the most in this world. Alaina and Abby. Abby was meant to be where you are right now. However, when I found out about his hot little affair with some new little snatch, I had to see for myself who this woman was that's apparently locked my son's balls up on a leash."

I laugh sardonically. "I have not."

Closing my eyes, I attempt to shut everything out. I need to find a happy place, a place where I can go to make me not want to end myself the next time I get a hold of a gun.

Kazimir chuckles, standing in front of me. "We must go."

I look up at him in between the hair that's falling in front of my eyes. "Where are we?"

He laughs, puffing on his cigar. "In Westbeach. Where else."

ADE NIXON

We're walking down the steps from Drago's house when my phone dings in my pocket. I swipe it open and see it's a message from Drago.

Drago: *Don't go to Russia. That was a decoy.*

Stopping in my tracks, making the gravel skid under my feet, I begin typing out a reply. I'm half way through when my phone starts ringing. I click answer, immediately.

"What do you mean, don't go to Russia. And where the fuck are you?"

"I know. I'm sorry. Look, we're working on something that I can't tell you, but it's good. They're not in Russia. I pulled up the CCTV footage from the Russian airport where that jet landed, and it showed too much of everything. So I zoomed in and the girl who they were escorting wasn't Alaina or Kalie. We did some more digging and as it turns out, the pings we are getting are actually coming in from Westbeach. We still need to sort out the exact location—"

Cutting him off I hang up my phone. *I know where they are.*

I begin running to my bike, letting off a whistle while I get on. All the boys start running out of the clubhouse, watching me while treading carefully. I know they're all waiting for the exact moment where I lose it completely, and they're all staying at a distance.

"The docks. They've been there this whole goddamn time."

Starting up my bike I speed out, with the rest of them following suit behind me.

The whole way there, I'm amped. My pupils are no doubt dilated, and I'm ready to kill anyone that's standing in-between Kalie and me. When we pull up, we park up at the front. There's no way I'll risk them hearing our bikes pull in. Taking off my helmet, I look over to Zane.

"They no doubt have this whole area covered in surveillance."

"Should we wait for some backup? This is the mafia," Ollie asks, getting off his bike.

I shake my head and laugh. "He's on my turf, brother. There won't be a whole lot of mafia here, and there's no way I'm fucking waiting."

We all begin walking up, ducking and hiding behind shipping containers.

"This place is fucking huge," Ollie says from behind me, "and has anyone seen Felix?"

I stop in my tracks and look to Zane. "Wasn't it Felix who gave you that last envelope?"

Zane narrows his eyes. "Yeah, why?"

I stand there motionless, trying to join the dots together in my head.

"Something doesn't add up. Why would Felix give me a hit on a man that had a connection with me as a kid?"

Zane shrugs. "Could be just a coincidence, brother. Can we stay focused now, get our girls back."

I shake my head while continuing to walk. "Nothing's a fucking coincidence in our world."

"Are we going to *handle* Felix?" I ask, looking to Zane for clarity.

"No. Get our girls back, and then we tread around what's going on with him."

"Why the fuck was he following Abby around like a lost puppy the other night?"

"She's been fucking him, that's why. Ollie doesn't suspect, or if he does, he knows he can't do jack shit about it. The man won't even talk to her."

"She's been fucking, Felix?" I whisper to him so Ollie can't hear.

We walk up to another shipping container, searching for a clue of where they might be located.

"If she has anything to fucking do with this," I say, eyeing Zane.

He shakes his head. "No, she wouldn't. She may be bitter about you and Kalie, but there's no way she'd do that. It was just them sneaking around."

"You sure?"

"Positive."

I look out in front of us and see a fishing boat floating in the water. Don't know why, but something tells me it would be big enough to set up camp for a week. There are three other boats that are similar surrounding it as well. Starting from the first boat, I make my way toward it drawing out my gun. Zane follows, hot on my footsteps.

I look behind us. "Blake, you and Ollie take the third boat. Harvey and Zane, you take the second. Chad and I got this one."

We all separate as Chad and I make our way onto the boat. Chad is exactly who you'd want at your back. He's ex-military, and he has no limits. I quietly make my way onto the boat and look around, watching my steps carefully. It's a shit hole and there are empty bottles everywhere. I look around onto the deck and see a box of fish bait. Shaking my head, I turn my finger around, just about to say it can't be this one when I hear a heavy slam come from under my feet. I stop and throw my finger up to my mouth at Chad.

"Shhh."

Drawing up my gun again, I round the back of the deck popping open the door and walking inside. When I see the stairs, we begin making our way down into the darkness. The smell hits me first. It smells like human decomposition. Once we hit the end, I look down to see a huge hallway. The walls are metal and there are six doors on each side. I can barely fit my shoulders down, it's that small. There's a door at the very end, facing me. I tilt my head to it and make my way down. Before I can reach it, the door swings open and standing in front of me is a ghost from my past.

CHAPTER 19

"No fucking way," I say in shock.

My dad laughs, lighting up a smoke.

"Well, you're a lot smarter than I ever gave you credit for," he answers smugly.

"You. You took Kalie and Alaina?" I growl.

"Yes. Drop the gun, Son." He points to my chest. When I look down, I see the laser dot aimed at my chest.

"Fuck," I yell, dropping my gun.

"Where the fuck is Kalie and Alaina?"

He motions toward the room, signaling for me to go in. I look to him and then back at Chad, nudging my head toward the room. The sight that I see when I walk in there will haunt me for all of eternity.

"*Fuucckk!*" I roar and fly myself at my father. "What the fuck have you done?"

I grab him by the throat, ready to end my deal I made with Sandra when I feel three other men pull me off him. I look behind me and see Chad being held up against the wall by two men the same size as him. I shrug them off me and start to run over to Kalie. She's hanging from the roof by her hands. She's in nothing but her underwear, her body is bruised black and blue, and her hair is sticky with blood dropping from her face. Her head hangs low, and I make my way to her. When I watch her face slowly lift up, meeting my eyes, I feel like her eyes have ripped my heart out of my chest. I can't cope with the turn of emotions I feel at this very moment, and they aren't good ones.

"Baby?" I slide my hand over her face and she begins shaking, her whole body convulsing.

I hiss and begin pulling at her arms. "I got you now. Fuck! I'm so sorry, baby."

All I want to do is take her away from everything and anything. I want to run off with her where it's just her and me so I can look after her for the rest of my life. I'm completely fucking heart broken. I fucking love this girl and I know it. There's no way I'd feel these feelings for her if I didn't—I'm inhumane, not stupid.

A hand wraps around my arm, and just as they are about to pull me back, I swing around and knock whoever it is dead in the face, putting all my force into that one punch. When I look down, I see one of my father's henchmen on the floor, knocked out cold. My father laughs, rounding the motionless body lying on the floor.

"Some shit never changes," he chuckles.

I point to Kalie. "Take her fucking down. Now," I grumble to him.

He looks at me, studying my eyes.

"Now!" I yell.

He clicks his fingers together and motions to Kalie. I watch as they take her down, and I catch her as she drops to the ground wrapping her in my arms and kissing her on her head.

"You will pay for this," I say, looking up at him from the ground.

He laughs, leaning against the wall. "I doubt that, Son. I'm untouchable. Even by you...*'The Executioner'*," he mocks.

I curl up my lip in disgust. "That's where you're wrong."

"Are you not wondering how I came to be here?" He motions around the room.

"No, I simply don't care. You're a dead man walking."

I slide Kalie's hair out of her face and kiss her on the lips. "I'm so sorry, baby. I'll spend the rest of my life making this up to you."

She chokes out a hollow laugh. It's the first sound I've heard her make since we got here. Frank moves across the room and pulls up a chair, taking a seat on it and propping his ankle up on his knee. The carelessness in his eyes is evident, and I cannot wait to watch the life slip from the depths of them.

"I am Kazimir Lyov," he says casually.

"I figured that, Pops. You can speak now. Make these words legendary. They will be your last."

He laughs, lighting up a cigarette and placing it into his mouth. "I've always been Kazimir Lyov. I was only Frank Nixon when I moved to Westbeach when I was in my late twenties." He takes a puff of his smoke again before continuing, "I had to move, live a double life. I needed a decoy from the feds, they were catching onto our family business and they were catching onto it fast. We all went our separate ways for a few years, with the knowledge that we'd reunite back together eventually when everything died down. I joined SS MC, it was the perfect cover for me, right up my alley and I didn't have to pretend to be a businessman or any bullshit like that. I could still kill, smoke, and fuck. I was supposed to go back to Russia a few months before I met your mother, and that was it. I feel in shit creek with her so fast I didn't know what hit me."

He looks between Kalie and me on the floor, smirking before he continues his talk. I wish I could say I'm surprised, but I'm not.

"I pushed my *staying in America* as far as I could, but eventually, I knew I needed to return to Russia. Therefore, I set up the accident to fake my own death and give me free passage back. Davey and Pete were collateral damage. I thought your mother would be fine. She had you after all. When I heard of her death, it ruined me. Maybe you will know how that feels one day, maybe today," he states casually as he gets up from his seat.

"What do you want?" I ask, squeezing onto Kalie.

"Isn't it obvious?" he answers smugly. "I want you. I need you on my team. I know how lethal you are Son, and I want you with me. Come back to your roots."

"Fuck my roots, my roots are here."

"Then I have no other choice, Son," he says, smiling at me.

I look down to Kalie before looking back up to him. "Where's Alaina?"

At the mention of Alaina's name, I feel Kalie's body go stiff under my grasp. I look down to her and stare deep into her eyes. She's different. When I look into her eyes now, I see nothing but emptiness.

I whisper against her lips, "What did they do to you, baby? They won't hurt you again. You need to trust me, okay? Do you trust me?"

She looks at me, a single tear dropping from her eye as her face goes dead straight. "No," she says sternly with absolutely no emotion whatsoever.

"Fuck," I mumble, placing her onto the ground.

I need to get away from her, I don't want anything that is about to go down anywhere near her. I push her hair behind her ear and kiss her lightly on the curve of her ear.

"I need you to stay against that wall, baby. Don't move. I will earn you back, I promise you. I love you Kalie-Rose, I fucking love you so much, baby. Please, trust me on this," I whisper.

When I bring my head back from her ear, I look down into her eyes and see they are pouring with tears. She nods and moves against the wall.

"Good girl," I whisper before standing back up.

"I'll come with you, on one condition," I say, pulling my shoulders straight, "you bring Alaina out here and let the girls and my men walk."

He nods his head, looking over to one of the men in the corner.

"Go, get the blonde."

The man walks out and a few moments later walks back in with Alaina draped over his shoulders. My heart slumps into my chest again as he drops her onto the ground next to Kalie. She murmurs and stirs and I see Kalie pull her up into her, brushing her hair away from her forehead. If I thought Kalie looked bad, Alaina looks like death. I look at her with worried eyes, the same worry a brother would look at his sister. When she opens her eyes slightly, she sees me and gasps.

"Ade? Ade, is that you? No. No. I'm dreaming again. It can't be…" she whispers off, coming in and out of oblivion.

They're both unrecognizable. These two sweet girls have now been exposed to such corruption that I don't think they'll ever be the same again. "Done, let's fucking go," I say to my father.

I look to Kalie, as everyone begins walking out. "I love you, baby. I'll be back for you. I promise." She turns her head away from me, obvious pain in her stare.

I look to Alaina. "Zane's outside, firecracker."

Glancing up to Chad I give him a small smile and a head nod, before following out the door.

We're walking back down the corridor and I begin to count how many men there are. In front of me is my father, in front of him is five other men, and I don't know if there are any others outside. I can take them, I fucking know I can, but not while they're carrying their weapons. When we reach the steps, we start to make our way up. Once the first

Amo Jones

man reaches the deck, a single gunshot rings out and the man drops to the ground. I look at my father and elbow him square in the face, making him stumble back. Pulling on the legs of the man that's in front of him, he smashes his face on the steps, and I stomp down on the back of his head, cracking open his jaw and teeth on the step. I spin back around and see my father's gun raised on me.

"Boys, now unless you want to be a valuable man down, I would let us out peacefully," he yells out to Zane.

Zane walks in front of the entrance, pulls up his gun and shoots the man standing in front of him square in the head.

"Zane..." Frank, or should I say *'Kazimir'* warns.

"Don't give a fuck what you say, Frank. I'll kill you all."

I look sideways at the gun raised to my temple, and in a split second I whip it out of his hands, flipping it around and shooting him in the leg. Turning around, and pointing the gun to the face of the fat fuck I remember from the video and drop it.

"You! Are you the fat fuck who had his hands on my girl?" I ask, walking up to him.

I hear two more gunshots ring out next to me, and I know damn well those shots came from my boys, so I don't bat an eye away from the target in front of me. Gripping onto his throat I push my face up to his. "I said…are you the sick fuck that hand his hands on my girl?" He laughs so hard his fat gut wobbles up against me. I look down at it in disgust before looking back up to him. "Think this is funny?" I push him back down the way we came, heading back into the room where the girls and Chad are located. Kicking it open, I see Chad wrapping his hoodie around them.

"Ade?" Alaina whispers.

"It's over, firecracker."

"That's where you're wrong," Kalie whispers out emotionless.

I throw the blob of fat to the ground before moving over to her.

"What do you mean I'm wrong, baby?" I grasp around her neck and pull her into me.

She pushes away from me. "This is not over, Ade. I will never be the same again. I've had men touch me in places that I only ever wanted *you* to touch me in." She wipes the tears that are dropping from her eyes and my chest constricts at the emotions in her voice and the words coming out of her mouth. "I will never be the same. I hate you, Ade Nixon. I hate you so much that I never want to see your face again." She stands from where she's sitting, wrapping the hoodie around Alaina and kissing her on the head. She wipes Alaina's hair away from her forehead, looking deep into her eyes.

"I love you, girl. I'm so sorry." She stands and begins walking through the door.

"Kalie!" I demand and she stops, whipping her head around to face me.

"What is it, Ade?"

I stand there, motionless. My mind is running one hundred miles an hour, there's so much I want to say to her. I want to drop to my fucking knees like a little bitch and beg her to stay with me, to promise her I would lay her world out at her feet and pamper her in whatever the fuck she wants until we both shall live. But I can't. I can't fucking ask this girl to stay with me when she's right. This is all my fault. She deserves more, she deserves someone that's not part of this life and I can't give that to her. I will never be able to give that to her because I don't just live with these demons daily, the fuckers dance with the devil in my sleep.

"Any last words to the fat fuck?" I ask, taking my hoodie off and passing it to her to put it on.

I'm looking up at her and trying to memorize her every feature in my head. I love her so fucking much, and that's why I need to let her go. I will never love anyone again. There was no one before her and there sure as fuck will be no one after her. I will always have a place in me for Kalie. That place will always be untouchable, and may God save the soul of whoever tries to touch that place again. She pulls my hoodie over her head.

"Kill him slowly," she mutters before walking out of the room, this boat, and my life.

CHAPTER 20

My jaw feels like it's going to crack from the pressure I'm putting on it, and when I look up to Chad and Alaina, I see pity in their eyes.

"Don't fucking look at me like that!"

Zane bursts through the door and takes one look at Alaina, swallowing hard with his eyes set in stone. "Baby?" he whispers out with raw emotion. Alaina bursts into tears, flying herself into Zane's arms. I look down at the fat shit sitting on the ground and I grip around his arms. Zane places Alaina down and walks over to me.

"This man touch you too, Lain?" he asks, not taking his eyes off the man on the floor.

She nods her head. "Yes, but mainly the young one."

Harvey walks in, dragging a skinny young guy behind him. "This him?" he asks Alaina.

She nods. "Yes, he also touched Kalie, Ade. He did horrible things to her."

I narrow my eyes at Alaina before walking up to the skinny young guy.

"Oh, yeah? Like what sort of stuff?" I ask while not taking my eyes off him.

"He...I heard her scream one time. She tried to stop him and another man from coming back into our room. I heard her yell *'no, leave her alone'* then I heard her scream out in pain while they were laughing. When they came into the room, they said that he fingered her up a wall while choking her. She almost died, Ade. They said she passed out and they had to perform CPR on her to bring her back."

Alaina barely finished her sentenced before I grasped onto this guy's neck and threw him onto the floor with the fat blob. I look to Zane. "How much time do we have?"

He shakes his head. "Not sure. I've locked Kazimir in the room next to us. We can deal with him last."

"We can't. These two, yes. However, I promised Sandra that she could have Kazimir. I didn't say he would come in one piece, though." I smile at Zane before my smile drops.

"How did Kalie get out?"

He looks to me uneasily. "Yeah, you're not going to like this. But he's a good dude Ade, he wouldn't try anything on her."

"Spit it out, brother."

"Trevor is taking her straight home. She doesn't even want to stop and pick up her stuff from the hotel," he says sadly.

"I'll get it. I'll get her stuff."

Alaina walks up to me and places a hand over my heart. "Honey, let me do it, okay? You're going to need to give her some time. Maybe a lot more than you're comfortable with. But that girl...she loves you too, Ade. I saw it in her eyes. Just let her mourn."

I swallow roughly. "Okay." Before looking back to the two tasks at hand.

"You!" I point, bringing the skinny one to his feet. I push him up against the wall.

"Wait here," I say as I begin to walk out of the room. Swinging open the door to the next room, which currently houses my father I say, "Give me your cigar cutter." He fishes into his pocket and hands it to me, and just as I'm walking out the door he stands from his seat.

"Son. I loved your mother, and you. I showed it differently to how most fathers do, but this is all I know."

I turn around to face him. "Maybe that's why I could never love because I saw from such a young age how dirty it was. That was until Kalie, then you took her from me. So trust me when I say you *will* pay for that," I berate slamming the door after I walk out.

As I'm walking back in, I get a text from Drago.

> Drago: *I know you're all in there. I can see you. Hello, big brother. Abby is giving you twenty minutes before she needs to intervene. Make it fast.*

I look up to the camera in the corner of the hallway and smirk at it, then reply.

> Me: *A lot can happen in twenty minutes. Kazimir goes to Sandra.*
> Drago: *Oh dear God. Abby said, please don't make a mess. And she knows they're working together.*
> Me: *Don't count on it.*

I shove my phone back into my pocket before opening the door again, to where everyone is currently standing.

"We have twenty minutes. So we need to make this fast."

I point over to Alaina. "You wanna see this, Lain?"

She nods her head, pulling her arms across her torso. "Yes. Yes, I do."

I continue making my way over to the skinny guy, yanking him back to his feet. Pulling the cigar clippers out of my pocket, I put them on his first finger and push down until I feel his finger drop, and hit the top of my boot. I maintain eye contact with him as I continue to go through each finger one at a time, smiling at each scream that comes loudly from his mouth. Once I've finished, he screams in agony while sliding down the wall, holding onto his fingerless hands.

I laugh. "That's not even the worst of it."

I take a cigarette out of my pocket and light it up in my mouth, exhaling a cloud of smoke and drop to him on the ground.

"Pull your pants down," I say smirking at him.

He looks at me with narrowed eyes and I laugh. "Oh, come on now. I don't roll like that. You got nothing to be afraid of. Well, where cocks are touching assholes are concerned." I smile and look up at the ceiling. "Oh shit! I just got an idea." I pull on his trousers so hard they fly off in one hard, swift move, and then make my way to his underwear. I put my cigarette into my mouth so I can use both hands, but when I see what underwear he's wearing I choke out in laughter.

"Oh bruh, didn't Mommy ever tell you that these don't get you laid? No wonder you force your shit on innocent girls."

I pull off his tight undies. What kind of man under the age of seventy would wear undies this fucking disgusting? I can feel Zane's anxiousness behind me, so I figure I should hurry this along so he can get his turn, too.

"I just need to do one thing real quick, and then I'll pass you onto my brother Zane. You know, time limit and all that," I say, reaching into my pocket and pulling out my knife. I slide the sharp side of the blade up his inner thigh, starting from his knee all the way up to his balls. Once I reach his balls, I lean into his ear, "Did I mention that I know how to completely dissect the human body? The genitals included," I tell him as I slice his sack open in one swift move causing his balls to fall out of the skin with nothing else joining them to his body, but the veins and tubes. He screams a blood-curdling scream before passing out.

Zane looks to me as I stand up. "Always gotta take the fun out of everything, aye?"

I shrug. "What can I say...I got a little carried away."

I turn my attention to the fat blob that's hyperventilating on the floor, his big gray beard running across his thick chest. "You're next flubber, get your ass up." I can see out of the corner of my eye as Alaina walks over to the skinny guy. She takes Zane's knife and cuts his dick clean off in one quick move. I look to Lain and see no regrets about her decision, she carried the task out with not a blink of an eye. Pain changes people, I understand that. And that's why I'm shit scared of what's going on with Kalie. I want to be there with her, fight her demons for her, so she doesn't need to. I will always put my girl on a pedestal, and I may give her time—but not much. How I need to deal with her loss during that time is undecided.

"We need to move fast. We have five minutes left," Ollie says from behind me.

I shrug, pull my knife out and slice him from ear to ear, watching as the skin on his neck splits open showing the white fatty tissue under the skin before blood starts to spurt out everywhere. I watch as he grips onto his neck, choking on his own blood. Once I know he's dead, I turn around to Alaina and Zane and see a horrific scene in front of me.

"Holy shit," I say with a laugh.

"Lain, you're a bit of an unbalanced bitch, aren't you. I'm impressed, firecracker."

The girl is fucking bad. When she was taken a few years ago from a man that was chasing her father, she stunned us all by shooting the enemy perfectly between their eyes. She's done that three times, to three different men. To some, that may sound unbelievable, but if you knew the story of her father you'd know that the apple just didn't fall far from the tree.

"We gotta bounce brother. Abby is going to lose her shit when she sees this mess."

I laugh as we make our way out. Abby is the Chief of Police. She's the youngest Chief that there's ever been, apparently. It's a good thing her connection to us is completely off the record. She's come in handy in more ways than I can count. We make our way outside, walking back around to our bikes. Before I start her up, I send a text to Sandra, giving her the location of Kazimir. I'm sure she already knows where it is, though, being with Abby. I'm not finished with him yet, but I know Sandra will let me have my way with him.

KALIE - ROSE

Once I slide into the truck, I look over at Trevor.

"Thanks for taking me home," I say, pulling on the bottom of Ade's hoodie.

Hearing him tell me he loved me moved me, but at the moment I'm too angry to go there, and I don't think I will ever be able to forgive him. Yes, it's not entirely his fault, it was only his connections, but I didn't really know the extent of what happens in this world. Maybe I should have watched more television shows. I look out the window, watching all the trees pass me by and thinking over the past week. I need to get a new phone. I don't even know if anyone knows what had happened. Probably not, it's probably all buried. Otherwise, there'd be media and the police surrounding us. I continue to glance out the window until, eventually my exhaustion takes over and sleep sets in.

⁓ ⌇⌇ ⁓

Opening my eyes to Trevor's voice. "Kal? Wake up babe, we're here."

Rubbing my eyes, I huff out. "Okay, thanks again, Trevor."

"I need to walk you up, Kal. I have orders."

Nodding my head because I don't want to cause him any trouble. "That's fine, come on."

Pushing open the door, I step out into the late afternoon sun. I glance around our apartment car park and notice people staring. Shrugging, I close the door. I don't really care what people are thinking right now. I lost my dignity this week, along with many other things.

I round the truck and take Trevor's arm in mine. He looks over to me, worried. He really is cute.

"Kal, do you want me to wait for you to take a shower then take you to go and see a doc?"

I shake my head. "I'll see her tomorrow. I just want to sleep."

He looks around nervously. "Ade, he wants me—"

"Don't fucking say his name, Trevor. Please. I don't care what *Ade* wants, okay?"

He swallows and nods his head. "I understand, baby, come on."

When we reach my door, I remember I didn't stop at the hotel and collect my things.

"Fuck," I swear out quietly.

"What's wrong?" Trevor asks me nervously.

"It's nothing. I just forgot that my keys and everything is back at the hotel."

I knock on the door and, both wish and don't wish, that Carter is there. He swings the door open, smiling until he sees me then his smile drops.

"What the fuck happened, Kalie!" He pulls me into his arms and sizes up Trevor.

"Carter...Trevor. Be nice, Carter. He's just dropping me off."

I turn to Trevor and pull him in for a hug. "Thank you, Trevor, really."

"No problem, Kalie." He smiles a small smile at me before he turns and walks away.

I walk in and shut the door, turning my body to a worried Carter. "Please give me time, Carter. I can't do this with you right now."

"No! Fuck that, Kalie. What the fuck happened?"

I roll my eyes because I really didn't expect him to take my answer as a legitimate response.

"A lot of stuff *happened,* Carter. I'm just not ready, okay? Please don't. I'm going to take a very long bath and sleep for a few days, and then I'm going to see a doc."

I walk out of the living room and make my way to my bedroom. I look around and something inside me aches. The last time I was in here was with Ade. They were happy times, times when I was only his. I think a part of me feels like I've disappointed him in a way. He loved it so much when he found out I'd only ever been with him after all these years, and even though the men who touched me didn't go all the way, I still feel disgusting. I feel as though he will never be able to see me as his innocent girl anymore. I feel dirty on the inside as much as I do on the outside.

Removing his hoodie that has the Sinful Souls emblem on the front of it, I fold it up and place it neatly on my bed. I tap it a couple of times before getting a towel out of my wardrobe, wrapping it around me and making my way to the bathroom.

The tub begins to fill as I turn the taps, then I pour every single bath salt I can see into it. Bubble baths, soaps, they're all are poured into the bath. Tears begin rolling down my cheeks again as I begin to get angry about what's happened. I'm a mess. There's no doubt about that. I sincerely hope there's some way that I can learn to live with what's happened.

I feel like an idiot in a way. Poor Alaina, she was treated much, much, worse than I was. Yet, somehow she handled it perfectly. And it's at that moment that I realize what Phoebe was talking about. She would always say how I was not cut out for their lifestyle. Vicky and her both said it. I understand that now—because I'm not. There's no way that I would ever be okay with living in a crazy world like that.

Once I am satisfied with the amount of soap in the bath, I take off my underwear and throw them into the corner. I place one foot into the scorching hot water before putting in my second foot. It's so hot that my skin tingles from the sensation of the heat. I suck in a breath, and quickly sink into the bath, biting down on my lip to stop me from crying out. The pain feels good. It takes away the pain that I feel ripping into the deepest depths of my soul, even if it is just temporary.

After a few minutes, the pain disintegrates and the warmth overwhelms me. I lie back in the bath, turn on my sound dock and push play on Evanescence 'Going Under.' I slide my head under the water and stay there for as long as I can until I've run out of breath. Floating on my back to the surface, I run my hands over my face to remove my hair from my eyes. While I just lie there staring at the ceiling allowing the lyrics of the song to float through my ears and dig into my now contaminated soul.

CHAPTER 21

Hours pass, and when I begin to get goose bumps over my skin from the temperature of the water dropping, I pull the plug out and stand as I get out of the bath. Picking up my towel, I wrap it around myself and open the bathroom cabinet. There's no doubt in my mind that I need something to help me sleep tonight. I see one of Carter's Xanax tablet bottles sitting there from his accident. They're begging me to pick them up—so I do. I pop the container lid open and drop two in one go then close the cupboard.

Turning to leave the bathroom, I stand on my old underwear that's on the floor. I look down at them briefly before bending down to pick them up. I instantly feel sick. I swing the bathroom door open, run past Carter and dash into my room, slamming my door shut behind me. I move quickly to my desk, open my drawer and pull out some scissors and begin cutting them up into tiny little pieces before dumping them into a plastic bag and throwing it into my trash can. Once I'm done, I look down to my shaking hands. Fat tears drop from my eyes again and I swipe them away angrily.

It's here and now that I decide that I will let this hurt for one night. I will cry for one night only. Cry for the girl I lost. However, after that, I will not let them have it. I'll see someone to help me work through my issues, but I will not let it bring me down. Throwing my towel off, I pick up Ade's hoodie again and shove it on then get under my bed covers.

I don't know why I did that.

I hate Ade at the moment.

The sound of his name sets me on fire, but the ignitor to that fire comes from a place that loves him so fiercely that it could burn down villages.

And that's where I'm fucked.

I open my eyes to the late afternoon sun. When I glance at my alarm clock, I see it reads five p.m. I moan and roll over, staring at the wall for a few seconds before swinging my legs over the edge and sliding into my slippers. I hope Carter is at work, or out. I really can't deal with his inquisition right now. I walk out my door, closing it softly behind me and slowly make my way into the living room. When I walk in there, Vicky, Phoebe, and Alaina greet me.

"Oh, um…" I say looking around at them nervously.

Vicky stands from the couch and runs over to me with her arms stretched wide, tears in her eyes, and her face raw and red.

"Kalie, I'm so fucking sorry. Oh my God, I'm so sorry," she says repeatedly.

"It's not your fault, Vicky. Don't do that."

"Come and sit down babe," Alaina says from the couch, her cheeks still puffy and red, the evidence from our assault apparent.

I swallow down the pain I'm feeling all over my body and walk to the sofa, wincing as I take a seat beside her. I know that after the week we spent together, I feel closer to Alaina than anyone else sitting in this room right now. Don't get me wrong, each of them are my best friends and I love them dearly, but there's some comfort I get from being with Alaina. She places her hand on my thigh and looks at me, right in the eye. Her tortured eyes to my tormented ones.

"We're going to get through this. I'm going to push you through this, too, okay? We're all here for you, Kalie. We're your family, the club, us," she gestures around the room, "we are yours to use as you please."

I shake my head. "I love you all dearly." I squeeze onto Alaina's hand tightly. "So much." A light smile touches my lips. "I really do," I say pointedly at her. "But, I can't do the MC club thing. It's not me, I'm just not that kind of girl. I'm weak, and I cannot deal with it."

Alaina smiles a small smile at me before looking at Vicky.

"Hon, you don't need to *be* strong. You just need to *love* strong. The intensity of the love you have for Ade? That is what will pull you through it. He's hurting too, and I know that doesn't consolidate you in any way, but he's there when you're ready. He loves you Kal, but he knows you need time," she whispers out honestly. My eyes are wet again, so I wipe the tears that drop onto my cheek.

"I love him, too. You know, I probably always will. But he needs to let me go."

When I look around the room, I see understanding. And when I lock eyes with Carter, I see the wrinkles lining around his eyes.

"Don't frown, Carter. You're getting wrinkles," I say with a small smile.

He laughs a quite laugh. "Let me in, baby G."

I nod my head and swallow, before telling him everything.

In the end, he's furious.

"This is your fault," he yells to Vicky. "If you weren't such a fucking slut, she would never had met Ade." Vicky drops her head in defeat and I jump up to her defense.

"Carter! Don't ever fucking say that again. I'm my own adult. I wanted, Ade. *Want* him. Do not blame her for that. So help me God Carter, I will move out," I yell at him.

He winces and steps back. That was probably a low blow because he has security issues, he needs stability and all that, and when he's not getting it from a partner he needs it from me. However, I can't have him lashing out at the girls.

I sit back on the sofa. "I'm sorry about that, Vick."

She shakes her head, waving her hand in front of her. "He's right, Kal. I'm so sorry."

"No, no, he's not right. It is not your fault..." I pause before continuing, "I'm going to see my doctor tomorrow, then I want my life as normal as I can get it."

They all agree and stand from their seats.

Phoebe pulls me into her arms. "I'm staying back in The Hills. I need to be near you. I'll be back at my old place, and I bought your stuff back with me along with a new phone," she says as she kisses me on the forehead. When I look down I notice it's a brand new iPhone.

"Phoebe, you shouldn't have!" I point to the phone.

She shrugs. "I didn't pay for it. It was a gift that I do not want. So I'm gifting it to you," she says casually.

I raise my eyebrows in surprise. "Okay, well, thank you."

Walking with them to the front door, I hug them all briefly before saying goodbye. Upon closing the door, I pick up my bags and take them back into my room. My head is thumping again, so I drop to my bed and pull the covers up over me, letting my sleep take over.

ADE NIXON

"Ade?" Haleigh says from beside me.

"What?" I answer, watching one of the new girls work on the pole while swallowing my drink.

She places her hand on my collar, running it down the front of me before dragging it over my crotch. I look up at her, eyebrows raised and a smirk on my face. Haleigh is cute, in that all-American girl kind of way, but she's new. There's no way this girl knows what she's getting herself into—she's about to, though. I grab onto her hand, push it down under my jeans, and bring my face up to hers. "Don't bite off more than you can chew, sweetheart," I say smirking at her while rubbing her hand all over the cock. She bites down on her lower lip and it pisses me off instantly.

"Don't do that," I say with my mouth set in a hard line.

"Do what?" she asks as she runs her teeth over her lip again.

I grip onto her lip and pull it out of her mouth roughly. "That. Don't do it."

The motion reminds me of my Kalie. The thought of Kalie has me picking up my drink and dropping it back fast. By this point, Haleigh is practically dry humping my leg. I push her off me forcefully before standing. Walking to the bar, I snatch a bottle of Johnny Walker and walk back to the table. I pull her by the hand, making her smile and stand. She begins following me to the room, the same room I snapped Gretchen off in, not too long ago. I close the door behind me while I watch as Haleigh lies back on the bed, removing her top and skirt, and then rubbing the spot next to her.

"Come on, big boy, show me if what I hear about you is true."

I scrunch up my face in disgust. "You got balls coming into my room and saying that."

I take another long pull of my drink, place it on the dresser and remove my top while unbuttoning my jeans. Her eyes look at me hungrily and I almost laugh. This girl is, first of all, way too fucking skinny. I hate fucking with girls this thin. They never have enough stamina because of their lack of calorie intake, and there's no way their bodies are built to fuck a man like me—or rather—let a man like me fuck them. Not fucking appealing to me at all, give me Kalie's perfect curves over this bullshit any fucking day. Fuck, thinking about Kalie again makes my dick rock hard instantly. I move over the bed and pull on Haleigh's legs roughly. I slide down her panties in one movement before pulling down my jeans. She wraps her hands around my neck, only for me to push them back down.

"Don't," I say to her.

Her face drops for a second until she sees my dick.

Cock-thirsty whore.

I pull open the drawer next to the bed and snatch out a condom wrapper. Ripping if off, I roll it onto my dick. I rub my head over her clit slowly, then ram into her in one strong movement. She screams out loudly, and I put my hand over her mouth roughly.

"Fuck up, or I stop. Got it?" She nods her head quickly so I remove my hand.

I pull out of her and then slam back into her. It's nothing but a motion, a routine. There's nothing to it at all, it's as though I'm fucking a faceless body. I would have more fun with my hand. The thought of this fucks me off, so I grip onto her neck while continuing to pound into her. I have to remind myself a few times to ease off my grip—the times when she starts to turn purple. When I feel her pussy clench around my dick, I flip her over and lift her ass into the air. I wrap her long black hair around my fist and yank on it so her head comes back. I continue to pound into her pussy again, trying to reach something—anything, that will push me over. Grabbing onto her neck with my hand that has her hair, the movement causes her to scream again in pleasure. The fucking sound fucks me off again and at this moment, I realize that I want to repeat the events of Gretchen all over again. I pull out of her as Kalie's beautiful smile comes in full HD display in my head, giving me a flashback of a memory of us on the beach.

"That good huh?" I asked laughing at her as she moaned, taking the first bite of her burger.

She nodded her head. "Really, really, good. Good enough to not want to go for a run just for eating it." I shook my head and wiped the sauce from the side of her lips, making that beautiful blush splash out across her cheekbones. Fuck, she's phenomenal, there was no one in the world that was like her, and she was all fucking mine.

"You're pretty fucking special, you know that?" I said honestly, sucking the sauce on my finger that I'd just wiped from her lip.

She swallowed and laughed. "Good special, I hope?"

My laughter died out as a foreign feeling tingled deep in my chest. "Real good, darling."

The memory fades out, and I look down to the girl on my dick right now, to see it's not Kalie. Our bodies are dripping in sweet. Having not come, nor do I want to, I pull out of her. Rip the condom off and throw to into the bin, before pushing her naked body off the bed.

"Get out," I say flatly. She stands up, putting her clothes back on.

"I can finish you off if you want? It wouldn't be fair for me to get three out of you, and you not get any?"

I look up at her. "Do you wanna know what happened to the last girl who refused to leave this very room when I asked her to?"

She laughs, looking around the room while pulling her hair into a ponytail.

"Yeah, what?" she answers excitedly.

I think she may just be the dumbest bitch I've ever met, and that's saying something. I stand, pull on my jeans, take out a cigarette from my pocket and light it up. I stalk up to her, leaning down into her ear. "I killed her," I whisper with a smirk.

Her curious face drops and she swallows down while making her way to the door.

"Thanks, Ade. I think," she says as she swings the door open and power walks out of there.

I laugh as I put my top back on.

Fucking stupid bitches.

CHAPTER 22

KALIE - ROSE

I look around the crisp white walls as I sit and wait for Dr. Oswald to come out. I know I need help, I know I'm not going to be able to work through my issues without a professional. The sooner I can get past this, the better.

A young African American woman walks out in a crisp white blazer and an immaculate suit, with heels that I would break my neck in.

"Kalie-Rose Reynolds?" she asks while looking around the room of people.

"Yes, that's me," I reply, collecting my handbag and following her into her office.

"Hi, I'm Dr. Maree Oswald, it's lovely to meet you. What do you like to be called?" she asks, with her hand stretched out to me.

I take her hand in mine. "Just Kalie, thanks. Pleased to meet you too."

She gestures to the seat in the middle of her office so I walk to it, sit down, and glance around. It doesn't look like the shrink rooms you see on television, it has a homey feeling to it, making me completely relaxed. One wall is lined with books. There's her office desk in front of a glass window overlooking the city, and it's decorated in white and soft gray. It really is a beautiful room.

"How can I help you today, Kalie?"

I begin fidgeting with my fingers. "Anything I tell you can never leave these walls, right?" I ask.

"Yes, that's right. Unless I feel you are going to harm yourself or others around you. Anything you tell me is one hundred percent safe within these walls," she responds with a soft smile.

"Oh boy, where should I start." I pick up the glass of water from the coffee table and take some small sips, and then I begin to pour sifted bits out to her. Leaving out information like the identity of the MC. I only tell her the parts that she needs to know, the parts of me that I know need to somehow repair.

Once I've finished, I look up at her and see a worried look spread out across her face.

"We can work through this, Kalie. We can do it together."

I hope so. I truly hope that we can.

I walk into our apartment and drop my handbag to the floor.

"Carter?" I yell out while walking to the fridge to grab a bottled water.

"Hey, baby G. How was your appointment?" he asks, walking into the kitchen in his Playboy robe.

"It was good. She was lovely, and my next appointment is tomorrow. She wants to see me daily for a while," I say then take a large drink of water.

"How are you feeling, though?" he asks with a worried tone.

"A little better, I guess. I just need to take it day by day."

I walk into my room, strip off, and wrap myself in a towel before walking to the bathroom and getting under the scorching hot shower.

"Yes, I am going to get better," I whisper to myself.

ADE NIXON

"Are we going to talk about the fact that Felix is a shady motherfucker who needs to be dealt with?" I ask Zane. We are at one of Zane's nightclubs in the city, just him and I.

"Yeah, I've been watching him these past couple of days. Watching his movements, his whereabouts and important shit like that. I want to make sure I have everything in line before I go out shooting," he says tilting his drink up to his lips.

"Fuck that. I don't need anything in line, I'll fucking shoot him right now. What he did was fucked up, there's no more to it than that. He knew more than what he made out he knew. Therefore, he's a traitor."

I watch one of the girls rubbing and grinding her shit on the pole. She does it fucking good. The door opens, shining in the daylight. Ollie walks in with Chad and Harvey behind him. Ollie and Chad take a seat, but Harvey is standing stock still, watching the girl on the pole.

I raise my eyebrows and chuckle. "Fucking good, huh?"

He doesn't hear me so I kick his shin. "Harv?" I laugh. "I said she's fucking good, huh?"

He laughs, rubbing his hand over his beard. "Yeah, not bad," he gruffs out. I keep smiling at him, not bad my fucking left nut. The man was hypnotized in minus two seconds.

"I need to fill you boys in on something," Zane says, pulling his seat into the table a little more.

"It's Felix. I'm not sure how good his intentions are anymore. One of Ade's jobs was given via Felix. The job that just so happened to set off the train of events that occurred with the girls. I need to tread carefully, though, there's still a chance that—one, it could be a coincidence, or two, he may not have had a choice."

I laugh, then take a swallow of my drink. "Your second point is not valid. You always have a choice. And if he didn't, he should have come to us and we would've handled it as a club. Not bitch out on us and almost have our girls killed."

"He wouldn't, surely he wouldn't," Harvey says in disbelief.

"I don't know. He's been acting a little strange lately. Someone who won't kill him. Ade needs to confront him," Ollie says.

"That's me, I will have no problem. I just need to give you boys a heads up as to what's going on," Zane states.

Blake walks in, with obvious stress around his eyes. "Fuck, this parenting shit is hard work. Vicky is fucking full time. She's killing me slowly. I shit you not," he says, waving over the bartender.

Vicky has been riding Blake, a little rough since the girls were taken. She wants him out and we all know it, even if she hasn't admitted that yet. There's no way I would leave the club, not even for Kalie. As long as you know what you're walking into, you have no excuse to bitch out. And if I ever get Kalie under me again, you'd have a higher chance of hitting the lottery five times before I ever let her go again.

Zane fills Blake in as he did with the rest of us, and by the end, Blake is ready for war.

"We go there now and ask him. No more fucking waiting around Zane."

I shake my head. "I got somewhere to be. I'll be back tonight."

Zane looks to me from the other side of the table. "Everything good?"

I nod my head. "Yeah." Standing up, I throw the rest of my whiskey back. "I have a ghost to bury."

Arriving at the destination where Sandra sent me, I look down to my phone before gazing back at the building again. It's a big industrial building. Looks average, and if you drove past it on the street, nothing would stand out. I walk up to the metal door and knock on it a few times. It opens up to Sandra standing there, her blonde hair tied in a tidy knot on the top of her head, with her pearl earrings and straight suit. She's exactly how you'd imagine someone in her line of power to look.

"Come in, Ade." She gestures inside the building and I walk in, removing my gloves and looking around.

"He here?" I ask, looking behind my shoulder.

She nods her head. "Yes, but I don't want you to mess him up. We need him, *alive*."

I laugh. "Yeah, we will see about that."

"I'm serious, Ade. Abide by these rules."

"You still have a thing for him, don't you?" I ask her.

Sandra Fisick and my mother were best friends growing up, some say she had a thing for my dad and that's why their friendship ended.

She tilts her head. "I never had a thing for him, Ade, and I need him alive. He's an asset. We can use him to bring down his entire family operation."

I nod my head, deciding to drop it because I can't be fucked with the drama of it.

She smiles a small smile at me then walks ahead. "Follow me."

I follow her through the empty space and it's large and cold. There are a few cars parked inside but nothing else. Once we reach the beginning of the stairs, I follow her up to a loft. She stops at the top and I move around her, putting Frank, or Kazimir in my direct line of sight. He's sitting on a sofa in front of me. When he sees me, he smiles and gets up from where he's sitting.

"Sit back down, this won't take long," I say moving across the room.

"Ade," Sandra warns from behind me.

I look over my shoulder and smirk at her, making her blush.

"I just want to talk," I say to her. Her body eases and she nods her head in approval.

Sitting down on the seat opposite to him, I throw my leg on top of my knee.

"Why Felix?" I ask.

"What do you mean, why Felix?" he answers in a confused tone.

"You get time with me, and you want to spend it gossiping about one of your brothers?"

I shake my head. "Don't fucking ignore the question. Why Felix?"

He clenches his jaw and raises his eyebrows before shrugging. "Was easy really. It's amazing how stupid men can be when love is involved. I ordered him to give you that hit."

"Why? Why would you be so theatrical with how you got me?"

He shakes his head. "I wanted the business Bruce Peyton had. It was like, killing two birds with one stone."

I stand from my seat and walk to him. Bending down to his level, I gather enough saliva in my mouth before spitting it on his face.

"You're fucking lucky, I can't kill you. I'm sure whatever these people here have in store for you, will make you wish I did, though," I say, getting up from my position.

I turn around and begin walking out, nodding at Sandra on the way. Pushing open the metal door I move out into the dim light of the day. I throw my leg over my bike and set off out of there. I want to drive to Hollywood so fucking bad. The past couple days have been fucking hard without her. Her innocence always calmed my demons and I wish now that I never knew how love felt. The feelings I feel for her consume me, and if I die from the suffocation of her love, I will die a fucking happy man.

Time. I just need to give her time.

Time I cannot be fucked giving.

On arrival, I walk back into the clubhouse and see Felix at the bar heading straight to him.

Grasping onto his throat I push him up against the wall.

"The fuck are you doing, Ade," he seethes.

"What the fuck are *you* doing, Felix? Daddy dearest came clean with me. Get the fuck in that boardroom *right fucking now*," I yell in his face.

The rest of the boys walk in through the door and Zane stops in his tracks.

"Ade? We had a plan, brother. You—"

"Fuck the plan. I just spoke to the devil himself who admitted he sent him to hand me that hit. He's a fucking traitor."

Zane's mouth sets into a hard line and he swings his eyes to Felix.

"In the boardroom. Now."

I let go of Felix, dropping him to the ground and follow everyone into the boardroom.

"Explain this shit, now?" Zane pushes back onto his seat.

"I didn't know, brother. I didn't know why he gave me that hit."

"You knew. You knew he was alive! You knew who he really was. You fucking betrayed this club and you will pay for that," I say walking up to Felix and pushing him off his chair.

"Ade...sit, now," Zane orders from his seat.

I look to him and narrow my eyes. There haven't been that many times where I have wanted to challenge Zane on a decision, but this was one of them.

"This is fucked-up Z, and you know it." I point to him before sitting back on my chair.

"Explain it all...*now*. And don't leave anything out. Ade is like a caged lion needing to get out and rip into his prey. I will unleash him on you if you do not spit everything out, *right fucking now*," Zane casually states while putting a cigarette to his mouth.

Felix looks between all of us, and I see the fear he has in his eyes, so I laugh.

He snaps his eyes back to me before he continues, "He threatened, Abby. I couldn't have him threaten her. I didn't know he was alive this whole time, only when he approached me to give you the hit. He gave me no other choice. I gathered he targeted me to hand it to you because I'm the eldest, and he knows I don't run the same way you lot do. I didn't betray the club. I had a plan to tell you everything, but I needed to wait for the right time to make sure he didn't find out."

I narrow my eyes at him and flip out a switchblade. "Something's gotta give, brother. You may not think you didn't betray the club, but you did. You could have told us what was happening and we would have handled it together, as a brotherhood." I lean back on my seat, spread my legs wide, and flick my knife around in my hand. I look to Ollie and see his mouth set in a hard line. That would have been hard for him to hear, the fucker has been chasing Abby since we were little.

Zane nods his head. "Ade is right. Left or right?" he asks, stubbing his cigarette out in the ashtray. I chuckle under my breath, bringing one of my hands up and rubbing my top lip with my index finger.

Felix scrunches up his face. "Fuck," he rips his hoodie and shirt off, "right."

Flipping my knife out that I've been playing with in my hand, I throw it across the table where he's sitting, stabbing him in the arm.

"F-f-fuck!" he spits, trying to hold down the pain.

I walk to where he's sitting and kneel in front of him, patting his knee. "See, this just isn't going to do it for me. This didn't scratch my itch—"

I watch Zane push his chair out and stand from the table. "*Ade,*" he growls under his breath.

"Relax, Z. I'm calm. However, this little wound here is not enough for me. You see it's your fault, my girl...well, girls were taken. Whether you like to admit that or not, you played a part." I yank the knife out of his arm and stab it into his left arm, pushing it in deep and circling it around.

He screams out in agony, no longer able to keep up his front.

I bend down so my mouth is up to his ear while still circling the knife deep in his arm. "This pain that you are feeling right now?" I whisper to him so only he and I can hear, "does not even scratch the surface of what those girls endured. And you are fucking lucky that I don't rip your fucking eyes out of their sockets." I yank my knife back out of him, snatch his top out of his hands and wipe my blade clean with it. I look up at Zane and he nods his head in a silent approval before I walk out of the boardroom slamming the door shut on my way out.

CHAPTER 23

KALIE - ROSE

It's been a whole week since I started seeing Dr. Oswald. I feel lighter, and although I know what happened will haunt me for a long time—if not, forever—I know I need to attempt to try to get my life back into a somewhat regular routine. So here I am, running my little heart out on the treadmill for the first time since I'd been back from my holiday. So, it is safe to say that I feel as though I'm running a one hundred kilometer marathon.

How the fuck I did this shit every day before, I do not know.

I'm letting the sweat drip from my head, with Eminem *'Till I Collapse'* pulsating through my ears. What can I say, I have anger to vent and there's no one better to vent with than Slim Shady. I'm pounding my feet on the rubber when I see someone walk in the door. Judging by the size of the person, I know it's Dominic. I smile, look up at him, and pull my headphones out.

"Hey," I say, slowing the treadmill down to a walking pace.

"Hey," he replies with worry lines around his eyes. My smile drops and I put my iPod down, pushing stop on the treadmill. I get off and grab my towel.

"Are you okay?" I ask, wiping the sweat off my neck.

"Shouldn't I be asking you? Fuck Kalie," he says with a little anger in his tone.

I pull my lips in-between my teeth and close my eyes briefly. "Who told you?"

"Does it matter? It's all the same." I see the worry in his eyes and it pulls at feelings I never knew I had there for him.

"I'm sorry," I whisper.

"Why are you sorry, Kalie? Fuck, if anyone is sorry, it's me. Come here," he says gesturing to me with his arm out. I walk into him, cuddling under his embrace. Feeling the light kiss on the top of my head, I sigh out in appreciation.

"Thank you, Dom," I say, looking up to him from his embrace.

He looks down on me. "Thank me? What for?" he asks, pushing stray hair behind my ear.

"For always being there. For this, just for being you. You're a great guy, Dom. I'm sorry I never saw it," I say shyly.

"Do you see it now?" he asks rubbing his thumb across my cheek.

"Maybe," I say unsure.

I know I want to try things with Dominic. It's hard not to want those things when not only is he hot, he's a great guy on the inside and has a big heart. I think over a few of the pointers Dr. Oswald and I went over this week.

"*Do things that make you happy in the moment. Try to normalize your life again.*" Her voice echoes through my head.

I look up to Dominic and see a small smile on his pouty lips.

"Maybe if we take it slow at first? See where it goes?"

He's searching my eyes, when his smile gets a little wider, showing his straight white teeth. He brings his face down to mine and kisses my nose.

"I can do whatever you need, Kal. Always."

I smile back at him and nod. "Okay, okay. Now what?" I ask, and he laughs.

"Now, I take you to dinner." I blush slightly and look out in front of me.

"Okay, dinner," I reply looking back to him to see he's still smiling.

"I'll pick you up at eight?"

"Sounds good," I say, fiddling with the towel in my hand.

He takes hold of my hand and kisses it before walking out of the room.

"Shit," I whisper under my breath.

My impulse decisions have been getting the best of me lately. That thought reminds me of Ade, and my smile drops. It doesn't drop because he doesn't make me happy—very much the opposite—it drops because after it all, I never told him that I loved him back, even though I obviously do. I can't have him, though, it wouldn't be fair to lead him on to thinking I can live the type of life that he lives. I'm just not that girl. I'm not strong, sassy, or badass like Alaina and Vicky. I'm introverted, quiet, and reserved. I hate confrontation, and I'm always worried about how people might perceive me. I'm the complete opposite of what any man in an MC club will ever want.

Ade Nixon, how can one man be so many kinds of difficult. How can I love such a complication of a man? That's why I need to do this, why I need to test it out. Dominic Abrahams is the type of man I should be with, and I owe it to myself to try.

I realize I have been standing in the same position since Dom left so I turn around, pick up my water bottle from the table next to the treadmill and make my way back home.

~ ∞ ~

Walking in the door, I head straight for the shower. Turning on the faucet, while I stand there waiting for the water to heat up. I'm excited about tonight, but there's a part of me that feels empty. It's a big part. It's the part that likes bad boys who have tattoos, ride bikes, and have something called a Jacobs Ladder on their penis.

"I'm fucked," I mumble.

I need to forget Ade Nixon and all his out-of-this-world beauty. Dominic is magnificent looking, and any other girl would be leaping at the opportunity to have a date with him. He gets hit on daily. Almost every woman he talks to will be twisting her hair in her fingers, or biting her lip at him trying to gain his attention. Dom's not like that, though. He's selective on who he beds, I've noticed that over all the years that I've known him.

He's always discreet and professional.

Complete opposite to Ade.

I need to stop thinking of Ade because it's becoming more of a problem. Maybe that can be mine and Dr. Oswald's next issue to work on—*How to stop thinking about ex-lovers.* I'm pretty sure you could write a book covering that particular topic.

Yeah, I doubt anyone could help me with that. I pour some shampoo into my hand and lather it into my hair before following the same routine with the conditioner. After I'm done washing, I turn off the shower and grab my towel that's hanging over the shower door, wrapping it around me and walking back to my room. I shut the door behind me and look into my wardrobe. I walk in and turn my light on as I start to rummage through all my clothes, trying to find something to wear. He didn't say where we were going for dinner, so I don't know how to dress.

"Shit," I mumble.

I walk back into my room and pick up my phone from the bed. I scroll down to Dom's name and press the send a message button.

Me: *You didn't tell me where you were taking me. #wardrobedilemma*

I cannot believe I just hashtagged in a text message. Nice Kalie, showing how much of a loser you are already. This relationship won't last.

Dominic: *It's a surprise. Dress how you want. You're perfect.*

Smiling at the words of his text message, I realize he didn't give me an answer. I'm just going to have to take a chance and play roulette with my clothes. I walk back into my wardrobe and carry on with my rummaging. I stop at a black dress. It's tight without being too tight, and it's plain—but plain is safe. I can match it with my nude pumps and it'll be a perfectly plain combination.

That's what he gets for being cryptic.

After I comb out my hair, straightening it out, and leaving it in little curls at the ends. I put on a light smudge of eyeshadow, some blush, red lipgloss and I'm ready. Standing in front of the mirror for a few seconds, I look at myself. Yep, I look good, but deep down there's a part of me that wishes I was dressing up for Ade. Where Dominic is sweet and gentle, Ade is rough, raw, and knows when *not* to be gentle. He was different with me, though, that much I know. He was an asshole to the world, but a gentleman to his girl. He's a beautifully flawed soul though and I have no doubt he's fighting his own demons. There's also a huge part of me that wants to fight them with him. I wanted to be his. He made me feel more than special, he made me feel, magical.

I sigh, looking down at my shoes before sitting on my bed. A knock sounds at my door.

"Come in," I say, trying to hide my sadness.

Phoebe pokes her head around my door with a smile. That is until she sees the look I'm pulling. "Okay, what's wrong?" she asks, shutting my door behind her.

I pull my bottom lip into my mouth and tilt my head. "I don't know. I should be ecstatic right now. I'm going to dinner with Dominic Abrahams, and he's my best friend. He's someone who's right for me, someone who is safe. So why am I sitting here all dolled up thinking about a menace!" I swing my arms up before putting my face in my hands.

I feel the bed dip next to me and an arm wrap around my shoulders.

"Menace being Ade?" she asks lightly. I drop my hands and scowl at her.

"No. Menace being, '*Don't be a menace in south central while drinking your juice in the hood*,'" I reply sarcastically.

"Okay, okay, be nice," she says with a hint of a smile. "Do you want to know what I think?"

I widen my eyes and nod my head. "Obviously Phoebe don't play dumb."

She narrows her eyes again and smirks. "Easy tiger. I think you need to do a lot of healing. I think that you're probably going to end up with Ade. But

I also think that you should take your time with that. Do you want to know why? Because there's no way in hell he will ever be letting you walk out of his life again. *Ever.*"

"But should I be going out with Dominic tonight?" I ask, looking at her.

"Yes. It's just dinner. Feel it out and see how you go. Take note of those feelings. After tonight, you should know what you need to do," she says calmly.

Damn, this girl is pretty bloody smart.

I smile. "Okay, I can do that. I miss him so much, Phoebs. It hurts how much I miss him, his company, and how he makes me feel. I'm addicted to him."

She smiles and pats my leg. "I know, love, I know."

She stands from the bed and stretches out her arms. "I better get going. I'm supposed to be back in Westbeach by now."

"Why were you over this way?" I ask, touching up my make-up.

She looks at me and claps her hands excitedly. "That's what I came to tell you! I took a job that could do tremendous things for me. I'm not sure what the gist of it is, at the moment, but I'll have to go on tour with some famous singers while they tour around the world. I'll need to dress them and all that. I'm really excited, but I hope I don't get a damn diva queen. I'll fucking kill it. I swear to God, I will kill the next famous person that plays diva with me."

I nod my head in agreement while standing. "Tell me about it, the Diva comment. I need to throw myself back into work. But, oh my God, Phoebs! That's so awesome. Don't forget me when you're famous and all that. I wonder who it is? The list is endless. If it's someone like *Eminem* you have to shove me in your suitcase with you. I swear I will play nice," I say gripping her shoulders.

She laughs, patting my hand. "Honey, I doubt someone like *Eminem* will give a flying fuck about the thoughts of someone like me when it comes to his apparel. Calm down."

She pulls me in and kisses me on the lips. "I don't head out for another two weeks. So we have heaps of time to catch up."

I nod my head. "Okay beautiful, I love you."

"I love you too, sugar cakes," she says while throwing up the peace sign, and walking out of my room.

Phoebe has this chillness about her. She's so sure of herself and knows what she's doing in this world and she doesn't give a shit about what people think of her. She races cars in four-inch heels for goodness sake. The girl is a goddess.

"Right," I mumble out. "Time to get this shit sorted."

I straighten out my dress, grab my clutch of my dresser throwing a few necessities into it before walking out of my room. Walking down to the living room I see Carter on the couch with a guy that I've seen around—twice now. Interesting. Carter usually only does casual and has a definite no double dipping rule. I look between both of them snuggled up on the couch.

"Hello," I say with a smile.

Carter pulls out a huge smile and rakes over my body from my head to my toes. "Damn, baby G, you are fucking flawless."

"Thanks." I look to the dark haired beauty next to him and pointedly look at Carter. Carter looks at who I'm looking at then looks back to me.

"Oh, shit! My bad. Kalie, this is Matt. Matt...Kalie,"

I walk over to them on the couch and shake his hand.

"Hi, nice to meet you!" I greet him with a huge smile.

"Nice to finally meet you, too, Kalie," he says kindly.

I'm not going to lie, seeing Carter with someone makes me extremely happy. Who knew? I look back at Carter and he's giving me evils. I snap my mouth shut and narrow my eyes back at him.

"Stop!" He points to me with a small smile.

I throw my hands up. "I'm not saying anything!"

"Where are you going anyway? You look to die for."

"I'm going to dinner," I say bluntly.

"Yes, I gathered that, but with who?" he asks patiently.

"With who is irrelevant," I snap nicely at him.

He narrows his eyes and lifts his arms off Matt. Just as his mouth opens to say something, I hear a knock at the door.

"Shit." I rush toward the door but fall on my ass in these huge heels, which results in Carter and his quick fucking feet jumping up and diving toward the door before me. He swings it open and smiles a big broad smile at me.

"Well, well, well, if it isn't Dominic Abrahams."

I walk to the door with a frown, pushing him out of the way with my elbows.

"Sorry about that. Carter is a little….fucking annoying. Shall we go?" I say innocently to Dominic. Carter frowns and kisses me on my head.

"Be safe kids. Kalie, do you still have those—" I walk out quickly, slamming the door in Carter's face instantly cutting him off. I blush and look to Dom apologetically.

"Sorry again. He can be…yeah, he can be Carter."

Dom shakes his head, trying not to laugh out loud.

"You two are cute."

I laugh at his comment.

He's anything but cute right now.

We walk out the lobby of my apartment as he leads me to his truck. Opening the door, he helps me in, before going around to the driver's side. Once he's in, I look over to him while putting my seatbelt on.

"So, where are we heading too?"

"The Rocks," he says smiling at me.

"The Rocks? Wow! I'm impressed."

The Rocks is a high-class restaurant in Hollywood Hills. It's hard to get a table there, and you usually have to book months in advance. So yes, I'm impressed.

He shrugs and glances over to me. "Not a big deal."

I smile and look down at what he's wearing. Tidy jeans, a white top rolled up at the sleeves, and Chuck Taylors. His hair is how it usually is shaved short on the sides with the top long and slicked back. Dominic has a body builder physic. He's huge. He and Ade probably stretch around the same. Only Ade stands around six three and Dom reaches around six foot. I look out the window and swallow down nervously.

I feel his hand grasp onto my knee. "You look amazing, Kalie. But you could wear a paper bag and still look fucking gorgeous."

I smile at him. "Thanks, you don't look so bad yourself."

CHAPTER 24

We pull up outside The Rocks and I get out before he can open the door for me. He rounds the truck, hands the key to the valet, and grasps my hand leading me inside the building. My heels clink along the glass tiled floor as we head to the restaurant. There's a young girl standing at the entrance behind a desk, and she gawks approvingly at Dominic. I almost laugh. It doesn't bring up any jealous feelings in me, and I note that because if she were looking at Ade like that we would be having a problem. I bite down on my lip and breathe out loudly in the knowledge that maybe this isn't such a good idea. Before I can let my thoughts go wild, I feel his large hand tug on mine gently.

"Come on." He nudges his head toward the tables.

I smile and follow him to a table near the glass windows. I take my jacket off and sit down looking around at the beautiful architecture of the interior. It's all glass and dimly lit with tea lights around the entire room. Picking up the water in front of me, I pour me a glass and take a few small sips. Dominic looks to me with a smile.

"You okay?" he asks.

I nod my head. "Yeah, I'm good. How was the rest of your day?"

"It was good. Yours?" He picks up the menu and scans through it.

"Meh, average," I say shrugging my shoulders.

He laughs. "You going back to work?"

"Maybe. I'm not sure what I'm doing yet."

I begin looking through the menu just as the waiter reaches our table. I end up ordering the eye fillet steak and Dom orders the triple meat combo. *Not surprised.*

"Anything, in particular, you wanted to do? Your plans I mean."

"I have a few ideas, but I'm not one hundred percent set on them yet."

He reaches over and grasps my hand. "I'm serious, Kal. I'm really happy that you decided to give this a go."

I smile at him. "I'm happy I did too."

I see an older woman walking up to our table, she must be in her late sixties.

"I'm so sorry to interrupt," she says looking between Dom and me.

"It's fine," I respond, smiling at her.

"You two remind me so much of my late husband and I. It's so sweet to see young love." My eyebrows shoot up and I start coughing, taking hold of my water.

"Thank you," I say into my glass.

"It's all new," Dominic adds, stretching out his collar. I notice his cheeks redden a bit and he looks adorable.

She touches my hand. "They all start new, sweetheart."

I smile at her words. Maybe she's right. Dom stands from the table before the woman begins walking away.

"Do you know how to take a picture on one of these?" he asks her, flashing his iPhone.

I roll my eyes. There's no way this woman knows how to take a picture on an iPhone.

She giggles. "Well, yes I do. I had to learn so I can take photos of all my great-grandchildren." Dominic hands her his phone with a smile then looks over to me with a mischievous glint in his eyes.

He sits back down and pats his lap. "Come on."

Amo Jones

I smirk at him, walk over and sit myself on his lap sideways so my legs hang to his side. I look down at him with a smile.

"You're such a dork sometimes. Do you know that?" He places his hand behind my neck, pulling my face gently down to his and smiling against my lips, before kissing them gently.

"Only when I'm with you."

We both start laughing against each other's lips. I forgot all about the woman with Dom's phone. I quickly stand and the old woman smiles.

"I got some good ones in there. Bless your heart sweet girl. He's a keeper."

I think that was the turning point for me. Dominic is amazing. Not only on the outside but the inside too. At this moment, I want to try with him.

"Thank you," I say shyly.

Dominic walks up behind me, taking the phone from the old woman. "Thank you," he says and she smiles. "Oh don't thank me. That was a pleasure to see."

My eyebrows shoot up. If she weren't such a sweet old lady I would have been creeped out by that comment. I look up to Dominic, and he's smiling a huge smile at me while flicking through his phone.

"What?" I say self-consciously.

He smiles. "You're so fucking beautiful. These are going on Facebook."

I shake my head. "Give me a look first. Shit."

I swipe his phone out of his hand. Flicking through the photos, they are actually great. We look like a couple in love. She snapped three of them. One was of us laughing against each other's lips. The other was a perfect snap of a light kiss on my lips, and the other was both of us looking deep into each other's eyes. We look like a happy couple. I smile up at him and pass his phone back.

"They're good. Maybe she should be a photographer."

He laughs. "Or maybe you should be a model."

I laugh, sitting back to my seat. "Yeah, nope. Never. Carter has enough model like behavior for me to handle."

The waiter comes back, placing our meals out in front of me and we chat and eat like the friends we are.

I'm tossing and turning in bed, thinking about what happened tonight. It feels as though I'm forcing myself into this a bit too much. I need to try it out, but I also don't want to lead him on.

Relationships are such a fucking mess. Now I could lose a friend as well. I close my eyes and let sleep drift over me, where my nightmares await.

"No. No. Get the fuck off me."

Who is that? Where am I? I try to open my eyes, but I can't, it was as though they were stuck closed.

"Get the fuck off me you pig."

That's Alaina. Oh my God, what the fuck. I began to stir around.

"Fuck up bitch!" I heard the sound of a fist hitting flesh, and then there was silence. The next thing I heard is a zipper and the slapping sound of skin-to-skin contact. I attempted again to say something, but it came out in mumbled words.

"Fuck...where am I?" I managed to mumble out in a sleepy haze.

The sound stops. "Fuck, Jason. Go put that bitch back to sleep."

I felt a hand come over my mouth and a pill drop on my tongue. He kept his hand covered over my mouth, forcing me to swallow. My eyes closed and darkness took over once again.

I wake up in a sweat with my arms shaking. That wasn't a nightmare. That was a memory. I look at the time on my phone, ignoring the two messages and see it's the early hours of the morning. There's no way I'm going to be able to go back to sleep. My body begins to convulse as tears start pouring down my face. "*Alaina*," I whisper out to the darkness. She endured horrific things. I bet that's not even the tip of what happened to her. Here I am moping about having fingers shoved inside me. I'm a shitty person. I pick up my phone, opening a new message and send her a text.

Me: *Can we talk sometime? Please.*

Placing my phone back down on my bedside table, I feel like a place in me has broken for her. That memory was so vivid. *Fuck.* I lay there for a couple hours until the tears have dried on my face and the early morning sun is pouring into my room. I hear a knock on my door.

"Baby G, it's me. Can I come in?"

"If I say no will you go away?"

The door swings open, and he prances in with his robe wrapped around him and in his *Hugh Hefner* slippers.

"Of course not," I mumble, rolling my eyes.

He sits down on my bed, placing his arm around me. "I heard you screaming last night. I ran in here, but you were asleep and you wouldn't wake up. What's happening? I'm worried."

"It was a memory...from that week," I say looking directly at the wall.

His eyebrows push together in worry. "What happened?"

"To me? Not much compared to what Alaina had to deal with. That's her story, though. I can't share that with you, Carter," I reply sadly.

"What about you? What did they do?"

I shrug, pulling the blanket up to my chin. "It only happened a couple times. He always used his fingers. He never came near me with his dirty dick."

Carter swallows and turns red. "I can kill them," he says with certainty.

I sit up on the bed and pat his hand. "Ade has already taken care of it. And Zane. I'm gathering, seeing as I left them there with both of the men who did this to us."

"Well, I'll unbury him and do it all over again," he says with a shaky voice.

I grip onto his hand. "Hey, don't. I didn't tell you for sympathy, Carter. Don't cry for me."

He wipes under his eyes. "You don't deserve all that, Kal. No one does. It's sickening to think men like that exist in this messed up world."

I nod my head and throw the covers off me. "I know. I need to make sure Alaina is okay. Every time I see her it's as if she's so strong, calm, and collected. She endured some horrible shit, Carter. I'm surprised Zane hasn't burned this entire earth down."

"Well," he begins, walking over to me, "it's probably that painful, that he's gone the opposite way you know. It sounds like some pretty dark and deep shit."

He's right, that's probably what is. Sometimes our coping mechanisms can change depending on how serious the shit is we have to deal with. Nothing can pull Zane and Alaina apart. They're the King and Queen of the MC world. She fits perfectly into it. I knew her pre-Zane and she was always quiet and reserved. Maybe Zane brought out a side of her that she kept hidden. It's like she has no fear now that she has her man by her side. I envy her in a way and I have an inkling of how that will feel because I felt it once—with Ade. Carter chuckles while looking down at his phone. I look behind me, taking my top off, leaving me in my panties and bra.

"What?" I snap at him.

I know that laugh. It's a tsk tsk laugh. I might kill him if he decides today is a good day to pick on Kalie. I have a video to do tomorrow, and I need to go out shopping today. He flashes his phone at me, showing me what he's looking at. I narrow my eyes, trying to gain a better look. I smile at the screen when I see Dominic has tagged me in all three of our photos from last night.

"Was a good night, huh?" Carter asks with a cheeky smile and a raised eyebrow.

I smile. "Yeah. Yeah, I guess it was."

Picking up my phone from the nightstand, I open up my Facebook app, and *'like'* all three photos. I toss over whether I should make one of them my profile picture. Then think, *not yet, too soon.* I check my Facebook wall while I'm on there, and Phoebe has left a comment, which sets off a conversation with the girls.

Phoebe Rendon: *Hey girl, lunch today?*
Vicky Rendon: *Yeah, not without me you're not.*
Phoebe Rendon: *We might.*
Vicky Rendon: *I sincerely doubt that, sugar puff. I'm leaving Westbeach now.*
Phoebe Rendon: *Nope, don't do the sugar puff thing again Vicky, makes me feel fat.*
Vicky Rendon: *Calm your tight size 0 ass down about it, sugar puff.*

Alaina Mathews: *I'M COMING! Vicky, if you leave me behind, I will set those Louboutin's on fire. Don't play.*

Vicky Rendon: *You're an evil woman. We need to sneak out. Because of you know who.*

Alaina Mathews: *Yeah, that was pretty obvious, Vicky.*

Phoebe Rendon: *Ade?*

I roll my eyes and laugh at their conversation. These girls are crazy, but I love them to bits. They don't have to worry about Ade, he's not on my friends list so there's no way he can see their conversation. I look through the photos from last night again, smiling. My smile drops when I see the little earth symbol near the privacy.

"Fuck," I whisper while clicking on the symbol.

Carter comes up to me, looking over my shoulder. "What's up?"

I point to the symbol. "These photos are public. Anyone on Facebook can see them."

It falls silent, and when I look over my shoulder I see his face is red from trying to withhold his laughter. I drop my eyes in a bored look.

"Carter, this is not funny. Ade will get the wrong idea from those pictures. They almost killed each other at the wedding. He will for sure kill Dominic now. Shit."

Carter waves his hand around his face. "Okay, okay, I'm sorry. Look, Ade is probably not even on Facebook."

I think over what he just said, and he may be right. There's no way Ade will have a Facebook. I check through Vicky, Phoebe, and Alaina's Facebook friends anyway just to make sure, and sure enough, none of the boys are there. I relax instantly. Carter rounds me, standing in front of me and taking my brush in his hand and he begins running it through my hair.

"The question is though, baby...why did that possibility bother you so much?"

CHAPTER 25

I swallow down and shoo his brushing away. "Because Carter...because I think I'm in love with him, and there is absolutely nothing I can do about it."

Carter pauses and spins my body around to face him. "You know what you need to do. You can't do that to Dominic. You need to let him go."

I look away from him, glancing at the door. "I know," I reply swallowing down a ball of worry. "I'll just...I'll call him today." I smile at Carter and he nods his head.

"Good girl," he says lightly kissing me on the cheek.

I don't know where I'd be without him. We balance each other out. God was apologizing for all men when he made Carter—as always, the good ones are either gay or married.

Fuck my life.

Apart from Dominic, he's special. I really hope I haven't ruined our friendship, I'll be heartbroken. I can't live without Dominic in my life. He's been there for so long that I've almost become dependent on him.

I take out some casual clothes, scrub fast through the shower before running back to my room. I end up settling on a black maxi dress that hugs my curves nicely, curves that have come back in full force after my week of no food. I swear my ass has doubled. I brush my long hair and leave it in natural waves down my back. I put on some *BB cream* then snatch my glasses and handbag from the dresser before I leave my room. I walk out to the living room to see all the girls in there and Carter playing with Phoebe's hair. She has incredible hair, Carter and I always fight over who gets to touch Phoebe's hair.

"Hey!" I chirp, walking over to hug them all.

"Hey girl," Alaina says cheerfully from the seat she's sitting on.

Vicky smiles up at me, although the smile doesn't quite reach her eyes.

"Please tell me those photos I saw today were just two friends casually kissing at a restaurant?"

I blush, sucking in a breath, before sitting on the couch and placing my hands over my legs. These girls are my life; they will tell me where to put it if I fuck up. They're real, and there's no way I can lie to them. Especially Vicky, she's scary.

"Um...before I left for your wedding, Dom kissed me. I said to him just to give me some time. When I came back, one thing leads to another and he asked me out for dinner, as more than friends. I agreed. And that's how those photos happened. I love Dom, so much. I really wanted it to work, but I can't do that to him. Not when my heart is currently riding a motorcycle." I breathe out in a rush and Phoebe adds in a mumbled tone, "More like riding his army of skanks."

I look at her, eyes wide.

Alaina kicks her softly with her foot. "He's hurting. It's how he deals."

I tilt my head and look to both of them. "He's fucking around?"

They all look to each other before Vicky stands and sits next to me. "He's hurting. He loves you, but you have to understand that this is how Ade deals with his emotions. He kills or fucks." She shrugs.

Carter's eyes shoot up. "Are you serious?"

Vicky looks to Alaina whose eyes widen as if she needs to cover what she's just let slip.

"No, I'm just using that as a figure of speech." She attempts to laugh it off.

I narrow my eyes at her. "I don't give a fuck who he kills. But who he fucks? Yeah. We have a problem." I stand from my seat and I'm one hundred percent aware that I'm being a total hypocrite, but I didn't have sex with anyone.

"Kal, you're thinking too much into this. One of the last girls he fucked ended up buried in the forest. Trust me, sex means nothing to him."

"Not helping...not helping at all."

I begin pacing around the living room. I spare a glance at Carter and he looks like he might be sick. I've never felt jealousy like this before. Oh no, this is a dangerous feeling. I've felt jealousy like, *she has nice shoes and I want them*. But this jealousy? This jealousy makes me feel like ripping his balls off and licking them, all at the same time.

"Okay, I'm going to be okay. I just need to forget about him. I think. Is that what I need to do? Oh my God, what the fuck do I do? I don't know how to cope with this knot of hate and jealousy I feel deep in my chest. This fucking sucks."

I slump back to the sofa, a bead of sweat dripping off me.

It's silent, I notice no one has said anything. I look up at all the sets of eyes looking at me in shock. "Wow," Vicky blows out. "Who knew you had that in you."

I look to the side before thinking about my actions and smile. "Let's just forget it. I need food." I stand from the sofa and make my way to the door, and when I feel no one is following I stop and turn around. "Are you guys not hungry?"

They all stand at once and follow me out the door.

We're all sitting at a new café we decided to try downtown, and I'm sipping on the fattiest, chocolate milkshake I could find. Everyone's voices die out. I think Carter and Vicky are having another debate about politics when I take my phone out of my handbag and send a text to Dominic.

> Me: *Can we talk?*
> Dominic: *Two pm? I can meet you at yours?*
> Me: *Sounds good.*

I huff out and throw my phone back into my bag. This is going to suck. Why did I have to meet Ade Nixon, he's toxic.

"I need to start heading back soon. Dom is coming up at two," I say to all of them.

Vicky pats my knee. "Be nice, please. He's my big brother. You're doing the right thing, though. I wish you two could be together, but I can see it in your eyes, we all can. You're already claimed by Ade, you just don't know it yet."

I laugh. "Oh, I know it. However, the slutting around thing is making it difficult for me to decide whether I want to love him or kill him. Jesus, how could he just…You know what? Don't care."

That was a blatant lie and we all know it.

I care too much.

"Are you girls heading back to Westbeach?" I ask them all.

"Nah, we've decided to stay. I heard about this new club downtown. Care to check out?" Alaina asks over her coffee. I smile at her with a mischievous glint in my eye.

"I accept. Give me an hour with Dom, then you guys can come up." I kiss them all on their head and walk out of the café, making my way back to my apartment.

Walking in and throwing my crap down onto the floor, I look at my watch and see I have ten minutes before he arrives. I begin giving myself a mental pep talk. Just when I finish pouring my wine, I hear a knock on the door. I run over and swing it open to Dominic in ripped, cut off jean shorts that hang to his knees and a white singlet. I'm so extremely disappointed in myself right now because I want to lick him.

"Hey, come in," I say stepping aside and gesturing to the open space beside me. He kisses me on the head and makes his way in. I shut the door and sit beside him on the couch.

"Do you want anything to drink?" He shakes his head then smiles.

"Just say what you need to say, Kal. It's okay."

I nibble on my lip, placing my hands on my lap. "It's not fair, Dom. I'm not ready to see someone right now because I have too many issues I need to deal with inside. And, I still hold strong feelings for Ade. I don't want to lead you on, you deserve better."

He leans his elbows on his knees and looks up to me. "I know. I'm sorry, I sort of pushed this on to you. It was a dick move."

"You didn't force anything on me, Dom. I wanted to try it."

He smiles, pulling me under his arm. "I hope I meet someone just like you one day, Kal."

I wipe the stray tear that has slipped from my eye. "I don't. I hope you find someone better."

He stands from the couch, pulling me up and under his embrace.

"If you say we can't be friends anymore I will understand, but I will also probably stalk you in your sleep until you decide that you have no other option than to be my friend," I say in a muffled tone in his arms. He laughs and pulls back from me.

"There's no way in hell I'd stop being your friend, Kal. That's crazy talk."

I smile up at him and he kisses me again softly on the lips. "You're a fucking special girl, Kalie. Always remember that," he tells me before walking out of my apartment.

An empty feeling creeps into my stomach, but I also feel lighter. I couldn't keep doing that to him, I should have never explored the idea to begin with, but it's Dominic.

That took quicker than I'd planned, so I decide to call my mom and check in with her. She picks up on the third ring.

"Hey mom, how are you doing?"

"He sweetie, I'm good. When are you coming to see us?"

"Real soon, I promise." I really should go to see my mom; it's exactly what I need.

"Dad bought a new pool, so you'll have to come and try it out."

I laugh. "Dad's always buying new things."

"I better go, Mom. I'll be back soon, I promise."

"I love you, darling."

"I love you too, Mom."

Hearing her voice is exactly what I need. Moms are angels sent from God, I don't know what I'd do without mine. I walk into the kitchen and pull out a bottle of wine. I'm eager to start this night with a bang. I feel free but slightly nauseated with the thought of Ade going balls deep into one of his skanks. I don't understand men. The saying is right, *'Men are from Mars and women are from Venus.'*

CHAPTER 26

I'm pouring my third glass when the door opens and in walks my life.

"Sorry, I sort of started without you," I say smiling up at them all.

"Well, fuck. I'll need shots to catch up then," Vicky states casually.

You would think becoming a mother calmed her, nope, not at all. She's just more discreet now, doesn't drink around Pipper at all.

"Shots! Yes," I say. Opening up the top cupboard in our kitchen, I unleash my friend.

"Absinthe?" Alaina says, looking at me in shock.

I nod my head. "Yes, I received it from...I can't remember who it was. But he gave it to me after I danced for him."

Vicky raises her eyebrows and laughs. "Girl, Ade has really worked one on you."

I shake my head in innocence. "I don't know what it is that you speak, child."

She snatches the clear liquid bottle of goodness out of my hand. "I thought Absinthe was green?"

I shrug. "He said this one is the *'real shit.'* Whatever that means."

She pops it open, taking the first swig. "Mmm, that's good. It tastes, different."

I snatch it out of her hands and swallow some down. "It tastes like my next mistake."

They all start laughing and Alaina comes up behind me while everyone takes their drinks, making their way to the living room.

"Are you okay? I never got around to asking you. Zane and I, we've been dealing with it little bits at a time," she whispers.

I swallow my drink and wipe my mouth. "I've been seeing someone, she's been really helpful. I've been getting memory flashes during my sleep too," I say looking at her sympathetically.

She shakes her head and smiles a fake smile at me. "I'm okay. We're dealing with it."

I nod my head and pull her in for a hug. "I love you, you know that?"

She squeezes me back. "I love you, too."

Vicky comes walking in. "That shit is amazing if I'm already getting to see some girl on girl action," she says smirking at us. I shove her shoulders and Alaina flips her off.

"Right," I say walking into the living room with every alcoholic beverage I can find, and a deck of cards. "We are playing thirty-one. Everyone know how to play?" I ask around the circle of Vicky, Alaina, Phoebe, and Carter. Carter and Phoebe shake their heads while Alaina and Vicky know how. *Surprise, surprise.*

"Okay, so it's sort of like Black Jack. Aces are eleven, all face cards are ten points, and all other cards are face value. The object of the game is to get as close to thirty-one points in your hand without going over. Each player is dealt three cards—one face-up and two face-down. Like in Blackjack, the play rotates for additional cards. At any point in the game, when you think your hand is high enough, say twenty-eight points or so, you can *knock*, which means everyone else has one last draw to add to their hand. All the hands are then laid down, and the person with the lowest point total has to drink a shot of Absinthe. If the person who knocked has the lowest point total, that player must also drink an additional penalty shot for poor play. At any time a player has a total of thirty-one in their hand, they immediately place their cards down and *everyone* else has a shot of Absinthe. Kapesh?" I look around at everyone and they all laugh.

"If I didn't know better, I'd say you were trying to get me drunk," Vicky laughs.

I look back at her and narrow my eyes. "Yeah, been there, done that."

I go to shuffle the cards before pausing, realizing what I've just said. I stop and look up at everyone who look shocked, except Vicky of course, she finds my verbal diarrhea amusing.

"Okay, fuck," I say, trying to think of a way to cover what I've just said. Instead, I pour a shot of Absinthe and shoot it back. "Let's just play the damn game, all right? Yes, Vicky and I had a semi-threesome with Blake. Done! Now let's continue."

Carter stands from the floor with an enormous smile on his face. "Oh hell, no! You're not getting out of this without explaining." I look to Vicky pleading for help.

She laughs. "It was a semi-threesome, the first night we meet Blake and the boys. Kalie was still a virgin and was only having a little play. However, it didn't get far because then our door was kicked down by a fuming Ade, and the rest is well...the rest is history."

I look at her. "Oh, but that's not all, you see," I begin, pouring another shot. I think I might not make it to town. "Vicky had another threesome that week." I smile at her. Her eyes widen and she looks at Phoebe who's smiling at her. I forgot about Phoebe and Ryder—the other man Vicky had a threesome with was Ryder Oakley. The lead singer and very, *very,* famous rock God from Twisted Transistor. He and Phoebe had a thing, but it was messy when they ended it. I don't think she would care.

"Oh, please, don't look at Phoebs. She wouldn't care," I mumble under my shot glass.

Vicky smiles at Phoebe and Alaina is looking anxious.

"Why the fuck do I not know what you two bitches are talking about?" Alaina asks pouring a shot. "Fuck, me. I'll be needing one of these for this discussion, I think." Carter takes the bottle from Aliana.

I shake my head at Vicky's silence. "She had a threesome with Blake and Ryder Oakley."

"What!" Alaina screams.

"Oh my God, it wasn't a big deal," she says looking nervously at Phoebe.

"Why are you looking at me?" Phoebe says turning red.

"It wouldn't be the first time he was being a fucking whore. If I never see him again, it would be too early," she spits, snatching the bottle off Carter and taking a drink.

"Well, at least you'll be traveling around the world with some famous person soon, and will be too important to worry about Ryder Oakley," I say to her and she smiles.

"Exactly."

"Do you know who it is yet?" I ask.

She shakes her head. "Maree hasn't given me the details yet. She will on Monday, or I'll lock her in a room until she does." I laugh and start dealing out the cards. "Here we go kids." I pick up my dock remote and turn on Qwote ft Pitbull *'Throw Your Hands Up'* while we begin our night. Vicky stands on top of the coffee table, pulling me up with her dropping it low to the blaring music. I laugh and drag Phoebe up with me while Carter stands from his seat and begins putting us all to shame with his ass shaking skills.

This is going to be a long one.

ADE NIXON

"So you want us to pause the plans?" Blake asks down the phone.

"Yes, I need it bigger."

"You don't need a bigger house, Ade. If it's just you…" he trails off in an asking tone.

"It's just me, but I want big. The same ideas but with a couple extra rooms. I have the land to do it, so I may as well use it."

"All right then, are you at the clubhouse?"

"Yeah, I just walked in. Call you back in a second."

I walk in to find Zane on his laptop so I walk up behind him. "What are you doing on Fuckbook?" I ask, laughing at him.

He looks up at me, eyebrows raised. "Well, I'm personally not on Facebook, but Alaina left hers logged in. When I opened the laptop to go through some accounts, Facebook it was open." He smiles pulling his lip into his mouth.

I narrow my eyes at him. "What? Spit it out Da Vinci."

He turns the laptop around to face me, showing me photos of Kalie and Dominic all over each other, kissing, laughing, him holding her on his fucking lap.

"Fuck!" I yell. "When the fuck were these taken?"

Zane looks down to the laptop again. "A couple nights ago. Kalie *'liked'* them too," he teases.

"I swear to fucking God, Zane. Shut the fuck up. Let's go."

He stands from his seat. "Where?"

"Don't play fucking dumb, we're leaving. I'm claiming what's mine. Now." I storm out of there smashing the door open. "I'm going to get my fucking girl back."

Zane laughs while following me out. "All right brother, I think they're heading out tonight. I'll text Alaina."

I wish I could fucking scrape those images out from my head, his fucking hands and lips all over her. I want to fucking annihilate him. The fact that I love her outweighs the feeling of wanting to slit her throat. It helps balance my feelings out.

"What are you doing?" Zane asks as I walk over to my bike.

"Taking my fucking bike. She can just get the fuck on and she can scream all she wants. It's nothing I haven't heard come out of her mouth before."

He laughs, shaking his head and taking hold of his helmet. "All right brother. *Shit!*"

The ride here was extra-long, long enough to work myself up. It's late, so no doubt their night will be well and truly flying ahead at full speed. If there's anything those girls know how to do, it's party.

I get off my bike and take my helmet off.

"They're not here," Zane yells from his spot across the road. "They're at Wired. It's a new club that's opened in town. And Ade? Alaina said that Kalie is wasted. By the sounds of it, they all are. Be fucking nice, brother. She's been through a lot."

She's about to be put through a lot more—a lot more of my dick.

"Where's this club?"

He points up the road. "Not far from here."

I jump back onto my bike. "I'll follow your lead."

He gets back onto his bike and we roar them to life, riding off to this fucking bar. Kalie has always been sweet and innocent, but she also has this mischievous side to her that only comes out occasionally. That mischievous side is going to be the death of me.

We pull up to the bar and there's a huge line out front, but the girls aren't there. We get off and ignore the gawking. Walking up to the bouncer, I take my gloves off, shoving them in my pocket and fluff my hair up.

"Here to find our women. That going to be an issue?" I ask.

He looks between Zane and me a few times before shaking his head and popping open the gate. We both walk in, in our usual get up. White T-shirt with our cut over the top, jeans that hang loose, and combat boots. Walking into the deep bass sound of some song with girls screaming and dancing, the place is huge and it's packed. Pushing through the crowd of people and ignoring the sultry stares coming from women all over the place, we attempt to find our little misfits. When I spot her, a fire lights in my chest and, *holy fuck*, I swear my whole world stops. The Weeknd *'The Hills'* is pumping through the speakers, and I'm watching her body do fucking amazing things to the base of the song. The girl dances dirty, about as dirty as she plays between the sheets.

I stand there stock still when Zane looks at what I'm watching and smiles.

"Damn, the girl can fucking move."

I bite my lip and smirk. "Yeah, she can."

My thoughts are interrupted by the attention she's drawing around her. I look around at all the men in this place and all eyes are locked on Kalie— *my fucking Kalie*. I begin walking toward them, pushing through everyone until I reach her, throwing snarls out at them on my way.

Who knew I could be such a predator, but what's mine is mine.

She has her back to me and is shaking her phat ass around the place. I slap it, and grasp onto her hips, pushing her into my groin. She stumbles and attempts to turn around. Obviously ready to push whoever it was off of her. But meeting my eyes instead.

"Ade?" she slurs.

"It's me, baby. Let's go," I say, grasping her hand.

CHAPTER 27

"Wait, I have an issue with you," she slurs again.

I bend down to her ear so she can hear me. "Do this outside, I can't hear you," I say nipping her ear while pulling her behind me to follow me out.

Once we're outside and away from the line of people, she pulls away from my grasp.

"As I said, I need words with sho—you. I meant you. *Shit*," she mumbles out the last bit with a small smile. I smile back at her, leaning against my bike and lighting up a smoke.

"Go on, you were saying?"

She puts her hands on her hips and narrows her eyes. Instead of it looking intimidating—which I have no doubt that is what she was trying to do—it looked cute.

"You've been a slut! I'm not cool with that. Fuck that. Yuck! Seriously, Ade, it didn't take you long."

I throw my smoke down to the ground. "Wait. So *that's* what your issue is? I fucking drove here because I saw the fucking photos, Kalie. Don't try and play the innocent card on me right now, because these lips right fucking here," I pull her into me forcefully and run my thumb over her lips, before bringing my mouth down to her ear, "are *mine*, and only *mine*, Kalie. Comprende?" Her breath hitches and her chest begins drawing in faster breaths. She looks down at my lips and I smile.

"Not here, baby. Get on the bike," I say letting go of her.

She shakes her head. "No Ade, I'm shit scared and you know that."

I pull her into me, picking her up and wrapping her legs around my waist. "Would I ever let anything happen to you?"

She looks deep into my eyes then shakes her head, making her long as fuck hair shake around. "Exactly. Now get that sexy fucking ass on my bike."

I hand her my helmet and she takes it hesitantly. "Pull your dress up, baby," I say while throwing my leg over. She comes up behind me, hitching up her tight dress, placing her hands on my shoulders before throwing her leg over behind me.

"Closer. Wrap your arms around my torso," I say with my head over my shoulders. She stops for a second before doing exactly what she's told. She grips on tightly. The thought of her on the back of my bike stirs crazy shit with my dick. This would be the first time a woman has ever been on my bike. I always knew that the only woman that would ever ride with me would be my old lady. The back of my bike is no seat for a whore.

I start it up, making it pulse under us both, then pull out with her grip getting tighter instantly. I almost want to ride off somewhere else just to have her gripping onto me like this.

We pull up to her apartment and I turn my bike off, waiting until she's gotten off. I swing my legs back off the bike, pulling her under my arm and kissing her on the head.

"Was that hard?" I ask.

She smiles and shakes her head. "Nope. I want to go again."

I laugh. "Yeah, of course, baby. Anything you want."

We walk into her apartment, and as soon as I've closed the door I pick her up and wrap her legs around me. I grasp onto the back of her neck and bring her lips to mine, kissing her slow and gentle.

"Are you done?" I ask her.

She tilts her head at me. "Done with what?"

"Done with fighting what we have here?"

"I am. But I have some issues."

I laugh, placing her back on the floor. "I'd be disappointed if you didn't, baby. Come on, we can talk about this tomorrow."

I pick her back up and carry her to her room. Seconds after laying her down, she's asleep. I start removing her dress and I look down at her body that's only partly covered by her little white lace panties and bra. I bring my knuckles up to my mouth, biting out a moan, "Holy fuck." She's going to be the end of me. She can bring me to my knees with one stare.

Kalie-Rose.

Who would've ever guessed that I'd want to settle my shit down.

I remove my cut and T-shirt, pull down my jeans, peel back the blankets and get in behind her then pull her into me. I brush her hair off her forehead and kiss her head.

"Fuck, I love you. You have no idea how much I fucking love you," I whisper into her hair.

"I love you too, Ade," she whispers a reply.

I stiffen, listening to her breathing, which is even. "Kalie?" I say.

No response.

Shit! She must have said that in her sleep. Those simple words are not so simple coming from those beautiful lips.

KALIE - ROSE

"Oh my God, my head," I moan into my pillow.

I hear a laugh beside me and I smile. I remember everything that happened last night, despite the amount of alcohol I consumed. It was a good night. Pushing my face off my pillow, I turn around to face Ade. His hair is all messy everywhere and his blue eyes twinkle.

"It's not fair. How can you look so perfect," I say, staring at him.

He brushes the hair from my face and squishes his eyebrows. "You're perfect, baby. Every single thing about you is what I crave. What I need."

I smile at his words, resting my head on my hand. "I missed you," I say dragging my finger along his strong jaw and up to his chiseled cheekbones.

He kisses my hand. "I missed you too, baby. But those pictures…they gotta go."

I laugh, pulling my hand away.

"Oh? You think this is funny?" he asks with a smirk and a playful tone.

I shrug. "Baby, you gotta cut the jealousy crap or this is never gonna work."

He grasps onto my legs, pulling me down the bed and bringing his body on top of me. I scream out a laugh and he kisses my lips briefly, chuckling against them. He brings himself back up so he's resting on his elbows, staring down at me. I stop laughing when I look up to him. God, he's breathtaking. This beautiful, sexy, dangerous man is on top of me, and he wants *me.* I feel untouchable. Searching his eyes, he smirks, rolling his hips into me. I clamp down on my lip and moan a little, reaching onto his forearms to stop the motion, and he narrows his eyes down at me.

"Don't do that."

I smile. "Oh, do what?" I rub myself up against his groin. "Don't do this?"

I bite my lip and smirk at him. I see his eye twitch before he matches my smile.

"Mmm, you shouldn't have done that."

He takes hold of my wrists, bringing them up over my head with one of his hands. His other hand reaches behind my back, unsnapping my bra and removing it in one easy motion. He brings his face down and licks each of my nipples lightly, so lightly it feels like torture. I roll myself into his groin again, trying to gain some friction.

"Keep still," he demands.

I turn my head to the side, attempting to keep still but needing a release. His hand continues its journey down my stomach and under my panties. I arch my back off the bed at the contact from his large rough hand covering my pussy. I've craved his touch for so long. I feel like a junkie that has just had my hit of the best damn heroin you could ever imagine. His hand sprawls out, slipping one, then two fingers inside me and I still for a brief second.

My eyes open and I look up to him. "Can we not do that yet, please? Just...anything but that," I whisper out to him. His face sets into stone and he pulls out softly.

"I'm so sorry, Kalie. So fucking sorry, baby. I will never ever let anyone ever come near you again. I promise you that on my life."

Tears prick my eyes and I nod my head. "I trust you, Ade, but it's not your fault. I know that now."

I bring my hand up to his face, running my fingers along his jaw, to his lips, lightly over the two rings that sit hooked around his lip perfectly. He smiles down at me, kissing me gently. I open my mouth, letting his soft pierced tongue slide in. He licks and tugs on my lips in the most seductive of ways. I've been kissed—a lot, but no one has ever kissed like this. I feel his hands come to my face, cradling it in his hands.

He reaches down, pulling his briefs down along with my panties. Sliding his hands back up my body while still never breaking our kiss. He runs his hand over my breast, lightly wiping over my nipple, igniting it to life. In one, slow, gentle move I feel his thick, long, pierced cock slide into me. I attempt to moan out against his lips only to have him intensify the kiss. He kisses me deep and hard, our breaths heavy, and our bodies working up a sweat. He pulls out, and pushes in slowly, putting pressure on my clit each time he pushes into me. He lets go of my hands with his other hand and I bring them up around his neck. We work up a pace that's perfect, our bodies joining, creating the perfect rhythm of love. He finally breaks our kiss, looking deep into my eyes, his breath hitches and he lays one tiny light kiss on my lips.

I know what he's doing—he's making love to me. That much I'm aware of.

I run my hands behind his tattooed neck, searching his eyes. He grips onto my thigh and lifts my leg up against his hip without breaking his grind. He brings his forehead to mine, resting it there, looking down to me. I pull his lips to mine, kissing him with all I have. I can feel my body building that familiar tingling feeling deep in my stomach. He pushes into me again hitting something deep inside me and I moan out as my orgasm racks my body, causing it to smash into me like jolts of electricity being shocked through me.

CHAPTER 28

He collapses down, putting all his weight onto me while we both try to catch air.

"Holy fuck," he says into my neck.

"Holy fuck is right," I answer back.

He gets up off me and swings his legs off my bed and sits there looking out the window. "Do you love me, Kalie?" he asks. The question throws me off. I crawl across the bed wrapping my arms around his torso from behind.

"Why are you asking me this?"

He turns slightly to me. "Answer the question."

I smile at him, bringing my body around and straddling him from the front. I run my hands over his face and look deep into his eyes.

"Fuck! I love you. You have no idea how much I fucking love you," I say with a smile.

He laughs, pulling me back as he lands on his back with me on top of him. "I do. I love you, too. I never thought I'd ever love anyone as much as I love you, Kalie. I never want to live another day apart from you ever again," he says with complete seriousness.

"I love you, but I have some issues," I say, pulling my hair behind my ears.

He wraps his arms around me and lies me next to him on the bed. "Shoot," he replies, pulling back so he can look at me.

"So you're a hitman?" I ask.

"I don't remember telling you that."

"You didn't, I overheard a conversation when I was taken. Also, Alaina and Vicky pretty much imply it all the time."

He pauses for a second before looking to me. "Do you want to know it all, or do you want to know nothing? We always ask this question, but the other girls have had more time to decide. We usually need an answer before the wedding day. But you need to tell me now before this conversation can continue. Do you want to know it *all*, or do you want to know *nothing*?" he asks uneasily.

I think over his words for a few seconds until I realize that nothing will ever be able to change the way I feel about him. My world began the day I meet him and it would end if I left him.

"I want to know it all," I murmur.

He gets up, propping himself on his elbows. "I am. That's aside from the club. It's how I earn. I have a large amount of funds because of it."

"And these people...are they bad?"

"I don't know. I get the slip and do the deed."

"Do you not care?"

He laughs. "No. Not a single fuck is given when it comes to taking someone's life. Does that scare you?"

I swallow. "No. It should, but I know you wouldn't hurt me, and I see how you are with people you actually care about. It's something fierce." I put my hand up signaling that I'm not finished. "I can't do the hitman thing, Ade. I can do the club, and will never, ever, expect you to leave. I love those girls in my life. But the hitman thing? Yeah, I have major issues with it." He lies back on his back, looking up at the ceiling.

"I thought you might," he says looking over at me.

"It's why I quit. I ended it all and invested some of the money into a few things. One being a tattoo parlor and the rest I put into shares. I want this with you, Kalie. I want it all."

I smile a wide smile. "Really? You've done that?"

He laughs and pulls me back on top of him, so I'm straddling him.

"Yes, but I can't guarantee I won't be doing stuff for the club."

I shake my head. "I can live with that."

He pulls my face down to his, kissing me on the lips.

"Move to Westbeach with me," he whispers on my lips.

"What?" I reply, shocked. "I can't, I have my job here…that I'm meant to be starting back at tonight."

He shakes his head. "Fuck that, Kal. Enroll into WBU, and get your Law Degree. Do shit you want to do. I'll support you through it all. All you will need to do is study," he says casually. I look down at him in shock.

"Ade, I cannot expect you to carry me like that."

"Kalie, I love you, and you love me. There's no way in hell I'm leaving this place without you permanently on my bike. We've been doing this shit for too long, and I'm not living without you ever again."

"Ade, let me just think about it? Please. At least let me apply to WBU and see where that goes."

"No. You can do that shit from Westbeach. Don't fucking fight me on this, you're coming," he says seriously.

I try to bargain with him.

"How about I come with you and apply, see how it all goes. But, I don't move in unless I get accepted and I get a job?" I raise my eyebrows at him.

He smiles. "That seems pretty fucking reasonable. Aside from the job part, fuck that. I will support you and that's final." He squeezes my ass and taps it. "Shower time," he hints with mischief.

"Oh, I'm sure it's shower time," I say laughing while getting off him.

Fuck. My life is about to turn upside down.

We pull up to his apartment on the back of his bike. I love riding with him now, and I'm almost certain that I want my own bike. We came straight from Hollywood to his house. I think back to the conversation I had with Carter before we left...

"So you're moving in with him?" Carter asked in a flat tone.

"No, I'm going there to sort out my options. I can't dance forever, Carter. I want a career."

"Please don't leave me," he said, dropping his lip.

"I'm three hours away. It's okay, you can visit whenever you want, and I'm not moving out yet,

all my crap is still here and I'll still cover my half of the rent." Carter looked to Ade then looked back to me. I see Ade's head shaking out of the corner of my eye, so I snap my head to him.

"What?" I asked Ade.

When I saw he was not going to answer me, I looked back at Carter.

"Spit it out, Priscilla, I don't have all day." His mouth dropped open and I heard Ade spit out some of his drink before laughing his ass off in the kitchen.

"Bitch," Carter sneered with a smirk.

"Since you asked, so nicely. Ade covered your half of the rent to last for a while," he added smugly.

"What!" I screeched. "Give it back, now!"

"Mmm, no. Now you can concentrate on sorting out Uni. It all makes sense, though. When you first handed me the cash I was confused," he added, walking into the kitchen to pour himself a coffee.

I looked to Ade. "You fucking bought me?"

He laughed, standing from his seat and pulling me into him. "That's a little dramatic, baby."

I pouted at him and he bit down on my lip. "What's mine is yours. Get used to it. I don't take no for an answer...ever."

Oh, fuck! What have you gotten yourself into now, Kalie? I thought.

I swing my leg off his bike and cannot feel my ass at all, but I'm not complaining. He takes my hand and pulls me toward his apartment.

"I'm almost scared to walk in here," I say as we move through the glass doors, where a door attendant stands to greet us. It's over the top flash. Do these people not wonder how a guy in an MC is living so lavishly?

When we reach the elevator, he punches in a number and it sets off.

"For the record, I've never brought anyone back to my house...any of my houses. Ever."

I smile at him because I know he's not lying. There's no way he'd have given any girl the time of day to bring her to his house.

"So you're building a house?" I ask.

"Yeah, Blake's doing it for me. I sort of interrupted his plans by throwing in a few extra rooms, though," he says with a smile.

"Oh? A few extra rooms?" I ask intrigued.

"Yeah, for all the kids I want you to have," he shrugs casually.

"Ade!" I laugh.

We've never talked about kids or marriage before, I guess I just assumed that they would come in time and I'm in no rush to do either of those things.

"What? I want six kids, five boys then one girl."

The elevator door pings open and he tugs my hand, pulling me down the hallway.

"Six?" I screech. "Yeah, no. No way. You're going to need to find another broad to give you your Brady Bunch." He laughs, reaching a door and swiping his key card through it.

"I don't want it with anyone else, I only want *our* kids. If it's not with you, then it's not with anyone." He swings open his door and I'm greeted with an immaculate apartment space.

"Holy shit," I whisper while glancing around the place. One would think someone who wears a suit lives here, not someone who wears an MC patch. However, it feels empty, as if he never spends any time here. It definitely needs a women's touch.

"What does *'holy shit'* mean?" he asks walking into the open-plan marble kitchen and dropping his keys on the counter.

"It means, I wasn't expecting you to be so...tidy? Classical? I don't know. It's beautiful," I say smiling at him. He walks to the fridge, takes out a beer and moves over to me, pulling me into his chest.

"It's just for now, baby. Once the house is done, you can do whatever you want with the space. I'll leave all that shit up to you." I look up to him, almost hurting my neck because he's *that* tall.

I pinch my lips together. "It all seems a little much? Doesn't it?"

He shakes his head, putting his beer back on the bench and picking me up as if I weigh nothing. But, in actual fact, I know I weigh at least, one hundred and thirty-eight pounds, and that's being generous.

"Baby, I've loved you since day one. My heart knew before my mind did. I should've guessed it because of the feelings I had for you. But for some people, it doesn't always work out like that."

I swallow and look into his eyes. "So this doesn't feel fast to you?"

He shakes his head. "Hell no. This is something that should've been done a long fucking time ago."

CHAPTER 29

He pulls my face down to his, kissing me long and hard. With his soft lips meshing perfectly with mine. He places me back down to the floor, grasping my hand and picking up his beer.

"Come, I'll show you around."

I follow him around, as he shows me all three bedrooms, two bathrooms, and a games room. The master bedroom is huge, with a super king sized leather bed and a massive walk in wardrobe. The en-suite bathroom that comes off the master bedroom is amazing and by far one of my most favorite rooms in the house. It's all black marble with a supersized tub that sits in the middle of the room. When we come back into the living room, he picks me back up and throws me onto his over-sized large L shaped sofa. It could fit ten Ades and

King Kong on it. I laugh and sink down into the huge cushions that scatter around the sofa.

"I think, I might just sleep on this." I pat the spot next to me.

He laughs and walks back to the kitchen. "Not happening."

Getting up off the sofa, I follow him into the kitchen. "I should probably tell you now," I say leaning my elbows on the bench, "I don't cook. Unless you want food poisoning," I say batting my lashes.

He pulls out a bottle of champagne Armand de Brignac out of the fridge, takes a glass out of the cupboard and slides it over to me pouring the champagne into my glass.

"Ace of Spades Rose?" I ask, lifting the glass to my lips. "I'm impressed."

He laughs putting the pink bottle back into the fridge. "So, I like good wine." He shrugs before continuing, "And it's a good thing I cook then. I can teach you."

I gulp down my first mouthful, licking the wine from my lips.

"You cook?" I ask in disbelief.

He rolls his eyes. "Don't judge. I learned at a young age. When your mom stops being a mom, you have to learn the simple things like cooking or you don't eat." My face drops and I round the bench, pulling him into me.

"The fact that you had to go through that breaks my heart. I could never do that to my son, I *will* never do that to my own son."

He smirks and leans down to my face. "We should get making then."

I push at his chest, stopping his movements. "Yeah, no babies. I need to finish Uni, and then we can start. For now, you just keep being the best uncle in the world to the babies you already have." He pouts and drops his lip. I swear to God, I want to eat him right here on the spot. How am I supposed to let this man out of the house when all I can think about is riding him through until next week.

"I want my own, though, imagine our babies."

I laugh, taking another gulp of wine. It's disturbing because the more he talks about it, the more the idea of having his babies excites me.

"What if we have six girls and one boy?" I ask with wide eyes.

His face pales and he shakes his head. "Nope, no way. There's no way I can pump out that many girls." He scoops my legs up from under me, carries me to his room, and throws me onto his bed. Before making love to me for the second time today.

He closes his hands around mine as I lay my head on his shoulder.

"You know that was the second time we didn't use a condom right?" he asks.

I turn my body to face him. "I'm on the pill, Ade."

He pulls back from me. "Not from now on your not. Throw that shit out. I'm serious, Kalie. Let it be if it's going to happen. I'll take care of you."

My eyes widen. I really don't think he's going to drop this baby thing.

"Ade, you haven't even met my parents yet," I say leaning up on my hand.

He gets out of bed and throws some jeans on.

"What are you doing?" I ask with a smile.

He throws on a T-shirt. "Get up. We're going to meet the parents."

I laugh. "Right now? You want to travel all the way to Las Vegas, right now? I'm tired of traveling. We will go this weekend," I say, getting up and grabbing onto his hand and pulling him back onto the bed.

He crawls up to me, licking my neck. "Promise?"

I giggle. "I promise."

My mom is going to eat him alive. Not in the way you probably think a mother would eat her daughter's new boyfriend who's part of a motorcycle club alive, but in the way a cougar would. My mom is going to drool all over him and it's going to be slightly embarrassing.

I cannot wait. Yay. I think sarcastically to myself.

Six Months Later

"Ade, why can't I take the blindfold off? I've seen the plans," I say as we drive out to our newly built home.

Ade has been adamant that he didn't want me seeing any progress on the house until it was finished. I started University two months ago, and it's been a busy time for us, but we're as strong as ever. Ade's tattoo parlor is a huge hit downtown and we've just opened a custom bike garage as well. He hired people to run both businesses because his main role lies within the club, that hasn't changed.

Vicky found out that she and Blake are having another baby—twins. So we're all happy and excited about that, more Ade than anyone. My scary, beautiful beast loves his niece and nephew so much. He's a big softie with the kids and he's going to make a great dad, one day, not today though. I have managed to keep him busy with other things to keep his mind off implanting his child into me. I took him to Vegas that weekend to meet my parents, and just as I suspected my mom embarrassingly ogled him. I think back...

We pulled up to my parents' extravagant home. It was well equipped with a maid and a cook. My father comes from old money and runs a successful business in new computer software that everyone uses. So to say my parents are wealthy was probably a slight understatement. Although they have money, they are the most understanding parents in the world. They don't come with the snotty attitude most of their rich friends have. My dad's old school, where my mom's very new school. They balanced each other out a lot, I think. Ade stopped the truck and opened the door. I swung my door open just as my mom walked out of the massive front door, passing the ginormous white pillars.

"Honey!" she squealed, walking down the steps.

"Hey Mom," I said hugging her tightly.

"Mom, this is Ade," I said, pointing to Ade, who was standing next to me.

Her face blushed and she pulled him in for a hug. "Well, well, well, my girl has taste. Thank

God. She gets that from me by the way." She winked at Ade.

He laughed showing his perfectly straight teeth. "I don't doubt that. Pleased to meet you."

My dad walked down with a big cheesy smile on his face.

"Dad!"

"Hey, princess." He pulled me in for a hug.

"Dad, this is, Ade. Ade...Dad." I carried the same introductions. They shook hands and began walking back toward Ade's car, with my dad admiring it.

And that was where I lost my parents to my boyfriend. He'd won them over in a matter of five minutes.

"The plans are nothing, baby," he says.

We come to a stop, and I hear the truck door open with the sound of gravel crunching underfoot. He reaches my door, popping it open and lightly grasping my hand pulling me out of the truck.

We bought a truck, an Escalade. I wanted to upgrade my car. So instead, he bought me this and left my Mercedes at the clubhouse.

I follow him until I feel him stop. His hands come up to my eyes, and he gently removes the blindfold.

"Holy shit!" All the air leaves my body and my legs shake. "Holy shit, Ade," I repeat and turn to him and he's smiling.

"I know," he says taking my hand and leading me to the masterpiece.

It's stunning. The house sits down a long driveway with a rock garden in the middle so you can circle around the front door. There is a huge wraparound porch. It's modern brick with so much flat land around the house you could almost build stables for some horses.

The house is still empty. He's set on the fact that he wants me to decorate it. As soon as you walk through the door, to the right, there's a flight of stairs.

He points to the stairs. "Seven bedrooms," he states then winks at me.

"Seven?" I ask.

"Six kids, baby. They'll have the best of everything."

Right, I almost forgot about the six kid's thing.

I follow him through to the open plan modern kitchen, and huge living room space that opens out to a massive back yard. The yard has so much potential and the living room is equipped with one of the biggest fireplaces I've ever seen. It's beautiful.

"I love it," I say to him with a smile and a tear pricking my eyes.

This is where we're going to build our family together. He takes my hand, moving the engagement ring on my finger.

"I want to get married, here. This weekend," he says.

I see he has that same look in his eyes. The look I've learned that means that this is final. I look out to the back yard and swallow.

"Of course, you do."

He smiles, pulling me into him. "Is that, a yes?"

I smile and kiss him. "That's a definitely."

The weekend after he met my parents, he proposed to me in front of all our friends and family. Making sure my parents were there.

"Where are we going?" I asked as we were driving into town.

"I told you, we're going out for dinner," he said casually.

"Dinner? You're wearing a suit, Ade. And I'm not complaining because, damn, that's a sight to see. But you never wear a suit." He looked edible. In a white crisp suit shirt, a black suit jacket was casually thrown over it and black pants with Chuck Taylors on.

He shrugged. *"No big deal, baby."* I narrowed my eyes at him and he laughed.

"Babe, chill," he said, taking my hand in his and kissing it lightly.

We pulled up to Vicky's restaurant that she owns, and everything was dimly lit. I jumped out of the truck and he took my hand, pulling me toward the restaurant. He pushed open the glass doors and we rounded a corner to the room. The whole place was empty, no one else was there, and when I looked to the center of the room I saw a long table stretched out with all our friends and my parents sitting there.

"Oh my God!" I looked to Ade and he immediately dropped to one knee, pulling out a little square box. He smiled his panty-wetting smile up at me and popped it open, showing a huge princess cut diamond sitting elegantly on a platinum ring.

"I love you, Kalie. There was no one before you, and there will be no one after you. Marry me?"

I nodded my head as tears streamed down my face. "Yes, of course, I'll marry you," I said and he picked me up and wrapped my legs around him, kissing me softly. A huge roar of congratulations sounded from behind us. And I looked at everyone with a cheesy smile, flashing up my ring.

Tainted Love

"I love you, baby," he mumbled into my neck.
"I love you, too."

CHAPTER 30

He smiles down at me, brushing my hair out of my face. "My world is complete with you by my side, babe. This is the first day of the rest of our lives," he kisses me softly.

I melt into his arms, where I want to live forever. I feel that feeling again. The feeling of being completely untouchable.

I know that with my man by my side, I can accomplish anything and anyone, his demons included.

EPILOGUE

Five Years Later

"Ade, I have to go to work," I say to him while he's trying to pull me back down to bed.

"You can work your case with me, baby. This is all the case you will need to solve," he says grabbing his crotch over the sheet.

I bite my lip and look down at him. Both his legs are now covered in tattoos. Both legs are all about our journey together as a couple. He's slowly added more ink to them as our lives progressed. Austin—the man we hired to manage our tattoo parlor—is the best in the state. His work is incredible, and people come to Westbeach just for him to ink them.

He pulls me down forcefully, and my papers fly up everywhere in the room.

"Ade!" I squeal loudly, pushing at his chest.

"Mommy? What's Daddy doing?" I hear a soft little voice ask from our doorway.

"Nate, baby. Go and get changed. Daddy's loving Mommy," Ade grunts into my neck.

Nate is our three-year-old little boy. When I found out I was pregnant with him, I was in shock. I'd just finished my first year of law school and everything was soaring, so seeing those two pink lines set my heart and life into full speed. When I told Ade, though, of course, he thought it was hilarious—fist pumps and all. I haven't seen him quite that happy before, except for the actual birth of Nate, and our wedding day, which was five years earlier...

To my beautiful Wife to be.

Hey baby, if you're reading this letter that means I succeeded in sneaking into your room late last night. I can't believe that the next time I see you, I'm going to be calling you my wife. You're my world Kalie, and I meant it when I said I would spend the rest of my life showing you that.
Starting with these. You have probably never seen them before in your life—well, you better fucking not have... :) I wish I could be there to insert them into your sweet little pussy, but

apparently, it's bad luck. Fuck Vicky and her controlling ways. They're Ben Wa balls. I think you have an idea on how to insert them, and I'll be waiting for you at the altar.

My love is yours forever.
~ Ade

I smiled down at the note, tears already in my eyes. I might need to go light on the makeup today; I was sure I was going to be crying a lot. Vicky bounced up from the bed.

"Todays the day!" She was clapping her hands together.

"Um, what is that!" She pointed to my hands where the Ben Wa balls laid.

"Ah, Ade snuck in our room last night and left them on my bedside table with a note," I shrugged. She walked over to me, wrapping her robe around herself with a smile.

"Still a kinky bastard, isn't he."

I nodded my head and laughed. "I don't think that will ever change." She slapped my ass and walked into the wardrobe where my gown was hanging.

"You better get that sexy ass into that dress." Phoebe pointed from the other bed in the room. I was actually surprised how Ade managed to *bypass all the girls in there. We decided on one big room with single beds throughout, so we could all sleep together that night. "Yeah, I guess, I should."*

I walked into the wardrobe and took the dress off the hanger. It was strapless, pure white, and hugged my curves perfectly, before dropping around my feet in a pond. It was beautiful and elegant, exactly what I wanted.

I removed my robe and Carter walked behind me, handing me my bra to put on. I took it off him. "Thanks, Carter." I slipped it on and he came from behind to help me put it on.

He's silent. I couldn't see the face he was pulling from behind me while he did up my bra, but I guessed he was having a moment. I took my corset off the rack and wrapped it around my tummy as he started pulling it in tighter.

"I love you. You know that, right?" I said to him. I heard a sniff and I turned around to face him. "Carter, don't cry, please, or I'll start."

He wiped his tears and waved his hands away. "Please don't cry. You're not pretty when you cry." I laughed so hard my stomach hurt.

"Shut up, Priscilla. I'm always pretty."

He chuckled. "Yeah, you are."

Once my corset was nice and tight, I took hold of my suspenders and rolled them up. I then took my dress and stepped into it. I almost stopped breathing when I realized what was happening.

"I'm getting married," I whispered. Carter picked up my dress and pulled it over my head and down my body.

"Yeah, you are, to a man that I'm pretty sure was God's way of apologizing for making ugly people in this world. Have babies, immediately."

I laughed, dragging my hair to one side so Carter could do me up. "That's not very nice, Carter. It's what's on the inside too, you know?"

He laughed and I could almost sense the major eye roll he was doing. "Bullshit. That's just a quote some ugly man made up because he wasn't getting any of the nookie." I turned around and pushed his chest with a smile.

"Pussy, Carter. It's pussy." He laughed and walked out of the closet.

After a few breaths, I walked out and saw everyone looking at me. Vicky, Alaina, Phoebe, and Carter. Yes, Carter insisted on being a bridesmaid, even though Ade said he could be a groomsman.

See, Priscilla—I told you.

"Holy fucking shit," Vicky whispered.

"Kalie, you look fucking insane," Phoebe followed.

I turned red and looked to Alaina, who was crying. "Lain! Don't. Please, no more tears. Shit. How am I going to get through today?"

Phoebe stood from her spot. "Oh! Look what I got." She pulled out a bottle of Absinthe from her handbag, the same one I had.

"Absinthe? How did you get this?" I asked.

She shrugged. "Oh, you know, the perks."

I laughed and shook my head. I knew exactly where she got it.

Alaina came up to me and kissed me on the cheek. "I'm so happy Ade found someone as special as you. Never, ever, underestimate your strength Kalie. Now with not only Ade but us," she gestures around the room, "and all the boys. You can do, and get through anything, girl. We got you." She pulled me in for another kiss. "Now, I need to go get our little flower girl and ring boy."

I shooed her out with tears coming down my face. "Great, the seal's been broken," I said laughing and wiping my face.

We stayed in the hotel last night only because Vicky insisted. It pissed Ade off like something chronic, but Vicky knew him too well. There was no way he would have been able to stay away from me.

Alaina walked back into the room, holding Pipper's hand on one side and Landon's on the other. I bent down to the two.

"Hey princess," I said to Pipper.

"Aunty Kalie," she giggled.

She was three going on fifteen. Landon pulled on my dress from below.

"Landon, no baby. Don't pull on Aunty Kalie's dress," Alaina said picking him up.

I wave her off. "Don't be silly. You can pull on my dress anytime sweetness."

These kids were seriously adorable. I couldn't wait to give them some little buddies, but that could wait.

My mom walked in and stopped in her tracks. "Oh my God." She ran up to me and pulled me into her. "You look so beautiful my girl." I wiped her tears and kissed her hand. "Thank you, Ma."

I turned around and looked at everyone in the room. I decided to keep my makeup on the classical side, and my hair was all swept to one side of my face in one big soft curl.

"Are we ready?" I asked.

They all looked back at me in their bridesmaid's dresses. I'd decided on red. Carter was wearing a red suit—even though I was sure he would rather wear a dress.

We pulled up to my home and there were cars everywhere. We decided to keep it small, with family and close friends, but that was actually a lot of people as it turned out. With everyone's plus one as well, it all added up.

The sun was going down and it was setting in a perfect light. We got out of the car and my dad greeted me at my front door.

"Come on, baby. Your groom is waiting for you."

Those words set off a cage of butterflies flying around in my tummy. He's mine, and I'm his. The thought still ignites me, like something fierce. I took his hand, letting the bridesmaids go ahead of me. When we reached the glass opening of our living room that had been covered in white sheet draping all over it, I heard everyone turn silent as the song we asked Twisted Transistor to do for us—with our lyrics—began playing softly through the speakers, with each bridesmaid disappearing through the white sheet.

"Holy shit," I mumbled.

I felt so nervous I could have spewed. I was nauseated and excited all at the same time.

"It's time, you ready?" my dad asked from beside me.

I nodded my head. "As ready as I'll ever be."

He pushed the sheet open, with my arm wrapped around his as we began walking down the aisle. It was lined with tea lights everywhere. The trees around the property had been draped with tea lights as well. On either side of the aisles, we had white seats where our family and friends sat. Finally, I look up to the altar which was also covered in tea lights, when I saw Ade standing there in a crisp, white shirt and black slacks. His hair was standing nicely around his face but still tousled.

He smirked and dragged his eyes up and down my body. I blushed and dropped my face for a second. Then looked back up to him where his usual cocky smirk had been replaced by the most sincere, soft smile I had ever seen on his beautiful face.

Once I reached him, my dad handed me to him and took a seat in the front row next to my mom. My parents love Ade, probably more than they love me. He's the son they never had, and I guess in a way, they're the parents he never had. Aside from Zane's mom. I looked down at Zane's mom and smiled at her. She had her tissues in her lap, sitting on the other side of my mom. They got on way too well, they were like old friends who drink and get into mischief with each other and it *drove Zane a little crazy. They both looked like proud parents and it warmed my heart.*

"You look fucking beautiful, baby. I can't wait to peel this sweet dress off you after I've made sweet love to your pussy in it," he whispered into my ear.

My face turned bright beet red and I laughed. He stepped back and we both looked at the priest as he handed us our vowels and the doors to our future opened.

THE END

If you are in emotional distress or struggling to cope, and are affected by any of the issues covered in this book, please contact:

The Samaritans USA 1(800) 273-TALK

The Samaritans UK 08457 90 90 90

Lifeline AUSTRALIA 13 11 14

Next by Author Amo Jones

Losing Traction
Westbeach Series Book One

Ryer and Pheobe's Story

My name is Phoebe Rendon. Growing up as the only girl surrounded by the Sinful Souls MC community has never been easy. Outside of the club, I had no life because my brother and his two psycho best friends kept tabs on me. My only out was racing at Point Hellers, the largest and steepest drift mountain in Westbeach, California. Cars were my life, and years later, that hasn't changed. Only now, I have the funds to support my habit.

My love life's been rocky. All I've known of love is twisted biker men from other MC chapters. Until I met Ryder Oakley, the lead singer and Rock God from Twisted Transistor. He showed me the world in two weeks. Then one night he up and left me, without so much as a note. Now, two years later, I've been assigned as a fashion assistant to go on tour with Alyx Munroe, pop princess and diva queen. Only my shitty boss Maree omitted to inform me that Alyx Munroe would also be touring with Twisted Transistor. Just when I thought I'd forgotten Ryder, he comes back into my life in full force, causing me to slowly lose traction of my feelings.

With my plans for building my own racing circuit underway, I finally have the footing to leave the fashion industry and concentrate on finalizing my circuit. Where we can showcase some of the best and hottest girl racers from around the world.

This empire is mine, but with power and money comes hate and destruction.

Welcome to Westbeach.

PLAYLIST

Akon "Dangerous"
Akon "Right Now"
The Weeknd "The Hills"
The Weeknd "Or Nah"
Vinylshakers "One Night in Bangkok"
Timberland "Bounce"
2pac "Thugs Get Lonely"
Metallica "Nothing Else Matters"
Evanescance "Going Under"
Eminem "Till I Collapse"
Beyoncé - "7/11"
Ludacris - "What's Your Fantasy"

CONNECT
with me online

Thank you for reading Tainted Love,
I hope you enjoyed reading it as much as I
enjoyed writing it.

Stay tuned for my new series "Westbeach" which
is coming soon, kicking off with Ryder and
Phoebe's story - "Losing Traction."

Thank you again to all my beautiful readers,
thank you for all your kind words and
encouragement.

You all inspire me to keep going—Thank you.

Goodreads

Add these books to your TBR list.
Perilous Love – Sinful Souls MC Series Book One
Intricate Love – Sinful Souls MC Series Book Two
Tainted Love – Sinful Souls MC Series Book Three
Losing Traction – Westbeach Series Book One

Website

http://www.amojonesauthor.com/

Twitter

https://twitter.com/authorAmojones

Email

amojonesauthor@yahoo.com

Facebook

https://www.facebook.com/amojonesauthor?ref=hl

Goodreads

https://www.goodreads.com/author/show/
14047384.Amo_Jones

Instagram

https://instagram.com/authoramojones/

ABOUT
the author
Amo Jones

A little bit about me. I am the mama bear to four little kiddos, two girls, and two boys. I'm also a wife-to-be to my partner of ten years. We were high school sweethearts, without the high school. My little (big) family are my rock, and I'm so lucky to have them with me through it all.

I am from New Zealand! Born and raised in a small town called Rotorua. It's a beautiful city, just smells a little. I'm currently living in Australia on the Whitsunday Coast (Great Barrier Reef) where we hope to settle down for a long time. I love the beach, and margaritas, and wine. Don't forget the wine. Chinese food is the best food.

One day I hope to travel the world, preferably the US, because I'm obsessed with it. I would travel now, but my bank account is like..."Dude, no." So I've put that in the goal bucket.

I love all my beautiful readers, you have kept me going. You're my inspiration to keep writing, with all your kind words and reviews. You are all amazing, and I write for you.

That's enough yappin' from me. See you all in Wonderland. x

Namaste.

Printed in Great Britain
by Amazon

46751803R00222